FROM ASHES TO BEAUTY

HEATHER CAMACHO

RENEWED HEARTS | BOOK THREE

FROM ASHES TO BEAUTY

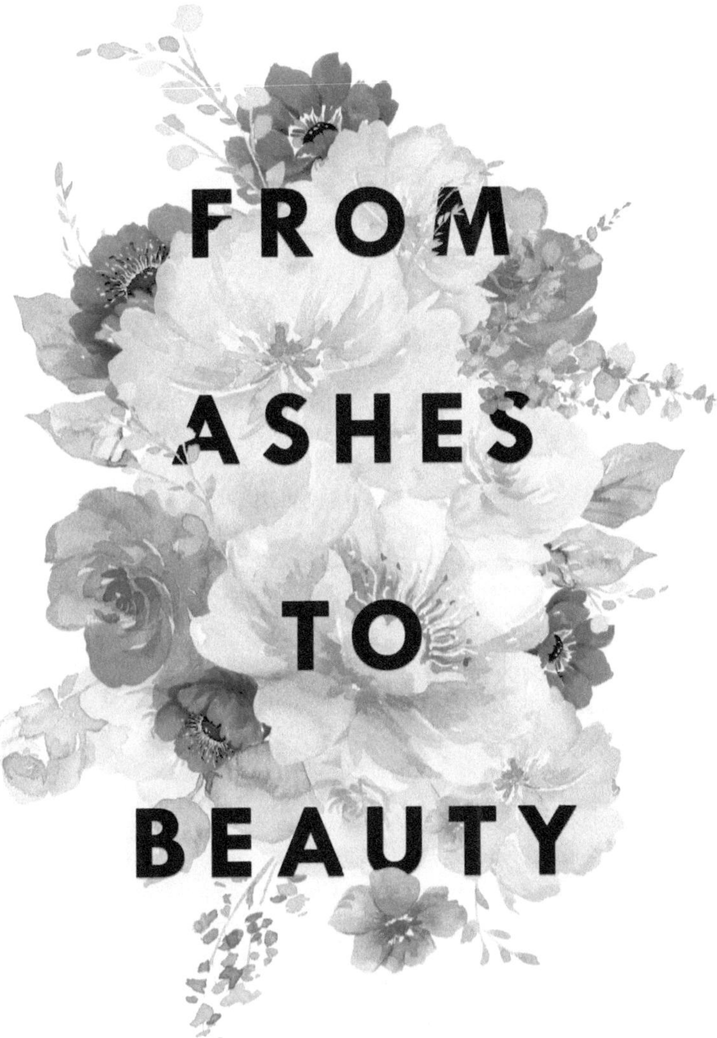

HEATHER CAMACHO

From Ashes to Beauty

A publication of Purple Morning Press, LLC

ISBN: 978-1-962902-24-3 (ebook)

ISBN: 978-1-962902-23-6 (paperback)

ISBN: 978-1-962902-25-0 (hardback)

Cover: Emilie Haney of EAH Creative.

Editing: Kendra Gaither of Kendra's Editing and Book Services.

For Gena Showalter — *Thank you for everything you do to uplift, encourage and inspire me. Russell & Birdie thank you, too. God bless you, sweet lady.*

For my God — *Thank You for holding my hand through every fiery step of this season. Because You love me, I have another book to share with the world, and to You I give all the glory.*

BIRDIE

1

I'd never been one for stage fright, but I was suddenly terrified I would die. My head pounded something fierce, but I couldn't let it stop me, not when I'd persevered through worse. In the past, I'd outperformed hundreds while sporting a fever, probably more than once. When I was fourteen, I had a broken wrist and refused a cast because it wouldn't have gone with my outfit. That one took a lot of grit and a whole lot more God, but I still completed my acro pass to perfection.

So yeah, I'd experienced the occasional bad day. But for the first time in my pageant career, standing behind the curtain only minutes away from my number, my heart raced.

But scratch over a little headache? Never. Not Birdie Jo MacLean.

Tonight there was an unnatural pounding in my head, stemming all the way from an intrusive ache at the back of my neck. I was a veteran beauty queen, yet I was shaking in my sequins, and *not* because I wasn't sure I had my routine down or because I might make a mistake—Because I did, and I would never. It wasn't nerves; it was something else.

During rehearsal the night before, while executing the same trick that I'd done hundreds of times before, and all perfectly, I might add, something tweaked my neck. Or something in my neck was tweaked. Whatever it was, it left me with an incessant pain I'd barely been able to mask with meds and copious amounts of cooling ointment.

Attempting to rub out the tightness in my neck, a pulsing spasm talked me out of it. I stretched my arms in big waves in front of and behind me, then shook them out like cooked spaghetti.

"Please, God. Let this go away. Just get me through one more. We both know I'm about ready to let go of pageants anyway. I don't have the time. So, if this is my last one, I'd like to go out winning. If not that, I'd just like to not make a total idiot out of myself in front of everyone I know and love." *Slow, deep breath in. Slow, deep breath out.* "At the very least, don't let me croak on stage. Okay? Can we be on the same page about this?"

The music had stopped. Applause for the girl before me had come and gone, and the announcer was about to introduce me, my queue only two minutes away. I worried the back of my neck, concentrating again on my breathing. *Slow, deep breath in. Slower, deeper breath out.*

"You ready, Birdie?" A hushed voice came from someone standing around a divider, their head peeking out of the corner of my eye. "You're up."

"I sure hope so then," I said to myself, mostly because the speaker was already no longer there. *Oh well, time to do this thing.*

On stage, I plastered on my signature smile, made it through the Q and A about my chosen talent and some insight into my self-made routine, and then got into the starting position. I even managed a quick wink and air kiss to all my people in the second row. Family, friends, boyfriend… they were all there, even my dad.

Push through, push through, push through. I can do this.

And I did. One eight-count after the other, I spun, leapt, and gave it my all like every other time before, ignoring the throbbing pain in my neck as it increased, making its way up my head. It soon left behind a fog I couldn't ignore.

As I flipped my head down to do an illusion, the same one that triggered me last night, I heard… I heard *bees?*

I forced my eyes open as best I could, but the only thing I saw was the ceiling. How did I get on my back? What was that buzzing noise taking over the whole world, and why wasn't it letting up?

God, I feel funny. I've lived as a beauty queen and, now, I will die as one. I'm not sure I approve of the irony, but points for creativity.

Disorientation moved to front row center, silencing the shouts of my name from the crowd. The next thing I knew, I was drowning in a quiet so severe that not even the bees survived, and the curtains closed all around me.

RUSSELL

2

In less than a week, I would be getting out of prison. That meant no more disgusting meals, no more public showers, and no more shrinks. A future was on the horizon for me, and sooner than expected, due in large part to plain dumb luck. While I *had* done a lot to curb my attitude since my arrest—being incarcerated was a starkly sobering experience—my good behavior only got me so far. A little thing called overcrowding got me the rest of the way. You couldn't beat a fifteen-month sentence coming to an end after only six.

My counselor, Dr. Alex Webb, was known as Alexander the Great among the offenders, since he was the only one any of us could stand. He really had his work cut out for him during our last session.

"You need to have a goal, a clear path to take," he told me, reiterating a previous conversation. "You'll be turned loose in just a couple of weeks, nine months ahead of schedule. What is it you want out of your freedom once it's gained?"

"To leave Corpus behind and never look back." It was the simplest and truest answer I could give, even after all this time.

The question remained: What the heck *was* I going to do with the rest of my life? It was a question everyone kept asking me, but a question for which I couldn't come up with a substantial answer.

Dr. Webb nodded. "Valid. But how will you achieve that? You have to back up your desires with attainable plans of action. One small step at a time leads to great distances."

The only thing I knew for sure was that I had nothing to go back to and no career aspirations to speak of. I might've had one or two friends left, but that remained to be seen, and I technically had my family, but how much support could *they* possibly be? Considering the fact that none of them besides my older sister had come to visit me during my time here, I didn't think it likely I could rely on them for all that much. Not that I would want to. They had left me to rot.

All I needed was a place to live, my car, and my own willpower, and eventually things would fall into place. They had to. If my only other choice was to someday return to another dungeon like this, I *had* to get my life together. No more prison for me, thanks.

I didn't respond, but merely watched my own thumbs twirl around as my hands rested atop my slouched chest.

Alexander the Great chuckled. "You know, Russell, you've been one of my favorite patients."

"Given your pool of choices, forgive me if I don't take that as a compliment."

His laugh was heartier this time. "I know you'll do great. You have an intelligent and amiable mind. Watch yourself while you're out there, and the answers will come to you."

Sure, and just maybe that was the truth, but I had to get home first. "I guess we'll find out."

My mom's shoulder was so ice-cold on the car ride home that I felt like I'd have been safer staying in my cell. I'd only been "free" for five minutes, and already, I may have opted to go back. At least while locked up, people were paid to care about you.

"Where's Dad?" No response or even the hint of one. "Matt didn't want to come?" Nothing. Not a thing. The only word she'd spoken to me was *'hello'* when I first got in the car, and she hadn't looked at me since. She didn't even manage to spare me a side-eye. I didn't expect a red carpet welcome or anything, but I was gone for half a year, and *this* was the greeting I got?

I sighed. "It's been a long six months, Mom. I just stepped foot back into the real world, and you already seem mad at me. Why the third degree?" Her incredibly bad mood was a red flag I should've heeded to begin with. I realized that I was calling on a foolish sort of bravery to raise questions rather than let it go, but I was unable to stop myself.

"You have the nerve to ask me that, when here I am driving my son home from *prison?"*

"It was just a question. Man, I haven't even done anything yet, and you're coming after me."

Her jaw set in disgust. "Funny that you say *'yet'* like you will though, huh? Are you just thinking about what's out there, itching for your next felony, or what?"

Wow. "You make me sound like some kind of addict."

She slammed on the brakes, propelling me forward against the locked protection of my seatbelt. She was sure looking at me now, and those eyes were like daggers.

"What else is it but an addiction when a person—with as near a perfect life as one can get, I might add—takes a repeated, dangerous, and *stupid* risk to himself and his family, by buying and selling stolen car parts of all things? You perverted the only thing you've ever seemed to care about, and for what? The only answer your father and I could come up with is that it must give you some sort of high."

Oh, brother. Exaggerate much?

Working for Tanner had started out innocently enough. Kevin and I were both part time employees of Blake Tanner Automotive when I caught wind of a special insider opportunity. I ran that for a year before Kevin finally joined me, and then it wasn't long before everyone got busted. But for a while there, it sure was fun. "It was just about the money," I muttered. *Lots* of money. Who didn't love money?

"Money?" she yelled. "You mean that green papery stuff that your father and I go to real, legitimate jobs to earn for this family every day? The stuff that provides everything you've never gone a day without in your all-too-privileged life? Ha! No, son, you stole because you enjoyed it, for God only knows what reason, but it makes me sick. I'm just *sick* about it all, and quite frankly, I'm ashamed to be your mother because what could I have done so wrong that resulted in my own son, the boy I carried, birthed, nursed, healed, helped, taught, bled for, worked for, and *loved* more than myself, would disrespect himself this way? Disrespect his parents? You let down everyone who loves and believed in you. I just can't understand it!"

I shook my head and turned away, unable to come up with a response to any of that. I let my forehead rest against the window where fat drops of rain caught against the glass. The view out there was a strange sight. Hurricane season was at its peak, and rain had made the usually dry, yellow vegetation green and overgrown.

She attempted to rage on, but I could no longer stand to listen. Eventually, from the corner of my eyes, I saw her give up and wipe away the salty evidence of her red-faced turmoil. As usual, my mom had everything all wrong but thought she was right, and she wouldn't be persuaded otherwise. I didn't even have the energy to try. This time, when she looked out to the road again, her silence was preferable.

Yeah, so I enjoyed the stealing. So what? It wasn't a big ole conspiracy or some depraved thing. It was just fun, and *really* good money that I'd earned myself, without the help of mommy and daddy for once. Big freaking deal. There were a lot worse things I could've been doing. I hardly thought stealing from rich, sleazy dudes and indulging in a bit of partying here and there was so bad.

But whatever. Delia Grandy didn't understand me when I was younger, and she wouldn't understand me now. It was all good. I just had to keep my head down and bide my time. The only thing that mattered now was arming myself for the most important battle to come, and that was getting out on my own.

Dr. Webb had meant well, but he'd clearly never met parents like mine. If my own mother and father treated me like a fugitive, how was I ever supposed to believe I was anything but?

BIRDIE

3

The large October moon shone brilliantly down on us as the soothing ocean tide flowed in closer and closer. Nick Benavides, the most awesome of boyfriends, had his chair wedged into the sand beside mine. We sat with our toes out, with a tray perched precariously between us on our armrests. A night of normalcy had never been more welcome.

I looked out into the dark waves. "Did you hear about the hurricane? This might be our last trip here for a while."

"They're already saying it won't make landfall here."

"Hope not. Not a fan."

"I love a good rain, but I'd rather spend more of my time at college doing fieldwork instead of bookwork. An active hurricane season will keep us out of the water a lot longer."

"I'm sure there will be plenty of both."

"Yeah, bet you're right." He reached over and clasped my hand. "So, how are you feeling?"

I led with a smile. "Perfectly fine." It wasn't a lie, but it wasn't the complete truth either.

His look was gentle but concerned. "And how are you *really* feeling?"

On a sigh, I deflated a little. "Still disappointed in myself, but I'll live. It's time I retired anyway. Pageants are so much work, and I am moving toward other things."

I was still feeling burned about bombing my final performance, but that was the last thing I wanted to talk about. In addition to having embarrassed myself, things were made worse when my mom insisted I take the ambulance to the hospital, and I was wheeled out of there like a side show freak. Drawing the curtain on my misfortune could only hide so much from the curious. Besides, folks talk.

My only consolation for the whole evening was that after a bunch of questioning and a physical exam, the emergency room doctors didn't find anything wrong with me. It was clearly a fluke, something I simply needed to rest after and monitor for recurrence, but nothing more.

"Don't blame yourself. You did your best. You couldn't have known something like that would happen. I'm just glad you're okay. It was scary to see you like that. It… it really put things into perspective for me."

I squeezed his hand and my smile softened. I guess if I were honest, I would say the same thing. I didn't really care that I was done with pageants. They were fun in the moment, but looking back, they seemed like a placeholder for what I should really be doing. Now I could focus all my time on work and school.

One chapter of my life had come to an end, and I was fine with it. Really. I didn't need to be a beauty queen when there were families to care for. But saying goodbye to years of my life like *that* had been unexpected at best, and a total train wreck at worst.

I accepted that it happened, but was it truly an isolated incident? I really hoped so.

Nick smiled back but then dropped my hand to clap his together, moving us along. He was always so good about sensing my feelings. "Anyway, this is a happy night, and you must be hungry."

"Sure am," I agreed, looking at the thoughtful spread. He'd garnished our club sandwich dinner with two pickle spears, sliced fruit, and a bag of chips to share. A single pink rose in a bottle graced the middle. Nick knew how to make something really count, even simple dates such as this one. Who else had a boyfriend who showed this much attentiveness and care? I knew what a lucky girl I was.

For my benefit, Nick prayed a small blessing over the food and handed me my sandwich, and we dug right in.

"Wanna know something funny? I can't even think of the beach anymore without thinking of you," Nick said between bites, patting his mouth. He carefully placed down his napkin, but the little table still wobbled. One wrong move and I could imagine the entire tray tumbling down.

I liked the idea that I could remind him of something so incredible. "It's one of my favorite places on earth, but it wasn't always," I said.

"That's hard to believe."

I laughed to myself at the memories of moving to Corpus Christi from Texarkana, when my parents were still trying to save their marriage, a plan which ultimately failed. The relocation and subsequent divorce not long after were only made easier when I fell into friendship with Sarah Stevenson, Samantha Ballard, and Jenna Rodriguez, and together, we spent a *lot* of time at the beach. It was a safe haven for my friends and me, but also a personal refuge for letting go of the way things were. My family was shattered, and it was hard work keeping myself together. To bury the hurt, I threw myself into friends, pageants, my grades, and ignored the rest. I could only focus on things that improved my life, not anything that would show exactly how torn up it was.

Through the years I spent in pageants, I'd developed some predispositions. It took many trips to these coastal sands, and to my dad's new ranch, for me to give up on keeping myself in order, my hair especially. The more time I spent in the great outdoors, either at the beach or riding horses, I had to learn that cuteness did not prevail where the dirt and winds were concerned, so I succumbed to ponytails or braided looks, for the sake of control over charm. To me, the beach was the only place that had no business in perfection. It just… *was,* and that gave me a freedom I didn't know I needed until I had it.

At least as far as my physical appearance was concerned.

Nick cupped my cheek, pulling my thoughts back to the present, to his warmth and his piercing dark eyes. "Do you want to know why?"

"Why what?"

He laughed softly, knowing my quirky, sometimes absent-minded ways and not minding at all. "I asked if you wanted to know why the beach reminds me of you."

"Sure, I do." I brightened.

"It's pretty simple, really. It's your golden curls slipping free and blowing across your face, the red tint across your cheeks, and all the floral sundresses. The way you looked the first time I saw you here is a core memory of mine. As far as I'm concerned, you're as much a part of this beach as the waves are."

His words warmed me from the inside out. The ends of my

mouth tipped, and before I could gush over his sweetness, Nick silenced me with a gentle kiss on the cheek, as respectful as ever of my personal boundaries.

"Birdie Jo," he whispered as he pulled back, rubbing his thumb along my jaw. I looked into his fathomless eyes, awed by the glimmer of the moon within them. "Will you marry me?"

BIRDIE

4

My heart was thumping at warp speed. I didn't know how much time had passed when he asked, "Birdie, did you hear me?"

"I'm not sure. Did you… did you just…" My throat dried up like a Texas drought. My tongue became so knotted, I couldn't form thoughts.

"I asked if you would marry me," he repeated with boldness, working to keep his smile alive.

Startled all over again, I stood abruptly, sending our picnic tray crashing into the sand. "You're proposing? Marriage? For real?"

Ignoring the spilled contents, too focused on me and my reaction, Nick rose slowly to his feet. Watching me like I might bolt any second—and honestly, it was a possibility—he spoke softly. "Of course, I am. I love you."

Love? Marriage? We hadn't said the actual words before, but we'd both hinted at them in our own ways. I knew we were feeling pretty confident about each other, but when did we get this serious?

"And you know how I feel," I said, utterly pathetic.

I had always wanted a husband and children. A big, happy family was my ideal happily ever after for as long as I could remember. But right here, now, being offered it like this, I just wanted to run and hide.

Admittedly, Nick was as close to perfection as a guy could get. Even though he didn't share my faith, he was understanding about it and never made me feel bad or weird. He knew how important work and school were to me and cheered on my dreams of becoming a social worker. He knew the importance of my friends and never badgered for more time than I could offer him. He concerned himself with my health as much as he did with all my passions. He had supported, wholeheartedly, every single thing I did since the day we met.

"But?" he questioned, calling out my hesitation.

"But this comes as a surprise. I mean, really? Marriage?"

Hurt contorted his features. "Isn't that what you've always wanted?"

"Yes?" All of a sudden, I wasn't even sure myself. It was like everything inside my head went completely blank. "But not right now?" All my confidence had been stripped away by my shock. I was lost in the haze of the conversation with no discernible hold on my own feelings.

"Birdie… This is what I want. You and me forever. I'm all in, and I really need you to be, too."

Forever.

"I thought what we had was perfect. I don't want to change anything."

"That would be going backward for me. I'm ready to start a life with you." He touched my cheek, looking me square in the eyes, so I couldn't look anywhere else. "I want to be your husband."

His words, once an intimate comfort and ultimate support, now caused me to crumble. Only my tears spoke now, and they weren't saying yes.

He looked longingly at me, silently searching for the answer that made sense, the one I had longed to say someday, but it never turned up. So, I spewed the first thing I could manage. "I'm sorry."

Pain dulled his eyes, pulling his signature good nature out of their gaze. It was my fault. I was the cause of this. This boy—this man—put his heart on the line for me, and I was refusing it. *Why* was I refusing it?

"All I know is I want to stay together."

"No, Birdie. I can't."

"But we don't have to break up. I don't want that."

"I don't either, but having anything less than forever with you would only kill me slowly. I'm sorry." His voice weak, he beheld me with so much regret it nearly brought me to my knees.

I was rendered mute. My jaw went slack, and when I once again said nothing, a dejected scowl overtook Nick's face as his own tears fell. He did nothing to stop them, even as he turned away and started packing things up.

This was it then. We were over. He was leaving, and I could do nothing to stop him.

That night, lying in bed, I was broken, left with nothing but the deep hollow of my own aching. Nick's apology rang through my head. Not even the roar of my raging headache could drown it out. The fact of the matter was, Nick proved something I'd known all along, ever since my dad left my mom and started his do-over family: I'm not worth staying for. And if Nick, the king of boyfriends, didn't think so either, then nobody ever would.

I cried myself to sleep, but my mind was made up. From now

on, I wanted nothing to do with love or anything that looked like it. I would focus on work, school, and friends, just like I always did, but a relationship was no longer in my five-year plan.

"Lesson learned, Lord," I whispered, my voice cracking like a broken mirror. "I won't come within a hundred miles of romance ever again."

RUSSELL

5

WALKING THROUGH THE FRONT DOOR OF MY HOUSE WAS NOTHING like coming home. It looked the same, even smelled the same, but any hint of belonging was nonexistent.

I found my brother sitting on the couch and waved. "Hey, Matty."

"Oh. Hey," he said coldly, like mother like son. He barely looked up from the small gaming console in his hands before he retreated up the stairs.

Awesome. I was zero for two so far. That made multiple rejections in less than an hour. As for my dad, I didn't see him at all, and my defensiveness wanted to count that as three.

"He's still at work," Mom said curtly, reading my mind. "Things like commissary and attorney fees really add up."

"Oh," I said, but the urge to tell her off was growing stronger by the minute. I didn't want to need their help, but what else was I going to do? Every cent I had saved up had been seized by the feds, even the hard-earned pennies I'd stashed prior to everything. What could be worse as a young adult than still being at the mercy of your judgmental parents?

"Go on and take a shower. I'm going to start dinner." Without another word, she headed through the hall and disappeared into the kitchen. It was like any other day, only worse, because it very much wasn't and nobody seemed to care. Whatever. That was the least of my problems. For now, a nice, hot, private shower followed by a delicious home-cooked meal sounded like Heaven to me.

My excitement was overshadowed by a startling new reality as I climbed the stairs and reached my room. I noticed it was missing a few key elements.

Like the *door!*

And my TV and PlayStation were missing. My laptop was nowhere in sight. All my posters and collectibles were gone, as were my shelves. There was a bed, smaller than the one I remembered. Opening a chest of drawers, I found it had a handful of clothes, only some of which were recognizable as my own. A small, wooden nightstand outfitted with a lamp, a Bible, and an ugly pair of shoes sat beside the bed. Everything was explicitly chosen to send a message, to create an atmosphere of punishment.

A terrible thought occurred to me, and I rushed to the landing. "Where are my keys?" I called down the stairs.

"Confiscated. Consider your car impounded until further notice," she returned. "Let's save the rest of the questions for later, when your dad gets home."

This has got to be a joke.

From the bitter reunion with half of my family, to the lack of anything I used to call my own, one thing was maddeningly clear to me. Released though I might've been, I was still imprisoned, and it was going to take a lot more effort to gain my freedom.

My bed may not have been what I remembered, but it was the best, most luxurious thing I'd ever slept on. Was it a really great mattress or was it the fact that I was finally not dirty, cold, scared, or starving, surrounded by armed guards and a hundred other guys? That could've been it.

My mood stayed at a steady elevation until my eyes adjusted and the reality of my surroundings came crashing back to me. Yes, I was home. The bed was great, I didn't stink, and the solitude was fantastic. But I was still a prisoner. No car, no phone, no entertainment, no *door*. I felt torn between gratitude and resentment, but one thing was undeniably true: the sooner I got out from under their roof, the better.

I padded from the bathroom—that nobody watched me use—and found my parents waiting for me in my room.

"Good morning," my dad said, his tone even. My mom watched on, standing by in silence. I hadn't seen either one of them since dismissing myself from the dining table last night, after stuffing myself like a pig on my mom's King Ranch casserole. My dad didn't have much to say then, so I'd been anticipating something more from him. But what or when, I had no idea.

"Hey," I said, uneasy.

"How was your first night back home?"

"Good." He waited. Did he expect me to say more? "Really good."

"I'm glad to hear it. Look, Russ, I know last night everyone was pretty tense, and we're going to have to feel our way through all of this. But we figured we'd get the uncomfortable stuff out of the way now. I know you're not exactly happy with the changes we've made while you were gone, but I'd like to explain so you can understand. First of all, and most importantly, our love is unconditional but our trust is not. You have a lot of work to do in earning it back."

"But my door? Really, Dad? I'm so tired of being watched all the time and having zero privacy."

"The only thing you're going to be doing in your room is sleeping, so what does it matter? And let's not forget, privacy is a privilege. One that you lost when you got convicted and sent away in the first place, so you can't really complain about how much it sucks."

I'm going to anyway.

"The last time you lived here, you did a lot of bad things behind our backs. What makes you think you deserve a door to hide behind now?" Of course, he'd counted on me having nothing to say. "When you have restored our trust in you, you may have your door back. It's that simple."

"What about the rest of my stuff?"

He cocked his head. "What stuff?"

Seriously? I spread my arms out. "Literally everything that isn't in here anymore. You guys left me with nothing."

"Oh, you mean all that stuff we bought you over the years? It's gone." His voice remained perfectly calm while every blood cell in my body became inflamed.

"Gone?" I exclaimed.

"We sold it to make your commissary deposits. Prison isn't just free room and board, you know."

Tell me about it.

"Speaking of finances, you need to get a job first thing."

"Finally, something we agree on," I muttered. He ignored it.

"There's a job fair downtown tomorrow with your name on

it. Just so happens it's right around the corner from the probation office, so after you meet with your new caseworker, I will drop you off on my way to work, but you'll have to take the bus home."

I'd already almost forgotten about the mandatory probation check-ins with some guy named Harold. "Hold on." Dread settled in the pit of my stomach as something else came to mind. "Did you sell my car, too?"

"We thought about it, but no, we didn't. It's in the garage. But you won't be getting it back until you're employed. And if you're going to start applying for jobs, you're going to need this." He reached into his pocket and handed me my phone. "Don't get too excited. It's not your old one."

I looked down, turning the device over in my hands. Sure enough, I didn't recognize it. If I had to guess, it used to be my brother's. "Where's mine?"

"Sold."

I should've guessed.

Turning the phone on, I thumbed through it. It was empty. A glorified paperweight. Child restrictions had been installed, and my contact list had been pruned with obvious prejudice.

"Why did you guys do this?"

"Do you really need me to answer that?"

No. I didn't need to hear an encore about how I'd broken their trust and didn't deserve anything nice and blah-blah-blah. "Forget it," I settled on.

"Look, things aren't going to be fun for a while. We know that. We expected you to have a bad attitude, but we also expect you to turn your life around. Make the changes you need to make and... be our son again." My dad's chest rose and fell. The first sign of emotion I'd caught yet. "I know things might seem harsh to you right now, but consider how we've felt during all this.

None of it has been easy, not the least of all for us. We love you, Russ."

My mom sniffed and drew my attention. She was looking away, fresh tears pooled in her eyes, threatening to spill over any second. How could someone look so angry while crying? I remained quiet, because what good would arguing do? They were already too set in their decisions about everything.

The best I could hope for was keeping them pacified long enough to coax my car keys back. Even if getting a job hadn't already been my number one priority, it absolutely was now.

BIRDIE

6

SINCE LIFE HAD TAKEN MY BEST FRIENDS AND ME IN SEPARATE directions lately, I had to settle for telling them about my news via group video call. It actually wasn't that bad, considering, if they were with me, there would be hugging, and I didn't want hugs. I didn't want sympathy and more tears. I simply wanted to inform them and move on, hoping against hope that Jenna, in particular, would be less herself than usual and let us keep the subject simple.

I should've known that wasn't how it would go down.

Jenna's voice rose above the others. "Are you kidding? Nick proposed and you said no? I don't believe it."

"Believe it or not, that's what happened." I sat crisscross on my padded chair as I faced my phone, which was propped up on my vanity. All of their expressions were varying degrees of disbelief and sadness.

"But you really said *no?* Like, N-O? That gorgeous, incredible Latino specimen treated you like a queen all this time, and when he gets down on one knee, you tell him no? You, the girl who wants the American dream of a white picket fence, blue-collared husband, with two-point-five children more than anyone else alive?" she probed tirelessly. "You've gone on and on about this for like, ever."

Annoying though she was, Jenna was right on multiple accounts. Nick was handsome, generous, sweet, and with him, I did feel like a queen, probably more than I ever did winning trophies and crowns. But something still made me turn him down.

And as much as I'd always been vocal about wanting a husband and family, when a potential husband suddenly stared me in the face, offering me his future, I had frozen.

It was one thing to be dumped by a boyfriend. I knew I would get over this, no matter how soul-sucking it felt at the time. But once I became a wife and my life depended completely on another person, that's when getting dumped would really hurt. I guess, in my own sad little way, saying no to Nick was about long-term self-preservation.

And it was a darn good thing I did say no because, at the first sign of struggle, he *did* leave me. Imagine how much worse it would've been years into a marriage with him.

I shuddered.

No, this was the lesser of two evils. I was hurting, but it hurt a lot less than it could've.

"He didn't actually get on one knee," I finally muttered, deflecting.

"Oh, whatever. That's not the point."

I sighed. "Jenna, the point is, he wanted all or nothing, and I couldn't give him all. So, he picked nothing. Not me."

Nobody would ever *get all,* I decided then and there. It just wasn't worth the risk to my heart and soul. No more dating, no nothing.

"It has to be some consolation at least to know that the only reason he left is because he was hurting, too." Sarah's voice cracked over the speaker of my phone.

If only the service would stop cutting in and out because of the stupid weather. As if the coastal bend had never had a storm before. The one raging outside at that moment was one of the many coming our way this month, apparently. It was awesome, because we could always use the rain, but I also needed the internet to hold out so I could clearly see my friends, please and thank you.

"If he was hurting so badly, he wouldn't have given me an ultimatum and then walked away for good." I could've said a lot more, because his pain was no consolation at all, actually. But since I was in no mood to defend my bad attitude, I held it back.

"I still just don't get why you said no to his proposal in the first place," commented Jenna.

"I'm not sure enough myself. But please, let's change the subject now."

Sammy nodded, rushing to cut off whatever Jenna was about to say. "You got it, babe. Just don't forget we're here for you, okay?"

"I won't ever forget. I love you guys." I really, truly did. Besides my mom and little half-siblings, these girls were the only ones safe to love. Nick had nailed that coffin shut.

And that was just fine with me.

"And we love you," Sammy said, reaching for the phone and pulling it into her arms. We all laughed and did the same. "This is the best group hug we can do until next month."

Jenna was the first to set the phone back down, freeing her hands to clap with excitement. "Ooh, I cannot wait for Friendsgiving this year! Do we know where we are having it?"

"At Kevin's, right?" Sammy propped her phone back up.

"I'm hoping so. It would double as such a nice *'welcome home'* event for Kevin, and you, too, Sam, for that matter. I'll iron it out with him and let everyone know as soon as possible, but I have a feeling he'll love the idea."

"Excellent. You know, after all this time, I don't think any of us have ever seen Kevin's house," Sammy mused.

We all exchanged looks, wondering the same thing. "I think you're right." I laughed, giddy for the distraction.

"Wait, Sammy. Are you even going to be home in time?" I asked. She was currently in the middle of a two-month mission trip in Mexico, doing God's work, but it would be hard to spend Friendsgiving without her.

"Should be. I may have to leave a few days early in order to make it, but I don't think it'll be a problem. Everything is going so great over here. I'll definitely be coming back anyway, so I'll more than make up for it."

"Maybe you could get Jared to go with you next time," Sarah said.

"I'm working on it, trust me."

I wished I could give Sammy a squeeze. "We're all so proud of you, girl. I can't believe one of my best friends is a real missionary."

"It's nothing. I love doing it," Sammy said, but she was smiling from ear to ear.

God, I want that. I want to take hold of my own purpose with two hands the way Sammy does. I want to be living it already, with no more uncertainty. No more guessing.

We continued with leisurely chatter and all the girlish laughter we could stomach until the night forced us to say goodbye. Despite feeling like my old self again while the girls were present, it was all too easy to revert to wallowing in my sadness once I was alone again. I felt utterly depleted. My head hurt by the time my brain shut down enough to let the tiredness creep in.

My well is dry, Lord. Please refill it with peace and joy so this pain will stop. Why must I hurt if I knew Nick wasn't the one? Shouldn't I feel relieved instead? Please just let me find the life I truly need. I'm ready to move on. Bring forward what You have planned for me.

RUSSELL

7

My dad waited in the car in front of a big glass-front building while I checked in with Harold and got a run-down of my dos and don'ts for the next six months. I may have been released, but the system still had a hold on my freedom. A block down, he pulled the car into a parking spot facing another giant glass building right in the middle of downtown. A folding sign with balloons marked the location of the event. The whole scene was framed by a gray sky of fast-moving clouds.

"It's super dark out," I observed.

"I'd be more worried about your mom than the weather right now, if I were you."

No kidding. "She's going to hold it against me forever." I saw him turn to me, but I didn't make a move.

"No, she won't. She needs more time to come around, but she will. She loves you."

I gave a half-hearted nod.

"Besides," he said, looking back toward the sky. "It's not going to amount to much out there. The hurricane won't be a hurricane by the time it hits. We've certainly seen a lot worse than the bit of wind and rain we'll get."

"Alright then." I reached for the handle.

"One more thing. Stand up tall, son. Make sure you shake a lot of hands and maintain eye contact. You're such a personable guy. Let them see that."

I hoped he didn't see me roll my eyes. "Sure, Dad."

Walking slowly to the door, I was aware when he drove away, and I considered bailing. I hardly believed there were any jobs inside for me, but I needed one, period. I figured I could browse around and fill out a few applications, but I definitely wasn't going to shake anyone's hand.

By the time I'd made my way through half the room, I had shaken a *lot* of hands. But something I'd found out the hard way? I needn't have bothered.

"Oh, just a minute," one man said as I was walking away. We'd just had a great conversation, and I was actually feeling good about my chances. "You forgot to enter your graduation information."

"I didn't forget."

"Do you not have a high school diploma?"

"No, sir."

"I see. Unfortunately, that is one of our minimum requirements for employment. In fact, I believe it's the same for every company here." He placed my application down, then flipped through a binder and pulled out a card. "But don't let this stop you. Reach out to our education director and discuss getting your GED, and then come see us again. These doors will all open." Which meant they were all closed right now. Which meant this was a waste of time, just like I'd expected.

The spear of rejection that shot through my heart let me know that I'd stuff that business card into my pocket and never look at it again. Being let down easily was still being let down. I should've bailed like I originally wanted. My own family wouldn't give me a second chance, so why did I expect anything less from complete strangers?

I'm out.

Long strides carried me the shortest distance to the exit when a burst of laughter brought me to a standstill. In a room dominated by stuffy suited men, where did that beautiful, feminine sound come from?

Drawn by some invisible force, I turned around, seeking out the source of what I just heard. On the hunt, I passed back through the crowds until her voice cut through everything else. My eyes finally landed on a girl in the corner, standing behind a booth that looked like all the others. Flyers, papers, clipboards, and even a goldfish bowl full of candies were laid out, beckoning hopeless suckers like me. But it wasn't the freebies that had me captivated. It was the fair angel, and the strange desire to hear her laugh again.

But I slowed my approach, willing my feet to the ground. What exactly did it say at her table? *"CASA volunteers needed! Be a child's advocate today!"*

So, she not only laughed like an angel, but she acted like one, too. I scoffed. I had no business looking directly at her, let alone going over and trying to strike up a conversation. Had I not already learned my lesson that there was nothing here for me, least of all an attractive girl with a heart of gold?

Turning away, I rubbed at the hollow ache in my chest. *If only I hadn't come.*

I WAS the only one waiting at the bus stop, and I hoped I hadn't just missed it. I wasn't sure how long it was until the next one if I had. The sky outside was darker and the wind had finally picked up. Any minute now, the clouds would overflow with rain, and I didn't want to be out here when that happened.

One by one, as tendrils of envy ate away at me, people poured out of the building, headed to the parking lot, and drove away. All those people didn't know how lucky they were. I was fixated on imagining all the things I would give to have my car keys back, when a certain curly-haired blonde stepped out. Her arms were full and the wind, which had not let up but instead gotten worse, drilled away at her and her cargo. The milk crate she carried was full and losing pieces off the top, print-outs and pamphlets from the look of it, at a rate faster than she could save them.

A release of compressed air snagged my attention, and I turned my gaze away from her. The bus was finally heading toward me and preparing to stop.

Turning my back on the bus, I made a snap decision I might later come to regret. Breaking into a jog, I left the idea of leaving just yet behind.

"Here, let me help you," I said, almost shouting against the wind. I bent down where her stuff had collected long enough to be grabbed, and had to ignore the rest. "Why don't we head back inside for a minute so you can adjust your things?"

As I propped the door open with my foot, I held my arms out for her crate. Her hair was beautiful chaos, the wind stretching her tight ringlets in haphazard streaks across her face. For a moment, she merely stood there, somehow doing more than just looking back at me. Something about the way our eyes met ignited me within, making me feel alive with energy akin to the growing storm.

I have to know this girl.

BIRDIE

8

THERE WAS SOMETHING FAMILIAR ABOUT THE BOY WHO HELPED me. Something downright captivating. It took me a minute of watching him like a fool to snap out of it and relinquish custody of my crate, after which I gratefully rushed back inside.

The wind *seriously* had it out for me. The moment I stepped outside of the building, arms fully loaded with everything I'd packed up from the table, a monolithic breeze blew right through me, taking some of my things with it. Not to mention what it must've done to my hair. *Ugh!*

But the gentleman who came to my rescue had left me more awestruck than the storm. Rain began pelting the glass just as the door closed behind him. He walked to the seating area and placed my crate down on a chair, and I couldn't believe I'd so completely forgotten my manners.

I held my hand out. "Thank you so much, Mister…?"

"Grandy," he said, accepting my delicate shake.

"Nice to meet you, Mr. Grandy. I'm Birdie Jo. You can call me that, or just plain Birdie will do." I smiled. "One more gust would've knocked me off my feet for sure. I thank you for your quick chivalry."

"Don't mention it." He rubbed the back of his head, looking flustered. It was cute. "I don't think you'll be getting your other pages back though."

"Lucky for me, they'll biodegrade. I'm not going to go running out there to fetch them." I smoothed out my hair and clothing as best I could, then began carefully piling things back in my crate, biggest and heaviest things on top. He hadn't moved, so he was still standing right beside me, his spiced cinnamon scent surrounding me, and his looming figure sending a chill through me. "Were you here for the job fair?"

Concealing his now free hands in his pockets, he stammered. Wow, he really looked sheepish, bless his heart. "Well, I, uh..."

The pinkish tint dusting his cheekbones gave him a vulnerability that his tough-looking exterior couldn't support. He was tall, dark, and handsome, if ever I'd seen it. Nearly black hair swept over his forehead, providing a stunning hooded contrast to stunning blue eyes. I couldn't put my finger on why he looked familiar, but that wasn't a surprise in a big town like Corpus Christi. Maybe he just had one of those faces, but that couldn't be. I'd remember a face like his, all sharp and perfectly formed. The more I stared, the more that—

Crap! Staring again, really? *That's enough of that, Birdie Jo.*

Maybe he didn't notice. I twisted away, fidgeting with my now-perfected crate. I was going to thank him and make a quick exit, but the words died on my tongue as our phones, one after the other, went off like a siren.

Because it *was* a siren.

Russell gaped at the words flashing on our screens. "Tropical storm warning, take immediate shelter."

Panic danced its fingers up my spine, heating my neck and face at the same time it chilled my heart. Storms were not my favorite.

I very specifically paid attention to the weather predictions, like how the hurricane brewing off the Gulf Coast was not going to turn into anything on shore except an unimpressive storm or two until the weekend winds kicked it out.

"Oh, Lord in Heaven. There's no way. The news said—"

With an electrical choking sound, the building went dark, and the loss of power quelled my statement. Outside, the wind howled. Debris scurried around the parking lot like an intrusion of disturbed locusts. We heard commotion down where the job fair was still closing up in the Convention Hall. A startling bolt of lightning struck as though right in the parking lot beside us, dispelling any doubt that this storm, whatever it was *supposed* to be, was now a bad one, and we were caught in it.

RUSSELL

9

I GUESS THE WEATHER AMOUNTED TO SOMETHING AFTER ALL, huh, Dad?

I pocketed my phone, taking in the disarray outside. "We need to go. It looks like things are about to get a lot worse up here."

"I need to get to my car," she said with panic, leaving behind her crate and bolting back toward the door.

"Wait, stop." I grabbed her wrist and she whipped around. "Sorry, what I meant was, we need to take shelter from the storm, not run out into the middle of it. You're going to have to stay with me for a bit. Okay?" I spoke gently while hoping to maintain a firm stance.

Her chest rose and fell with a heavy, determined breath. "Then we need to look for a basement. We need to be at the lowest point possible."

I nodded. Then, instead of letting her go, I threaded our fingers together and walked her beside me to the help desk. I tapped my free hand against it. "Do you have basement access here?" I asked the unnerved man behind it.

He looked a shade or two lighter than I presumed was

normal, rightly petrified like the rest of us, but he nodded. "Yes, down the hall."

"Well, you heard the lady. Let's go."

The receptionist grabbed a flashlight from under the desk and came around it. "This way."

Following close behind him, I was soon met with resistance.

"Wait, I don't know—" Her protest was cut short by shattering glass and the shrieking of the storm, blowing in through the now broken front doors behind us. Wrapping myself around her like a shield, I felt a couple of sharp nicks in my back.

Birdie Jo was shivering. "Hey," I said, standing back, rubbing my hands down her arms. "You're okay. We're all fine here. But the rest of that glass is next, and there's a whole lot of it left. We need to go downstairs now."

By then, there was a line of stragglers behind us.

"It's this way," the receptionist called out, before finally taking the lead.

Keeping Birdie Jo tucked safely into my side, I ignored the stinging in my back. It was probably fine, and I didn't want to scare her further. The girl was absolutely freaked.

When I arrived at the job fair earlier, I pretty much knew I would be rejected by every employer in sight. But after that, after deciding to leave the bus stop and stay behind to help a girl I didn't know, I couldn't have guessed how anything else would play out. As we began the descent into the basement, and she burrowed closer to me, I smiled into the darkness. Today didn't feel like a total loss after all.

~

"Careful," I said, pulling her along behind me. I could feel her strained breathing against the back of my neck. "We're fine down here."

"Maybe we shouldn't actually go to the basement. What if it floods?"

"We're not in a surge zone here, but we've gotta pick our battles, and my gut says glass wins. We are best off away from all those windows." She didn't respond, but I felt her falling curls tickle my skin as she nodded.

Right as we stepped back onto solid ground, she dropped my hand to hug herself. At my side, I flexed my palm and fingers, shaking some feeling back into them. Both of us moved out of the way for others to pass.

The light downstairs was dim, but from what I could see, there was a bunch of junk everywhere. Old school desks, stacked chairs, chalkboards on wheels, crates, and boxes upon boxes. There was only one small, rectangular window at the far end. Squealing, scraping noises of whatever was being dragged against it added to the creep factor.

"Then I'm going to stay as far from *that* as I can get," she declared, going over to the furthest corner. She slid down the wall right as another strike of lightning lit up the entire room. The loud boom that followed made her yelp, hands flying to cover her ears. "I hate thunder," she whispered into her knees. Poor thing was terrified. "Is this because I was eager to leave? Did you hold me back because I was wrong to not have stayed behind longer?"

I don't think she's talking to me.

I walked over and sat down beside her. "Thunder doesn't bother me. It's just a storm and it'll pass. We've seen worse, haven't we?"

"Not in a long time." Her voice got quiet, spurring my curiosity. "We always go back north to wait out the hurricanes."

"But you have some experience with big bad storms?" She was quick on the draw when it came to knowing how to find shelter upstairs. And she seemed shaken up enough to prove this wasn't her first rodeo.

"Yes. Mostly the ones that come with tornadoes. I don't hate much in this life, but I *hate* them."

That would explain her adorable little accent. It was a soft twang that definitely didn't come from around here, and neither did tornadoes. "Sounds like you've got some stories."

Another flash of light and boom of thunder had her pressing herself into me again, taking refuge against my shoulder.

"We're okay. This isn't even a hurricane or tornado, just some rogue tropical storm. It'll be over soon." I tried to sound confident, though I wasn't sure. It seemed to make little difference in how scared she was. Succumbing once again to the urge to protect her, I was raising my arm to cradle her again, but she straightened up abruptly, startling me instead. The movement had me wincing at the mild pain I'd nearly forgotten about, which, of course, she noticed when I leaned forward some.

"Oh! Are you hurt?"

Not wanting to sound whiny, I tried to shrug it off and deflect. "Not much. I'll be fine." But she was already carefully turning me around to inspect my back.

"You *are* hurt. There's blood on your jacket. Can you take it off?"

I thought it was ridiculous, but I did as she asked.

"Can you, uh, lift your shirt a little?" Her tone was soft and earnest. Not the typical fashion in which I was used to being propositioned.

"Really?"

"There might be glass stuck in your skin."

Reluctantly, I pulled my shirt from the back of the neck and hoisted it to my shoulders, questioning my sanity a little bit. This was just a random basement, not some war triage. It wasn't that serious. But my pretend nurse gingerly swiped her fingers over two sore spots, and surprised me when she said, "I got it. Make sure you clean those when you get home."

Nodding, I turned and shrugged my shirt back down. "Thanks. I'll take care of it."

She cleared her throat and looked to be picking lint off her dress. "So… Did you come for the job fair? You never got a chance to say."

Either she only just truly noticed what she was doing, or she was opting for distraction. But, no more storm talk. Got it. "Didn't I?" But I didn't really want to talk about me either.

"No."

"Oh, well, yeah, I came to the job fair."

"Are you a STLR graduate?"

"What's that?"

A cute smile budded across her face. "That answers that question," she said. "STLR stands for South Texas Life Recovery."

"Gotcha. It must be one of those religious *'get your life on track with Jesus'* places, right? I actually did hear about it while—" I swallowed what I was going to say next. There was no reason to tell this girl my life story, no matter how cute she was. "—a while back. Wait, are *you* from STLR?" She didn't look like someone who belonged there, but maybe she was its most glowing example of success.

She smoothed down her wayward locks. "In a way. I started

off as a volunteer, but I'm on the payroll now. I was manning a booth for one of our partnership programs."

Right. So, not a fellow degenerate, but an employee. Lovely. The fact that I'd ever, even fleetingly, entertained the idea of pursuing her made me want to melt away. At least in the darkness, which had become more intense as we spoke, I could hide embarrassment as well as I could a smile.

Her back went rod-straight right as her head shot up. She patted herself down, checking all her pockets. "Oh, no."

"What?"

"My phone… I guess I dropped it when I left all my other stuff behind."

"That sucks. Did you need to call someone? Do you want to borrow mine?"

Her fathomless doe eyes peered right through me. "Could I, if you're sure you don't mind?"

Retrieving it from the inside pocket of my discarded leather jacket, I unlocked and handed it over. "My phone is your phone."

She smiled gently. "Thanks." Then, she stood up, brushed off her dress again, and took a few cautious steps in the other direction, and I ignored her while she made her call.

I leaned back against the hard wall as the little pains in my back reminded me of how ridiculous I was. I felt ashamed of myself for all the things I would've happily given her the moment she looked at me with gratitude and appreciation, and all she'd asked for was my phone.

Had *anyone* ever looked at me with that much sincerity before?

I could answer that—nope.

And I doubted anyone ever would again.

BIRDIE

10

I paced back and forth, my mind whirling and temples starting to twinge. I may not have grown up in the Great Plains, but I'd seen my fair share of dangerous skies. There was nothing like hearing a warning siren blast through the town, knowing you only had minutes to get below ground. It haunted my dreams even still, and I considered myself grown, but every time I heard that stupid sound, I became a scared little girl again. Even if it was a fraction of what it used to be, as it came out of a cell phone instead of from big sirens outside.

But right now, being scared was not serving me. The pain in my neck that I'd first felt a few weeks ago had come back, only going away when I was distracted. "Everyone said this storm wouldn't last long, Lord. Yet here we still are, trapped down here like rats. What is that about?" I asked God.

"Why don't you try to take a nap? It might help pass the time." My handsome hero kept his voice even, watching me as though I were on the verge of complete self-destruction. He was another shocking point of contention for my poor brain to process right now.

"I couldn't if my life depended on it." Since the storm first hit, he had been by my side, offering comfort and support. It was a strange feeling, almost causing me guilt because of how much I liked it. It hadn't been all that long since Nick and I broke up, but there I was for half the day, nestling up against someone I didn't even know out of petrified desperation.

And he was so good at letting me nestle.

Onward I paced, the fingers of one hand rubbing my aching temples. My heeled sandals hit the cement floor with anxious speed. I directed my voice to the One above again. "To top it all off, You trapped me down here with a bunch of strangers." I practically whispered the last bit, hoping not to offend anyone who might be listening to my rant.

"Ah, but you and I aren't strangers. We introduced ourselves upstairs."

He was right about that, and it only proved how far my manners had really slipped today. "Now that you bring it up, I don't know anything but your last name. Why don't you tell me more about yourself?"

"I need a job."

With deteriorating patience, I ceased my walking back and forth to shoot him a pleading look.

He chuckled, and the sound was as soothing as it was lovely. "Fine, I'll play. I'm Russell Benjamin Grandy, nineteen-year-old firstborn son of Delia and James, born and raised here in Crapus Chrusti. My favorite color is red, and I'm a Virgo." Smirking at me, he urged, "Now you."

I channeled my pageant voice. "I'm Birdie Jo Rene Lewis MacLean, and I am eighteen years old. I originate from Texarkana, Texas. I love every color, but pink is the best, and I'm a Christian." The last one was a smidge poetic, if I did say so myself.

"Wow. I've never met anyone with a name that long."

"Are you jealous, Russell Benjamin Grandy? Do you wish you had more than the standard three?"

"Nope," he said on another wave of quiet laughter. "I'm good."

Studying him, I still couldn't shake the feeling that I knew him from somewhere. "You know, you look awfully familiar."

He peeked at me from under his fallen hair. "I do?"

"What school did you go to?"

"CCHS."

"That must be it then. I'm sure we saw each other in the hallways. What year did you graduate? Who are your friends?"

On a shrug, he said, "No one you'd know."

I wanted to challenge him, because how could he be so sure about something like that, even if we did have a huge graduating class, but it seemed like a hot-button issue for him. It would do no good to poke the bear right now, not when I needed his support and the peace he gave me.

While he fidgeted with a pencil he'd plucked from a nearby box, I calculated my next move. The storm outside continued, and service on his phone had been spotty. I doubted we'd get much entertainment out of it, and it was best to preserve his battery. But at least my mom knew I was okay, and I knew that she was okay, too.

Choosing friendly over fear, I swung my arms and sauntered over. One spot was as good as any, so I billowed out my dress, carefully taking it down with me so I could sit on the back and cover myself with the front. I blew up a bit of dust and we both coughed. "Sorry," I muttered.

He was looking down at my wrist where I'd placed my hands

in my lap. His face scrunched, and I realized he was checking out my charm bracelet. A gift from my parents after our move. A guilt gift of sorts, perhaps, but I loved it.

"What all do you have on there? Is that a horseshoe?"

"Sure is. I've been collecting these for years, since before my dad left. I have different ones for various things I love and important times."

"That sounds nice. Want to tell me about them?"

I took the hint and dove in, talking about the charms to divert myself, and Russell seemed interested enough. After, it got quiet again as the storm raged on, and I soon felt my anxiety ramping back up.

I dared to look at him and saw he was gazing pensively across the room at our co-inhabitants. "What do you think their stories are?" He nodded to them.

Taking them in one by one, I came up blank. There was one lady and three men, all with matching expressions of boredom. They looked like normal folk to me, anyone who might want a job in this congested town. "I don't know, I've never been good at storytelling. What do *you* think?" He definitely appeared to have something in mind.

He rubbed his chin, eyes narrowed. Then, he lowered his voice. "I think she's recently divorced with two kids under five. She's here because her ex-husband ran off with her best friend, and they refuse to leave the house she got in the settlement. Now she's forced to start over. She'll probably fall in love with one of those guys, in fact."

I gasped, properly sucked in. "Oh, yes! The storm is their Meet Cute!"

He looked quizzically at me. "Their what?"

"Meet Cute. It's an unofficial literary term for how the main characters in a romance meet each other. It always happens in some kind of cute way. Something often unrealistic but totally memorable."

"Didn't we just meet like that?"

His eyes were on me. I could feel his stare like a ton of bricks, and I had to play off my sudden shiver. "What about those two guys?" I ignored his comment, gluing my focus onto something else.

When he finally looked away, he got back into character. "They're long-lost brothers, but they won't know it until they strike up a conversation."

"Those two don't look close to talking." In fact, they were on opposite sides of the room, fiddling quietly on their phones. The third guy—the single mom's future man, apparently—was sitting against a wall like we were, his arms folded as he snoozed. The woman kept sneaking glances at him, and for a second, I wondered. I couldn't stop myself from smiling a little. The idea was adorable, as I, for one, as a voracious reader could attest to, but things like Meet Cutes and Inciting Incidents and Third Act Breakups just didn't happen in real life.

"They already did talk, you just didn't see it. Right now, they're angrily texting their parents for lying to them for the last twenty-some years."

In my excitement, I grabbed hold of his arm. "What if they're actually plotting their own parent trap right this very minute?"

"They probably are. Look at the way they're typing." We did. And in the meantime, I realized I was touching him and hastily dropped my hand.

"Oh, yeah, they're definitely conspiratorial," I agreed, feeling cold yet oddly warm. I glanced at where my hand touched him a second ago. "Hey, I just now noticed you have tattoos." Flames began at his wrist and climbed up his forearms, all the way around. I studied them, wondering if he had any more. "Very cool looking. Do they mean anything?"

"Not really."

"That's a bummer. Tattoos are permanent, so shouldn't they have some kind of meaning? I mean, if they're going to be stuck on you for life, at least make them special, right?"

"Well, gee whiz, ma'am. Next time I get one, I'll be sure to do that, just for you."

"Oh, yeah? That's exciting. What will it be?"

He rolled his eyes, as if that would ever happen. "Why don't you pick?"

"That's easy. Roses."

"Flowers, really? You think that's the kind of thing I want *permanently* applied to my body?"

I innocently raised my shoulders, a silly grin on my face. "You said I could pick."

"And I look like a flower guy to you?"

"Actually, roses happen to suit you perfectly. They smell and look good, but their built-in defenses will get you if you don't handle them carefully."

"You think you know me that well already, do you?"

"I could be totally off-base, but I don't believe I am. Regardless, I think it would be a neat contrast to those flames of yours. A compliment and a contradiction."

He hiked a brow. "Kinda like what you just said about me."

His teasing banter left me to let my mind wander a little too much. Even if I were one of those people who believed in such fairytale nonsense as love at first sight or Meet Cutes, this would not count. Besides, no matter how appealing or interesting a guy was, they all had the power to hurt and abandon.

You know the best way to avoid being hurt and abandoned, Birdie Jo? Stay focused on anything and everything else. Do not lose focus on what matters!

At long last, the storm was starting to lighten up, and we'd be on our way soon. As attractive as he was, and as much as his gruff attitude fascinated me, I would never see Russell Benjamin Grandy again after today.

RUSSELL

11

I DIDN'T LIKE ALL THE QUESTIONS, EVEN IF IT WAS *HER* ASKING. AND yet, when she asked, I found myself answering. I didn't mean to get as close to spilling my sordid story as I had, and narrowly escaped telling her just enough to scare her off. Although, maybe that wasn't such a big deal. After this, we would go our separate ways, and this whole storm-basement experience would be nothing but a memory to look back on. At least I could make myself interesting to her, less easily forgotten.

"I'm sorry, Russell, I didn't mean to make any judgments with the whole tattoo-flower thing."

"No, it's fine. You're pretty spot on. I do smell really good."

She looked horrified until she realized I was teasing her. Then she nudged me with her shoulder. "Very funny."

"You really want to know why I was at the job fair today?"

"If you want to tell me."

I didn't, but I would. "I just got out of prison not too long ago, and I really need a job."

She looked at me. "I don't believe any of the employers here discriminate based on criminal history. That would disqualify so many. Half the people who come to these events and apply for jobs are former STLR graduates."

I shook my head. "I didn't even get far enough to tell anyone about that. It's the fact that I don't have a diploma."

She made a sound of understanding. "So, you need your GED. That's no problem. I can get you in touch with people. We can make it happen."

"No, thanks, I really don't want any charity."

"It's help. It's what I do. Here, give me your phone again?"

Skeptical, I handed it to her. She fiddled with it, tapping at the screen for a moment, then handed it back. "Well, I tried to put my number in, but it won't let me. Says I need a passcode or something." She looked around, eventually digging into one of the boxes we sat beside. She happened to find a stack of pencils and spiral notebooks, which she tore a page from. "I feel kinda bad. I hope they don't miss one sheet."

"I don't think anyone has bothered with these supplies since our parents were kids."

She giggled, scribbling her number down before handing it to me. "Let me know when you're ready to study, and I'll personally make sure you pass."

Momentarily diluted by her enthusiasm, I accepted the paper. Her name, Birdie Jo MacLean, was written in a feminine script, seeming to me very appropriate for a girl like her. And there was her phone number, something I planned to forget completely about. "Yeah, sure," I said, lying through my teeth.

Rather than subject myself to more humiliation, I would find my own way to get a GED and job. Birdie Jo was a Christian, so that was strike one. She was unearthly beautiful, which was strike two. And because of those two things, she was probably stuck up once you got to know her—strike three. She was simply not my type, so it was best if I didn't indulge myself—I mean her—any further.

After the storm passed enough, Birdie Jo and I, along with the other stragglers, started the long-awaited journey topside. Of everyone who grew weary of hiding out down there, she was the first one up the stairs. Aside from being wet with random trash and tree bits everywhere, things seemed good and quiet outside. Certainly quiet enough to get the heck out of there.

With my jacket draped over one arm, I ascended behind her, then walked with my free hand on the small of Birdie's back, just in case. Though everything looked quiet, you never knew. Plus, I had to be sure she watched where she was walking. It wasn't that I wanted to stay close before never seeing her again.

"Be careful where you step."

Picking a careful path, I led us to her crate. "Let me check it for glass first," I said, breaking apart from her to walk ahead. Digging through it carefully, I removed anything that didn't belong. In the process, I plucked out her phone and handed it over. "I believe you needed this. It looks fine."

With palpable relief, she snapped it up fast. "Oh, thank you!" Then she hugged me, as though I had anything to do with it. When she pulled back, our eyes were drawn together once again. In the small streams of sunshine that broke through the dissipating clouds, she became even more ethereal than before.

"Uh, I think I got all the glass. But just to be safe, I'll carry it out for you. If you want."

"I would appreciate that."

"Well then," I said, picking up her box. "After you."

Taking the lead, Birdie traversed away from the shards that were now being swept up. When we crossed the invisible threshold of the building and onto the sidewalk, scattered debris and a cool breeze with partial cloud coverage was all that remained of the storm. Hopefully, the roads didn't give her any trouble getting home.

We stopped in front of a silver Volkswagen. "This is me. I'll get the trunk."

Once I had the crate placed in there, I closed it and turned to her.

"Thank you so much, for everything. You were really good to me today. I'm sorry I was such a scaredy-cat." She laughed nervously.

"It was nothing."

"Could I give you a ride somewhere? It's the least I can do."

"No thanks, my dad is already on his way." I fibbed.

"Are you sure?"

"Yep. It's all good."

"Okay. Well, get home safely and don't forget to take care of your back. And call me when you're ready for that GED." She winked and it made a twinkling sound. Or those were her keys coming out of her pocket. Either way, she was mesmerizing. "Bye, Russ."

Russ. I nodded, stepping out of the way of her departure. "Bye, Birdie Jo," I said to her empty parking spot after she'd driven away.

Looking toward the bus stop, I released a deep sigh. She might have appeared genuine in wanting to see me again, but her offer was probably only made for one reason, borne of a *'Christianly duty'* to fix people or whatever. I knew better than to think differently. I couldn't bother to get mixed up with people who thought—accurately—that they were better than me. I needed to stick to people my own speed.

Turning my back on the bus stop yet again today, I decided that mode of transportation wouldn't do. I would need a lift after all. Heading back toward the building, I found the receptionist just as he was leaving.

"Hey," I called out with a wave of my hand. "Could I possibly get a ride?"

"Where you going?"

"To the west side." To Kevin's house. It was time I got reacquainted with old friends and reminded myself who I was.

I had been dismissed a thousand and one times at the job fair, and then treated like a charity case by Birdie Jo Whatever-Whatever, after being stuck in a basement by a freak storm we weren't even supposed to get, so I thought I deserved a moment to unwind.

After the receptionist, whose name was Raul, dropped me off in front of Kevin's house, I was finally able to breathe. Things were normal here in this neighborhood where my best friend lived. I could make things make sense again, and work the beautiful angel out of my system. But the longer I knocked, I was forced to accept that Kevin wasn't home. His truck was in the drive, but he had to be out. I couldn't call him so decided on another route. There was one place I could go where I knew they'd be home, and it wasn't too far.

I set my sights on Dominick's house and got to walking. I had no idea what he would be up to after a day like today, but I sure hoped he had enough to go around.

BIRDIE

12

My mom was in the driveway before I could get out of the car. "I'm so glad you're home! Are you okay?" She hugged me too tightly, pushing more blood through my pounding head.

"I'm fine," I said, patting her back.

"I know you don't like storms. I was so worried, and you weren't answering your phone."

"I told you what happened. I just forgot my phone in the craziness."

"I know, but I'm glad you're okay." She held me at arm's length to inspect me. "*Are* you okay? You look a little pale."

"You just squeezed the life out of me. Of course I'm pale." I laughed. "But besides really needing a shower, I'm totally fine."

"If you're sure..."

"I am." *Liar, liar, pants on fire.* "I'm going to shower and then call the girls before I dig into some homework."

"All right. I will bring some dinner up when it's ready."

"Thanks, Mama."

I thought if I didn't get inside and run my head under some

soothing heat, it might explode. That was far too much excitement for one day.

I LAID PROPPED up in bed after my shower, my head showing marginal improvement. Pressing on and accepting no less than the *'fine'* I claimed to be, I went ahead with our weekly FaceTime call, clipping my phone onto my nightstand and calling the girls.

"So, how are you guys?" Sarah asked Jenna and me, the only ones who were in town. "Kevin told me there was a pretty decent storm today."

"You can say that again. I still have no power," Jenna griped.

"It wasn't so bad at my house, but it made landfall right over me while I was downtown, and it was crazy."

"Oh, yeah! You had that expo thing today, didn't you?" recalled Sammy.

"Job fair, yes. And it went great, too, until the storm hit right as I was leaving. Literally, I felt the wind change and then *bam*—there it was. I hadn't even made it all the way out the door before all my stuff started blowing around."

"That sounds intense," Jenna remarked.

"It was. But then a Prince Charming showed up and helped me get my stuff back together, and everyone's phone alarms went off, and then part of the glass blew out, and he—"

Sammy had her hands up, waving for me to stop. "Wait, wait, wait! You're going too fast. Rewind. Who is Prince Charming?"

"Just a guy from the event who came rushing to my rescue when the wind tried to blow me away."

"Ooh," they all squealed, in typical female fashion. I couldn't help but laugh with them.

"Tell us more," they insisted.

"We introduced ourselves, and... Where was I? Oh, yeah, so then the glass blew out and flew everywhere, and this guy seriously threw himself against me, and then those of us left in the lobby went down into the basement and sat there for *hours* waiting for this thing to pass."

"Wow! That's some adventure," Sarah remarked. "I'm glad you're okay."

"Me too." *Is Russell? I hope his cuts from that explosion aren't bothering him.*

"Some rando meat-shielded himself for you? Dang, girl."

Sammy's fascinated question made me laugh. "I know, right?"

"What was his name?" she asked.

"Russell Benjamin Grandy," I said primly, almost giggling to myself.

Sarah gasped. "You said Russell Grandy? Tall, dark hair, blue eyes, surly attitude?"

"Yeah. Do you know him?"

"That's Kevin's best friend. Don't you remember him from that awful party at Dan's house?"

"*That's* where I knew him from! I knew he looked familiar, but I couldn't figure out why."

"I don't want to burst your bubble, Birdie, but be careful. He's the reason Kevin got tangled up with Tanner's shady stuff in the first place."

"Oh." Oh, *crap*. "Well, it's not like I'll be running into him again."

"I hate to say it, but for your sake, if he's anything like he used to be, you're better off that way."

Just when I was enjoying the conversation, when I was finally feeling like my lighter self, the darkness came rushing back in again. Of course, the first guy who made me forget about what a loser I was becoming wasn't all that truthful about himself. Why hadn't I questioned more about why he had been in prison? Did I truly possess so little awareness or instinct?

At least it wouldn't be hard to stay away from him. I didn't know where he lived (and I wouldn't be asking) or how to get in touch with him, as I'd only given him my number. And if the look on his face when I gave it to him was any hint, he wouldn't be dialing it anytime soon.

RUSSELL

13

My parents could remove phone numbers from my phone, but not memories from my head. I still knew where my friends lived. I scaled the familiar steps, knocked, then stuffed one hand in my pocket as I waited, jacket still draped lazily over one shoulder. The door, featuring an outer crack in the glass and an unforgettable hinge squeal, was soon thrown open as Dominick's little sister greeted me.

"Wow, look who it is. We heard about your arrest. Don't tell me they let you out for good behavior." Kimber crossed her bangle-adorned sassy arms over her spaghetti-strapped chest. Her face was made up with black eyeliner and dark lipstick. At seventeen years old, she never did a good job of looking her age.

Part of me couldn't help but compare her to Birdie Jo. The two of them must've been only a year or so apart, yet there was nothing else similar about them. Not physically, and definitely not spiritually. Kimber was the kind of girl I normally went after, and who went after me. People as different as Birdie and me had no business mixing.

Anyway, if *she* was opening the door, that confirmed their

parents weren't home, and I was already late for the party. I side-stepped her, welcoming myself in. "They did, actually."

She scoffed, "Don't know you at all, do they?" She smirked, her teasing expression a reminder of memories past. "He's down-stairs." She waved before turning away, having already lost interest in teasing me.

"I know," I said, forced to follow her.

"I know you know," she called over her shoulder.

Down we headed, into the second basement of the day, through a portal of sorts. How could so much change at my house in six months, yet everything was still exactly the same here?

I could smell what Dominick was doing before I saw him, but I soon reached the bottom of the stairs and there he was, indulging away on the couch. A small pang of envy shot through me, almost taking me by surprise. I'd thought since being forced to dry out in the last six months, I didn't miss any of it, but maybe I did.

Kimber plopped herself down on the other side of the couch, so now they were both facing away from me. Her clueless brother still hadn't noticed me yet. With spirited intent, I slapped Dominick on the shoulders. "Hey, Dom!"

He jumped, shouting a choice expression while nearly burning his lap when he dropped what he'd been holding. "Russ, man! I don't believe it. When did you get sprung?" He held his hand out for our long-used bro-bump.

"Recently."

He exhaled a puff of smoke. "Wow, so fresh. How was it in there?"

Disgusting. Lonely. Terrifying. "Nothing I couldn't handle. But tell me, what's been going on around here? Who's hanging out lately?"

"Hardly anyone in a while. Believe it or not, it's been pretty quiet."

"No way. You're holding out on me."

"Nah, for real. It was different this summer, and a lot of the old crew has moved on." Dom worked on another puff, and when he offered the next one to me, it was second nature to accept it. Pressing the familiar to my lips, I filled my lungs to the brim, overdoing it on purpose. I coughed and sputtered like a noob, thanks to my imposed sobriety. Kimber snorted a judgmental laugh, barely deigning to look at me from over her phone.

"Jeez, can't hold your smoke anymore?" Dominick inquired with his own gritty laugh. "It really has been a while."

Yeah, it sure had. Nothing in my world was the same as I left it six months ago, not even my own lungs. Was there really nothing I had control over anymore?

He patted me on the back, and I jerked. "Whoa, what did I do?"

Standing up, I peeled out of my shirt and tossed it on the arm of the couch. I turned around to show him. "How does it look?"

"Dang, boy. What happened?"

"Is it bad?" It couldn't be. My leather jacket had taken the brunt of it all.

"Go look." He waved his hand over toward a full-length mirror, where his tattoo clients could admire his handiwork.

Kimber unfolded herself from the couch to hand me a wide hand-held mirror. "Pretty impressive."

Angling the mirror, I took a look for myself. There seemed to be a lot more cuts than I would've guessed, most of them already clotted over. One right below the shoulder blade was still leaking, leaving a smudged trail of new blood, but none of it looked deep or concerning. Birdie had removed the glass, so these cuts were just an irritation more than anything.

"It's fine. Nothing a shower won't fix."

"Feel free," Kimber said. "I can help."

I grabbed my shirt, bunching it up to dab away the worst of it. "I'm good. Thanks." She shrugged, going back to the couch.

I tossed my shirt into the trash bin and took another look at myself. I noticed a splotch of red on my arm, intermingling with my monochrome flames. Roses suited me perfectly, Birdie Jo told me. I remembered her saying, *'They smell and look good, but their built-in defenses will get you if you don't handle them carefully.'*

Thought my tattoos ought to mean something, did she? Okay then. *Thanks for the idea, angel.*

"Grab your gun and some red ink, Dom."

"Get a sudden burst of inspiration?"

"You could say that."

I TOOK my time walking home, constantly aware of the burning sensation around my right forearm, tucked securely inside my jacket, and I laughed to myself. Since I wouldn't see Miss Birdie Jo again, it's not like I'd have to answer to her about it. But something about her had stuck with me, and now, there were her red roses, forever intertwined with my flames that would always serve as a reminder that we'd met.

My house finally came into view. The living room light was on, and I already knew I was in for it. Walking through the front door, I met the angry glares of my parents. *Ooh, I was in troouuble.*

Mom put her hand to her nose. "Even if you didn't smell as terrible as you do, did you really think we wouldn't find out?"

"Find out what?" I made a quick play for innocence, just for fun.

"We watched your location the whole time you were gone. You were supposed to come straight home."

Dad stepped forward. "Do you have any idea how this will affect your probation? And what happened at the job fair?"

"It won't. It'll be a month before I have to see Harold again. As for the job fair, a whole lot of nothing, which is fitting, because that's exactly what I am."

Dad was not amused. "Why would you say a thing like that?"

"Because it was a big fat *'NO'* from every single company there."

"Explain."

"Apparently, my hand-shaking, shining personality wasn't enough to persuade anyone to hire me without a diploma. Thanks for making me go, Dad. I hadn't fully grasped the level of my stupidity until then."

He glared at me, his gaze growing hard. "I'm not going to continue this conversation while you're like this. Go. Come see me when the fog clears from your brain." And then he was gone, disappearing down the hall and into his study.

Part of me wanted to laugh and part of me realized I shouldn't. For once, my reasonable side won out, and I traipsed down the same hall and into the kitchen. From the cabinet above the coffee maker, I grabbed the first pod I touched. If it was coffee, it would do.

While that brewed, I glanced around for something to eat, spotting a loaf of bread. Score. Carbs. *Mmm.* Tearing into my mom's homemade sourdough, my eyes closed in reverence. This stuff was so good. Probably one of the things I missed the most while locked away, but I would never tell her that. Why give her the impression I appreciated the things she did? Mom hated me, so I would continue hating her, too.

This bread sure did taste good, though.

The coffee was done and smelled amazing. I took my bounty to the island table and sat down, resting on my elbows. The way my jacket rubbed against my skin reminded me I had no shirt on beneath it. I ignored that.

Sugar would make this mug of brew taste better, but it wouldn't do anything for my head. I needed grounding. I needed simple and straightforward, so I nursed my black coffee and chewed my bread.

The minutes went by, and the more I drank, the hotter I got. I wanted to take off my jacket, but I wasn't ready to explain my shirtless-ness or expose my arm. I wanted to keep Birdie's flowers a secret for a little bit longer. I liked nobody else knowing it was there. At the moment, when I didn't know I needed any, its presence gave me a small amount of comfort. Roses weren't me, though they were an ironic contrast between her and I. She was the beautiful, sweet rose. And I was the thorn, as well as the flames that surrounded us, threatening to consume.

Why was I even thinking about her still? Why did I get this tattoo? I sighed, hanging my head over my mug. Maybe I shouldn't have gone to Dominick's.

Darn you, Kevin. Why weren't you home?

The more my head cleared, the more I felt like crap. I hadn't indulged in anything in so long. Rather than feeling excited about that, like I got to experience something exhilarating for the first time again, I actually felt… disappointed. If I were being honest with myself, no part of the night was any fun, except for my new ink. That, I somehow knew, I would never regret.

Rising from the stool, I left my mug behind. No sense in putting my dad off. Better go face the music. Heading to my father's study, I flicked a glance upward. Years of portraiture spanned the walls on the way there. My senior picture from last fall was the last one of me they'd hung. My own reflection taunted me, looking like a façade of what I was supposed to be. What my parents had wished I was.

I came up to the study and didn't have to knock.

"Come in and close the door," came my dad's voice. I stepped into the room and backed up against the door until I heard it click. My face was resigned to the doom I was in for.

"So," he said, staring me down with his hands folded over his lap. "You went to Dominick's." I felt his eyes on me but kept my gaze on the floor at the foot of his desk. "You don't have anything to say?"

"I should've known." I should've known they'd be tracking me like a wild hog. I should've known there would be no semblance of a second chance even from my own parents.

I should've known I'd let them down the first chance I got.

He released an audible breath. "Is it that you enjoyed your time in prison so much you're that eager to return?"

The eye-roll I had been barely subduing finally escaped.

"No, I'm serious. Look at me." He waited until I did. His gaze was demanding, nailing the shadow of my guilt to the floor where I stood. "We asked you for a sliver of responsibility, Russell. It's only been one week since you got out, and you're already betraying that freedom. What were you thinking?"

"I was thinking that the day royally sucked and I just wanted to get out."

"There won't be much *'out'* to enjoy if you keep going back to everything that got you in trouble in the first place. You realize that, right? And that's exactly what your behavior is going to get you if you don't fix it. You're trying to get a job and get through probation. Do you even care about *any* of this? About your own future?"

If it's my future and life why don't they let me live it? "Yes, I do."

"Don't say it if you don't mean it. Don't tell us what you think we want to hear, because words alone will do you no good. This is something you're going to have to want for yourself because, apparently, keeping out of trouble is going to require a lot of actual work on your part."

"I got that."

"Does that mean you're going to work with us and not against us? And stop sneaking behind our backs?"

"Will I get my car back?"

"Eventually. Let's see if you can walk before you run this time. And again, only if you mean it."

"Yes, Dad. I mean it."

"All right then. Let's talk about the job situation. You need a GED, so you'll focus your efforts there. Did you happen to collect any information about how to get it while you were there today?"

"I did actually." Blonde curls flashed across my mind. "But..."

"Well, what is it?"

I reached into my pocket, pulling out the crumpled slip of paper Birdie gave me. "You'll have to add this number to my phone," I grumbled, handing it to him.

He nodded supportively. "Okay, but go take a shower. You really do smell awful." His anger having finally ebbed, he gave a fatherly wink, a sort of peace offering of his.

If there was only one up-side to everything, it was that I would be talking to my pretty blonde muse very soon.

RUSSELL & BIRDIE

14

RUSSELL

Hey. Birdie?

BIRDIE

Is that you, Russell Benjamin Grandy from Crapus Crusti?

RUSSELL

The one and only. How'd you know?

BIRDIE

You're the only person I've given my phone number to recently.

I admit, I didn't think I'd hear from you. I am surprised.

RUSSELL

Well, here I am. And as you might have guessed, I would like to take you up on your offer to help me get my GED.

BIRDIE

That's wonderful! I'm excited for you.

RUSSELL

My dad wants to know how much it'll be.

BIRDIE

Oh, I'm not charging you anything. It will be my honor to help you.

RUSSELL

Oh… kay… Thanks… I'll let him know.

BIRDIE

When do you want to start?

RUSSELL

As soon as possible. GED = Job = Need.

BIRDIE

Got it. I will let you know more after I talk to my boss. I have to see what kind of schedule I can arrange between work and school commitments.

RUSSELL

Sounds good, Birdie Jo. Talk to you soon.

BIRDIE

Yes, you will!

BIRDIE

15

I COULDN'T BELIEVE WHEN I HEARD FROM RUSSELL, BUT FOR ONCE, I didn't mind being wrong. Keeping my focus on him and his problems would help keep me from my own, which didn't even exist according to my doctors, but didn't go away according to my pain. So, really, I not only welcomed the distraction, but I was determined to thrive in it.

I sighed, resting my chin on my palm, twiddling a pencil with my other hand. I wondered who exactly would be sitting down at the table with me. Would it be the grumpy Russell who gave short, clipped responses when I asked questions, or would it be the personable and shockingly adorable Russell who gave me protection and peace in a unique moment of need?

Regardless, we were strangers, so it didn't make sense that my heart was doing silly loop-dee-loops in my chest as I waited, blood pumping at the thought of seeing him again.

'Didn't we just meet like that?' His words replayed in my head ever since he'd spoken them, and I had to physically shake myself to dislodge the thought. Russell and I did *not* have ourselves a Meet Cute.

And we were totally not about to have a second one.

Whatever did or didn't happen, I wished it would be soon, because the anticipation was killing me. And how could I forget even for a second about Sarah's warning that if he were anything like he used to be, I was better off never seeing him again? Oh, well. My offer to help happened first.

So, it made sense why he was at the job fair. Why I didn't remember him from graduation but still recognized him. He was Kevin's best friend, the one and only who got him into trouble with the law over Tanner's illegal business. It wouldn't be smart to overlook that. So why did he keep creeping into my thoughts?

I checked my watch for the tenth time. I had just decided to pull my book out and read until he decided to show when I saw a tall, dark figure come around a stack. Looking up—yep. It was him.

Shoving to my feet, I smiled brightly at him as he approached, and when his acknowledgment of me dawned, my throat felt tight. *Ridiculous. Lock it down, now.*

"So, it really is you. Birdie Jo Rene Lewis MacLean," he rasped, and a sly smile had formed.

He remembered. "As I live and breathe." I held my hand out to him. "Russell, it's really nice to see you."

"Is it?" he asked, either ignoring or not seeing my hand, before slugging his backpack onto the large wooden table. Then he sat down, only to look up at me.

I promptly sat in my own seat. "Of course it is. How have you been? How's your back?"

"Fine. And my back's fine. Just ready to get all this going."

I scrutinized him, absorbing his quick, deflecting comments. "You don't actually want to be here, do you?"

"What gave me away?"

I sighed, smiling with a reserved sort of sadness. "Look, Russ. We don't have to be best friends, but the least you could do is come with a better attitude. I'm here to help you. I want to be here. We can make it fun, or you can make it miserable. Without me. Which sounds better?"

"Oh, come on. It's not that serious."

"Which sounds better?" I demanded, my gaze piercing into his.

"Fun. Fun sounds better."

"Good, then I want your word that you'll try."

"Sure."

Not good enough. "Let's make it official." I held up my curled fist with my pinky sticking out.

He looked at my hand as though it were an alien. "You can't be serious. You want me to pinky swear?"

"I prefer the term pinky *promise,* and I don't just want it, I demand it." I held his questioning stare. Eventually, he sighed, sitting back in his chair with his arms crossed.

"No. That's dumb."

I started collecting my stuff. "Then I'm out. I'll apologize to your father for not being able to work with you. Good luck with your studying, Russell." He waited until I had pushed out of my chair and breezed past him to finally stop me.

"Wait." He gripped my wrist. The touch sent a tingle through me, but he only looked mad. I could practically see the fumes escaping his nostrils as he admitted defeat. "Fine."

"Fine what?" I asked with a downward flick of my lashes. I could accept no less than a direct, honest commitment here.

"Let's do the stupid pinky thing."

"I could refuse at your calling a solemn vow *'stupid',* but I won't hold it against you. *This* time." I held my hand out and smiled when he reached out his and linked our pinkies together. I stood taller, radiating with satisfaction. “All right then, now that that’s done…” I said, dropping my hand to let him off the hook. Literally. “How’s about we take our time and just hang out for a bit today. We’ll save diving into the deep end for tomorrow.”

“Sounds good to me.”

RUSSELL

16

I didn't release my breath until Birdie was once again sitting down. That was close. I'd never seen anyone get so passionate about something so ridiculous, but she truly wasn't going to back down. The girl wanted my word, and my pinky, so I gave it to her. I couldn't have her walking away when I'd already lowered and prepared myself to doing this in the first place.

As much as I had wanted to see her again, I didn't love the idea of her having to actually tutor me, like I was some dumb jock who couldn't keep my grades up long enough to play the homecoming game.

"What is that on your arm?" Birdie suddenly asked, her tone looking to confirm rather than question.

I'd actually been waiting for this moment. "You mean this?" I held my arm out, putting the new addition on proud display.

"Yeah, that."

"Well, you can see for yourself what it is. Looks nice, doesn't it?"

"I've never been one to admire tattoos before, but I would say it does look nice. But, um... Why'd you get it?"

"A little Birdie told me to. And it turned out to be a really good choice."

"You seriously took what I said and turned it into an actual physical permanent tattoo on your body?"

I chuckled. "Yes, why is that so hard to believe?"

She just kept staring at it. Her hand reached out tentatively. "May I?"

"Be my guest," I said, extending my arm. Nervously, she ran the pads of her fingers over the raised skin. It created the most intriguing tickle that crawled all the way up to my neck, heating my ears. The longer she lingered, the warmer I felt. Eventually, I gave a nervous chuckle and withdrew my arm, severing our connection. She drew back with a wince.

"I'm sorry."

"Nothing to be sorry for. It just tickled."

"Oh?"

"Yeah. Do you have any tattoos?"

"No way." She laughed, her hand fluttering away the notion. "No tattoos for me."

"Because of religion?"

"Because of *needles*."

"I see. Well, when tattoos are healing, the skin tends to itch like crazy, that's all."

It's true it had tickled as she'd touched me, but it hadn't actually begun to itch. I just didn't know how to withstand another second of her touch.

Coward.

"Honestly, I thought you'd forgotten about me the second you walked out of the building that day. I had no idea I'd made any sort of lasting impression, but it doesn't get more lasting than a tattoo."

"You had a good idea, what can I say?"

"I have so many good ideas," she said, tossing her hair over her shoulder. "That being said, don't get mad at me, but I do need you to do this teensy weensy practice test so I can get a baseline and am able to adjust our timeline and subjects to accommodate your individual needs."

I must've made a face.

"Don't worry, it won't take long at all. It'll just show which subjects you're better at and which we'll need to work on more," she assured me.

At least I would have a temporary distraction from her brilliance.

By the end of our first hour together, Birdie had given me a double-sided practice test and graded it. Then, putting it aside, she gave me a fresh smile. "So… We still have a few minutes. Tell me the story of Russell."

So much for not diving in the deep end. "You don't really want to hear all that."

"You must have one if you were browsing employment opportunities at our event. There aren't usually many young people at those things. Trust me, I'm usually the only one under thirty."

"My dad made me go."

"Ah, that makes sense." She watched me, waiting for me to continue.

"You really want my story? It's not anything great."

"Absolutely. I want to get to know you. The real you."

What did she mean by that? "As opposed to the fake one?"

"I don't want to judge you by hearsay. I want to know who Russell really is, not what I've heard about him."

"Let me guess. You saw the news reports in the spring?"

"Not quite. But I do know about Tanner's."

I resisted my instinct to slouch down in my chair. I was already at a disadvantage, needing her help, and I didn't want to look as pathetic as I felt. As my *'story'* was about to make me look. "Well then, you know it all. I did the crime, so I paid the time. End of story."

"Yeah, you and Kevin Sloan and a few others."

"Do you know Kevin?"

"Sure do. He's my best friend's boyfriend."

I blinked in surprise. "You're best friends with that Sarah chick?"

"With Sarah Stevenson, yes. Well, she's one of my best friends. In total, I have three. You know her?"

Wow. Was it just a small world or was it a cruel one, too? "I remember Sarah. I can't believe I don't remember you," I mused thoughtlessly, my eyes trailing from her soft face to her unique blonde curls. When she tucked a section behind her ear, I was alerted to her watching me. "What?"

"Nothing." She brushed it off, but she was hiding a smile. "So, have you seen Kevin since you both got back?"

She already seemed to know more than me. "Nope. Haven't heard from him at all."

"I'm sure y'all will reconnect soon. Coming home after what y'all went through must be a huge adjustment."

I gave a small nod, blocking out the reality of her assumption that we were held in similar accommodations.

"You should be glad to be where you're at now, Russell."

"And where's that?"

"In the right here, right now, with a bright and shiny clean slate."

"If you say so."

"I do, because it's true, and you should act like it." She made it sound so simple. There was no scorn in her voice, no judgment, but I scoffed, looking away. Was this girl for real?

"Was that too harsh?" she asked, the bridge of her nose wrinkling with anticipated regret.

"I know I caught a lucky break. The prison's overcrowding problem is the main reason I'm out right now. They needed my bed for somebody worse than me." I shrugged. "It's whatever. I'm here now."

"Let's try something less serious," she said, as cheerful as ever. "What do you do for fun?"

Fun? When was the last time I claimed I had fun doing anything? There was only one thing that came to mind. "Cars."

"Oh, yeah? What is it about cars? Driving them? Looking at them? Fixing them?"

"Yes."

She smiled. "Fair enough. Do you have a bucket list?"

"No."

"Really? Nothing? You don't want to visit the country's largest potato chip or ride the world's scariest roller coaster or something epic like that?"

I had to snicker a little. "Those are some very different extremes, neither of which are my speed."

"Maybe something in between then, like dancing the robot in public or bungee jumping."

"I don't really care about goals or lists or any of that. I just want to get a job so I can live my own life. Plain and simple."

"Then it's a good thing you have me now."

I nearly squirmed under the weight of her joyous declaration. "What do you mean by that?"

"I'm going to help you reach your goals, of course. Because whether or not you thought you were a goals-guy, you totally are. And that's really admirable, actually. You know what you want, and here you are going after it." She waved her hand to where I sat.

"I guess," I said, but it felt like saying nothing at all, and I almost felt bad. There she was, trying to make me feel better about my lame situation, and she didn't even know me, not really. But maybe it didn't matter if she did. Maybe that might even be better. I could be something, somebody, new to this girl. As much as I didn't want to read too deep into the idea, I couldn't deny the intensity of its appeal.

BIRDIE

17

I COULDN'T BELIEVE IT. INTELLIGENT WORDS ESCAPED ME AS I TOOK in the deep red images on Russell's arm, tucked artfully between the licking tongues of fire that encircled his wrist. Talk about making a lasting impression. I knew from the fact that he'd called me for tutoring that he hadn't forgotten about me after all, but I couldn't have imagined my silly storm-feared suggestion in a dark basement had any impact on him whatsoever. The idea was kind of intoxicating, if I was being honest.

But we weren't here for that. Russell had a GED to pass.

"After grading your pre-test, I can safely say this should be a breeze for you. You obviously remember a lot of what you learned in school, so you should have no trouble getting through the material. This will take about a month, focusing on one subject each week, and then we'll schedule your tests over four days."

"A month?" He did not sound happy. "Is it possible to get it done any faster if I commit more time?"

"Unfortunately, between my other commitments, I can't really do more than a couple hours a day if we're lucky. I'm sorry. But we'll get through it as quickly, yet efficiently, as we can."

"What are your other commitments?"

Why did he want to know?

"Well, in the mornings, I work at STLR, and in the evenings, I go to school. And now, in the afternoons, I work with you."

"How'd you get involved with an ivory tower like STLR anyway? You seem much more down to earth than they do."

"How so?"

"Most people who work for companies like STLR don't care about the people they claim to help. It's all for show, and as long as they get their tax kicks, what do they care? It's all corporate sell-out with a pretty charity ribbon tied on it in the end."

I laughed. "You're wrong on so many levels, but allow me to elaborate on my part in this *'ivory tower corporate sell-out'* first. I started as a volunteer, I think I told you that, but do you know what I was really *doing?* I worked alongside the caregivers, taking care of patients. I've helped mothers do everything from detox to give birth to write desperate apology letters to their estranged families. I've advocated for children in the court systems and seen them reunited with their moms once they've gotten clean. I've even witnessed a kleptomaniac surrender her life to God, and now she holds down a successful career as an author of children's books, and that's just one of the many.

"Me? I'm not a corporate anything. I just love people, and I'm doing everything I'm capable of to help them. As for my co-workers and bosses, they all feel the same, from the lowest on the totem pole—me—to the highest person in charge. That's why we're all part of this program. We very much do care." It was a little soap-boxy of me, but I felt happy with myself.

"If you like working with the people going through the

program so much, why would you split up a whole month just to help some loser study?"

"Don't call yourself a loser. You pinky-promised to have a good attitude."

He gave me a smug yet playful look. "Yes, ma'am."

Let it go, Birdie. Just let it go. Pay no attention to the knot in your gut. "I'm studying to be a social worker, so everything I do now is valuable experience for the long run."

"And you're in college, too? Jeez, do you ever do anything fun?"

I laughed. Something told me his idea and my idea of fun would not match up. "I know it sounds like a lot, but it's manageable. I'm enrolled online to make things easier. Besides, this *is* fun to me. I'm glad to be here doing this." *With you,* my mind dared to add, as if the defining factor in my joy to tutor someone had anything to do with the fact that it was *him* I was tutoring. As if I didn't know better than to admire him, even in secret.

"Hats off to you, chica. I didn't want anything to do with more school. Thought I was done when I got arrested, but it turns out the world has other plans for me."

"You're not the only one. I'm pretty sure Kevin got his diploma while in juvie."

"Good for him," he barked.

I was only slightly hesitant to speak again. "Well, you could have gotten yours while you were away, too."

"No one told me that, and I didn't know or care to ask. I just minded my own business so I didn't earn any more time." He stared at a small dent in the middle of the table.

"It worked out for the best, seeing as how we're working on it together now. You did really well on the practice exam. The prep course will make sure you pass it on your first try, if you put in the effort."

His pensiveness was slipping him into his old, pre-pinky promise ways. With a reproachful look, he asked, "Why would you do all this?"

"Weren't you paying attention? I like to help people. It's my calling."

"I don't like it. Sounds like pity to me."

It was my turn to scoff. "There's nothing pitiful about education. You need the certification, and I have the study materials that'll help you pass. That's all. I thought we settled this already."

He studied me like I was a two-headed zebra. "Still, it sure seems super *nice* of you."

I smiled, folding my hands gingerly in my lap. I had to get him off the negative train. "Nice is what I do best."

"I'm sure," he said, rolling his eyes. "Let me just ask you one thing first. You're not hitting on me, are you? Are you hoping to live out some kind of tutor-student fantasy or something?"

I wished I could laugh about it, but the idea brought Nick's sullen face to my mind and a burning sensation to my cheeks. "Absolutely not! I happen to have just gotten out of a serious relationship, and fantasies are the last thing on my mind." Swallowing the lump in my throat, it took a lot more than I thought it would for me to say that to him.

"Yeah, you look like the serious type."

Choosing to ignore his dig, I continued. "I am immune to any and all charms anyway, so don't *you* get any ideas about trying anything."

"No problem," he smirked.

I did not like that. And I did not like that I didn't like that.

Move on, Birdie. Just move on.

"Believe it or not, Russ, I really just want to see you succeed."

He eyed me for a moment. Not in a way that a snake watches a mouse, but… similar. "We don't even know each other."

"Aw, that's not true. You're Mr. Grandy, and I'm Miss Birdie Jo, your amazing study partner." I smiled wide, so wide he couldn't possibly refute me. I was sure my blue eyes sparkled and my blonde locks gave off just the right impression, even under the unflattering fluorescents.

"Sounds like a blast," he finally said with a teasing look. Every time I thought I had the upper hand with him, he had only to look at me to show me I was wrong.

RUSSELL

18

ON THE NEXT DAY OF STUDYING, MY DAD WAS IN A TERRIBLE MOOD when we arrived—late—to the library.

"You know, if you'd just given me my keys, I could've brought myself."

"Pass your GED and start behaving responsibly, and we will. You'll have to get yourself to work somehow." He wasn't much for chatting that afternoon, as he quickly left the moment I got out.

Getting dropped off at the library like this made me feel twelve again, and as I made my way through the entrance, a flood of memories surfaced.

My friends and I spent countless hours messing around on the computers, trolling the chat rooms, hogging them away from people who might actually have reports to research or essays to type. Sometimes, we'd just set up at a table in the back and eat, something you weren't allowed to do, and laugh too loud, the quintessential no-no of libraries across the globe.

A time or three, I met up with a cute girl from school, under the guise of working on a project together. Those were my favorites. If I wasn't mistaken, my first kiss took place behind the shelves of the autobiographical section.

What was her name? Eh, it didn't matter.

Yeah, the library held a lot of memories for me, but in all that time during my formidable pre-teen to teenaged years, one thing I'd never gotten around to doing there was studying. This was a month of firsts, and not the awesome kissing kind. I mean, I'd be down, but even a blind man could tell Birdie wasn't that type of girl.

Too bad. She's cute.

Alas, I wasn't there for girls or fun today. I had a stupid GED test to pass.

That car is as good as mine.

I turned a corner, finding Birdie at one of the smaller tables in the middle of the study area. I had liked our table in the back, where I wasn't subjected to people behind me, but whatever. She was already situated, with neat stacks of books and spiral notebooks, and an assortment of pens, pencils, rulers, and calculators.

Boy, this ought to be fun.

Birdie didn't see me because she had an open novel in her hands. I couldn't make out the title on my approach, but once I sat down, eating up the space across from her, Birdie jumped and threw her book face down against the table.

"Well, hello," I said, not trying to hide my amusement. Suddenly, I hoped more than anything for a better look at that cover.

"Hey. I didn't see you come in."

"I noticed." I tipped my head. "Whatcha reading there?"

"Just a book."

"What kind of book?" Her face flushed with pink, and I mocked a gasp. "Why, Miss MacLean, are you reading smut?"

She looked horrified. "Not at all!"

"Then why are you hiding your book from me and blushing? That makes you look pretty sus."

"Because..." her confidence faltered.

"Because why?" I pushed.

"Because you'll just make fun of me," she snipped.

I will? Hm, yeah, I might. But I'd become too curious. "Try me."

Her nostrils flared, accentuating her reddened cheeks. Then, she flipped her book and tossed it at me. I tilted to look it over. It was some kind of... *Amish* romance? Seriously, this was a thing?

Just as she had suspected of me, my mind didn't have to press too hard to come up with half a dozen remarks, but I had decided to prove her wrong. I wasn't able to stop a slight laugh from escaping, however, and at that, she rolled her eyes.

It was so fun to get that little rise out of her; I really couldn't help but enjoy it. Her embarrassment was cute. Her frustration was cute. And her cuteness was heart-shockingly adorable.

"See?" she demanded, as if one laugh equated making fun of someone. She didn't know the damage I could do if I actually tried.

"Sorry, but I've never seen anything like this. I didn't know anyone wrote Amish romance novels, let alone read them."

Reaching over, she snatched her book back. I caught a whiff of her shampoo and suddenly wanted to lean in and inhale deeper. The thought struck me as insane, and I steeled myself, remaining firmly in place.

"Well, they do, and *I* do. They're lovely and a very interesting insight into the different Amish communities. Plus, you can guarantee this kind of story is free of cursing and—what did you call it?—*smut*."

"Doesn't sound all that interesting to me."

She gave me a little glare, and I had to bite the inside of my cheek to keep from laughing again.

"Whatever, I love it. I don't want to feel ashamed of what I consume."

"Yet you tried to hide it from me."

"For a very different reason." She tucked her book away and then folded her hands on the table. "So, I see that you've come empty handed, which is fine. I planned for such a possibility."

Judging by the piles of supplies sitting between us, she planned on top of her planning.

She plucked a spiral notebook from the top of one pile, and a pencil from another, then handed them to me. "You can use this one for math, which we'll be going over first."

So today will not be another chill day. Fun. "Sounds good." It sounded boring, actually. But perhaps I could make things a bit more interesting…

"WELL, that's it for the day. Do you have any questions?" Birdie closed the heavy book and pushed it aside. We'd spent the last half hour correcting my worksheet. I wrote down every equation, operation, and definition she threw at me.

However, I had other things on my mind. "Yeah, just one. You wanna go out with me this weekend?"

"I'm sorry. Do what?"

"Do you want to go out with me, Birdie Jo?"

Her brow furrowed. "I thought you didn't even want me hitting on you."

So did I. "Ah, you're overthinking it. All this studying stuff gets so tedious. Let me make it up to you with some food or something." I hoped my smile was really as devastating as she looked like it was.

She pasted on a smile of her own before responding. "It's okay, I'm not hungry. And believe me, I live for this kind of thing. You don't owe me at all."

"It might be normal for you, but it's not for me. I'm not used to people doing me favors. Just let me take you out so I'll feel better."

"I… Well, I mean…" She rattled her head, appearing to talk herself out of possibly considering the idea.

"Take a chance, Birdie. Why not? It's only a meal."

I really thought I had her. But then, with more force and determination, she said, "No, I'm sorry. I can't."

What she meant was, she wouldn't. That much was obvious. But a guy could tell when a girl was interested, even despite herself. I had no plans to let her off easy. "You seem unsure about that."

"I'm very sure. Your question just took me by surprise."

I studied her, unable to prevent myself from feeling satisfaction from the way she nervously fidgeted with the charms of her bracelet. A floral horseshoe. A cowboy hat. A crown. How fitting for this little country princess. "I don't totally believe you, but okay. I'll let this go." *For now.*

"Thanks anyway though. It was a kind offer."

I shrugged. "Anytime." *And I mean that, Sweetie Bird.*

RUSSELL

19

Later in the week, I was deep in concentration, more or less, when the music coming from my ear buds paused between songs, and something different trickled into my ear. I peeked up, finding that Birdie was muttering to herself.

"...aware that some things we want are outside Your Will, so there's that," her low chatter continued, with her face down on a worksheet she was grading and a red pencil resting against her temple. "But I know that you know what this family has been through. Those kids deserve—"

Once again, my curiosity got the better of me, and I couldn't keep quiet anymore. "Birdie, who are you talking to?"

My voice startled her, and the pencil fell from her grip. Her hand flew over her heart. "Jeez, Russell."

"I'm sorry. I didn't mean to scare you."

"It's okay, it's not hard to do." She laughed airily at herself.

"So, who were you talking to?"

"God."

"Ah. You don't say." Undoubtedly, my tone gave me away.

"I hope I didn't make you uncomfortable or anything. It's just something that I do sometimes. A lot of times."

"Why do you do it?" I hadn't given a lot of thought to my relationship with God, if He were even real, but I knew it would never be so… vocal and public, if I had one.

"Why do I talk to God? Oh, for so many reasons. Sometimes, it's about praying for someone or something. Sometimes, I need to unburden my heart. Sometimes, I just want to share something awesome that happened that day. I just talk, really, like I would to anyone else who was special in my life."

"I meant, why do you do it out loud?"

She blinked like she couldn't understand the question. "I talk to everyone else out loud, don't I? Why should God be any different?"

Maybe because He was invisible, and she looked like a lunatic talking to herself? "I don't know."

She smiled and dipped her head like she agreed with me. "And I don't either. Now, as you were. You need to have that done soon, or I won't have time to look it over before we leave."

"Yes, ma'am."

With her trademark preening smile, she waved me back to work. As I readjusted my ear bud and returned to my music, I think I grinned. There was something so cute about her eccentricities. Every day we spent together, I learned something new, and so far, I hadn't found anything I didn't like. She was so genuine a person, it had me locked in. I would do a thousand worksheets, and listen to a hundred of her one-sided conversations, just to spend time with her.

20

IT ACTUALLY SEEMED LIKE MY EFFORTS WERE STARTING TO PAY OFF. Russell appeared a little less surly every day, and he was on time today. He even brought a backpack with his own supplies in it. Granted, asking me out the other day was a curveball I hadn't seen coming, though I wondered if I should've known better. Working in close proximity with him every day like we had been was doing crazy things to my own head. I seemed to look at him a little bit longer, smile a little wider every time I saw him. A little bit more each day, he was usurping my focus.

As I was sitting in a live lecture with my class in the evening, my phone vibrated, skidding across my desk. Flinching, I quickly grabbed it. How could I have forgotten to apply Do Not Disturb settings before logging in? Only a couple pairs of eyes glanced at my video stream, but it was enough to make my face heat. After covertly swiping my phone on, I peeked down at the text.

RUSSELL

Hey, so what were you talking to God about earlier? Or can you not tell me because it won't come true?

BIRDIE

It's not like that at all. God is not a birthday candle. You can tell Him anything at any time, however you want. But I was just discussing a family I'm assigned to at work.

RUSSELL

Uh oh. Are things not going so well?

BIRDIE

Actually, they're going great! This family has court tomorrow to re-affirm custody. It's my first time seeing a case from start to finish, and I'm very excited for them.

RUSSELL

Oh, okay. So, you talk to God about good stuff, not just bad stuff?

BIRDIE

Yep, I talk to Him about everything.

RUSSELL

Oh, really? What have you told Him about me?

Panic mode activated! Deflect! Deflect!

BIRDIE

What I mean is, sometimes prayer includes praising, begging, crying, asking, thanking... But it's always a two-way conversation.

RUSSELL

Hm. I will take your word for it.

BIRDIE

Hey, I have to get back to my class. But if you ever have any other questions about stuff like this, I'm your girl. Okay? 🙂

RUSSELL

Thanks. I look forward to having you as my girl.

BIRDIE

THAT IS NOT WHAT I MEANT

RUSSELL BENJAMIN GRANDY

RUSSELL

Relax, Sweetie Bird, I'm only teasing you. But I am not teasing right now about looking forward to seeing you on Tuesday. 😉 Until then.

My mouth slid to the side so I could bite my cheek, hiding my distracted smile from my video feed. The man was incorrigible. Pressing my phone closed, I flung the device onto my bed, ridding myself of it like a torn sock. My professor talked on and on and was finally making the rounds for questions. My turn was almost there, and my mind was a million miles away from Clinical Psychology at the moment.

I rubbed my temple. *Distractions don't pay off. Boys like Russell don't stay. Nobody wants commitment. Get him out of your head and pay attention to your own commitment!*

That was the most he was going to get out of me. I couldn't afford to let him have anything else. Hopefully, I could still say the same when I had to look into his beautiful eyes and see his intriguing tattoos next. I sincerely hoped he wore a dark pair of shades and a jacket.

BIRDIE

21

My gut was always in knots on court days, even if I wasn't there for personal reasons. I snuck a glimpse at the familiar courtroom as we herded the children through the hallway to the little room where we were to spend the duration of the hearing. The double doors were held open by little kickstands as people continued filing into the crowded room, one after another. This particular defendant was one of the lucky ones. Unlike many that went through the South Texas Life Rehabilitation program, she had a lot of friends and family still on her side.

The kids and we, their entourage, made it to the child waiting room just in time to hear staff close the doors to the courtroom. The judge had already had his time with them, both individually and then together, and now it was up to the rest of the people in the case to get their turn.

Their mother, an awfully sweet woman who just so happened to have a terrible addiction, celebrated almost one full year clean since going through the program and was now fighting the state for the right to keep her children while she finished.

I always loved spending this time with the kids, keeping

them comfortable and lighthearted while their futures were being decided in the next room. It came so naturally to me, maybe because I was still close enough to childhood myself to acutely understand their fear. One never forgot the feeling of being held in a waiting room like this, sitting at a table across from a CASA advocate, no matter how clean or messy the case might've been.

Today, there were two of us. Me, an entry-level case aide, and Serenity, the Lawrence children's Court Appointed Special Advocate.

The eldest was a seven-year-old girl just as sweet as her mother, and her five-year-old brother always seemed to be the happiest little tyke I'd ever seen. He rivaled my cousin Tay as cutest kid alive.

My boss, Stephanie Hallows, was needed in court today; otherwise, she would've been there, too. The official caseworker was always present for the ruling.

"How much longer do we have to be here?" little Christopher Lawrence asked, propping his head lazily with the back of his hand.

Serenity checked her wrist. "Until they finish," she replied practically.

I didn't think that response would cut it with two young kids. "I hope it's long enough for *me* to finish." I bent over and reached into my backpack, then proceeded to slap a coloring book and a pink plastic box of supplies on the table. "I'm almost done with my latest picture."

It worked. Their elbows on the table, I knew I had them. Chairs scraped the floor as Christopher and his big sister Corrine drew nearer. The kids were now intensely absorbed with seeing all my stuff, their anxious boredom completely forgotten. I suppressed a smile so I could pretend to only care about my little art project.

The kids were so engrossed and each had a finished page of their own by the time the doors opened. Gia Lawrence's face came into view, red and tormented. I stared, praying, the pit in my stomach growing deeper every second. Just no way. There was no way she lost.

In my time at STLR, I'd seen her complete her program with zero infractions, zero relapses, and one hundred percent commitment. She could be the perfect poster child for the entire program. There was no way the state would do better than her at raising her children. She was clean. She was committed. She was loving. She was ready to live her life with her kids in the real world again.

The kids leapt up and ran to her. "Let's go home," she said, to the audible relief of us all. I *knew* she was ready! *Thank you, Jesus.*

The children cheered, and Serenity and I clapped, joined soon by Stephanie. Congratulations abounded. The kids presented their masterpieces to their mom. There were papers, words, and hugs exchanged, and Gia and the kids were allowed to leave together. We wouldn't see any of them again until the upcoming graduation ceremony.

After all our goodbyes, I rode back to the office with Stephanie. The hearing had taken up the better part of the day, but I still had some paperwork to help her finish up and my dad's car was back there. I was just sighing into the window, leaning my suddenly tired head down, when Stephanie turned the volume down to barely audible.

"So, how are you feeling after your first start-to-finish case? It's different, isn't it?"

"Very different, and yet exactly the same."

"I know just what you mean." She nodded, both hands firmly on the wheel in front of her as the highway stretched on ahead of us. "I admit I was a bit worried about this ruling. I haven't seen a judge take so long to decide since my last removal."

Removal. Every social worker's worst nightmare, especially from STLR, where mothers are allowed to keep their children while going through the program. It's part of the deal, a natural way to show struggling mothers that it's safe to join. It's safe to trust us. We were not out to take children away. No, that's one thing that set us apart from other rehab facilities.

Curiosity got the better of me. "When was that?"

"Oh…" She rolled her shoulders as though knots of cases past were still lodged deep in there. "Last year."

"Really? I thought you were going to say it was much longer ago."

"I wish it was, but unfortunately, these things do happen. Not everyone who passes the program makes it to graduation, and not everyone who graduates makes it their first year. And as much as I hate to say it, sometimes it's for the best when they lose custody. Sometimes hitting rock bottom is the only way people can find their way back up."

Her sentiment put a cold weight in my chest, yanking my heart down. "Putting it like that makes it sound like the whole program doesn't work. Like none of it is worth it."

"It's all very worth it, but it's just the simple nature of people. Some of them fail and that's a fact."

"But some don't," I said, clinging to any shred of positivity I could.

"Exactly. Many don't. Many more succeed than fail, and that's the idea. That's why I bust my rump day in and day out for these women. They all have so much to live—clean—for, whether or not they have children."

That was more like it. That was why I joined, too. I wanted to be part of something small that turned into something huge for somebody. I didn't want anyone to credit me for saving lives or any such thing, but to have had even the smallest part in the reason why someone improved their life for the better was what brought me to volunteering at STLR in the first place. I wanted to witness God's greatness in this program, and to help foster His cause.

And today I did just that. God's love and greatness was with Gia and her sweet children, as evidenced by the judge's good ruling. They had the same faith in Gia as a recovered addict, and in our program being a success, that I did. It was a beautiful show of family and how right it was to keep them together. A testament to God's design of mother and child at the very least, if there was no earthly father in the picture. And if I knew anything, it was that family meant everything.

RUSSELL

22

My mom forced me into every clothing store the mall had to offer. When she was at last satisfied that I had enough interview and proper work attire to last me a lifetime, we found ourselves sitting in the food court with half a dozen bags full of socks and ties and everything between. Sore feet, too. Something about the mall just added to the exhaustion of life, and it all seemed to congregate in one's feet. Hanging out in this place had never been my scene. At least that meant the chances of me running into anyone I knew were slim to none.

"Russell Grandy?"

Was that... Birdie? You have got to be kidding.

The familiar voice hung like a haunted melody in the air, causing a ripple of chills to slide through me. Did Mom hear it? I couldn't bring myself to look. Maybe if I ignored Birdie's call, she would go away. Like a T-rex. Just don't make any movement and they won't see you.

But the footsteps got closer, and soon, the voice boomed from beside me rather than across the food court, where it belonged. "Hey, Russ. I thought that was you. How are you doin'?"

Backed into the corner of inevitability, I finally looked up. "Hey, Birdie." My shoulders sagged. "What's up?"

"Oh, you know. Just doing a little shopping." She held up a small blue and white checkered bag, barely bigger than a smart phone. Noticing our loot, she nodded. "Looks like y'all were doing the same."

I let the moment go without a response, and then my mother cleared her throat. "I'm so sorry for my son. Russell obviously lacks manners he didn't learn from me." She extended her hand. "I'm Delia Grandy, this perfect gentleman's mother."

The two exchanged a pleasant handshake. "Oh, well, it is a pleasure to meet you, ma'am. I'm Birdie Jo MacLean, this perfect gentleman's GED tutor."

"Ah, that's wonderful. I'm so glad for the opportunity to meet you. And how is that going, would you say?" she asked in wonder, as though I wasn't even there. As though she and Dad didn't ask me constantly.

"Going great! He's very bright and has all the necessary skills. It's just a matter of keeping focused and applying himself when the time comes. I know he's going to pass with flying colors." All of that was said without even a glance at me, without missing a single beat, as if she actually believed all that.

Mom's smile was laced with unshed tears. "You have no idea what it means to hear that. Thank you. We're so appreciative you're doing this."

Birdie's cheeks blossomed with a fair pink. Ha. Cute. I doubt she could get as squeamish as I was to run into her while sitting at the *mall* with my *mother*, but she wore that shade so well.

"It's no trouble. I'm happy to help," she said. "Really."

My mom smiled, something I hadn't seen her do much of since I got home. "Are you busy at the moment, or would you like to sit down and have lunch with us? We were just discussing what to eat."

Shock zapped through me, targeting my chest and frying my heart. "Mom, Birdie is busy. Don't bother her. I'm sure she has more shopping to do."

Birdie finally looked at me. A strange sort of smile spread across her face. "I'm actually done, and I'm totally famished. I would love to stay for lunch."

"Perfect, I'm so glad. Russell?" My mom gave me a pointed look, expressing with a tip of her head what I should do.

With a heavy sigh I would've been smart to suppress, I lumbered to my feet and pulled out the chair next to mine. "My lady," I flourished with a wave of my hand, bending into a deep bow.

"My, my. There's those gentlemanly qualities. Who knew they were truly in there somewhere?"

My mom's laugh told me she loved Birdie already.

With a teasing smile, Birdie pulled her dress skirt forward and sat like the lady she was, reminding me of the day we first met, when she sat beside me in the basement. That already seemed like a decade ago. It felt like I'd known her for years already, but it had really only been a few weeks, hadn't it?

After a quick discussion about who wanted to eat what, I went to one end of the food court to get my mom and Birdie their Chinese orders. Then, avoiding her for as long as possible, I went to the opposite side to get myself a chicken sandwich. While waiting for the food, I tried not to watch them converse without me. The urge to know what they were saying was getting on my nerves.

Once I'd collected everyone's lunch, I carried the loaded trays back to the table.

Folding her hands under her chin, my mom studied our lunch guest. “So, Birdie Jo, how did you come to do tutoring?”

“My boss recommended me for it. It’s just one of the many hats I wear at work.”

“And you work with the recovery program?”

“Yes, I do.”

“That sounds very nice. I hadn’t heard about it until James found the job fair.”

“It’s huge. They have campuses all over the state. I work mainly at the women and children’s campus here in town.”

“I imagine that can be hard work at times.”

Birdie nodded thoughtfully. “It really can. But other times are magical. Getting to see people give their hearts to Jesus and put their families back together after years of suffering with addiction... there’s nothing else like it.”

“Sounds like a powerful experience, indeed.”

“Absolutely! And what do you do, Mrs. Grandy?” she asked between bites. She had a hearty appetite; meanwhile, I had yet to touch my Chic-Fil-A.

“I teach second grade.”

“And you thought my job sounded tough.” Birdie giggled. “I love children, but I could never be in charge of so many.” She tucked hair behind her ear, and my mom’s attention was drawn to her charm bracelet.

“What a lovely bracelet. May I?”

“Oh, sure!” Birdie extended her arm so my mom could pick through each and every charm, offering admiration, and lingering on a cross.

“Do you go to church around here? My husband and I have been looking for one to attend.”

"Since when?" I asked, skeptical. She only glanced sideways at me.

"Sure do," Birdie said, and I couldn't tell how oblivious she was. "I can text Russell the location pin. It's a wonderful church. We've been members ever since we moved to Corpus."

"Where are you from? I guessed it wasn't here because of your accent."

"Texarkana. It's very different from here, but this is home now. I love the beach and these crazy winds more than I ever thought I would."

She and my mom chatted mostly amongst themselves while I primarily ate my food in silence. The more they carried on, the more I felt awkward about their natural camaraderie, and yet, something about that very thing also put me at ease.

At least until after Birdie left and my mom confirmed, "I really like that girl."

Mom sat with her legs curled up on the couch with Abby in her ear later that evening. I was taking my time cleaning the dinner dishes, once again content to let the ladies talk so I could be left out of it, but that didn't last long. When I turned off the faucet, I could hear her voice trickling from the other room toward me.

"Oh, he's just in the kitchen. Do you want to say hi?" Pause. "Okay, I'll tell him. I love you, baby. Give Miguel and the littles a hug for us. Alright. You too. Bye." Finished in the kitchen, I crept my way to the stairs, but Mom turned to me, snatching my attention before I could escape. "Hey, Russell, Abby's going to call you."

She was way ahead of her. From inside my pocket, my phone

vibrated against my thigh. Without slowing my ascent, I held the device up and waved it so she could see, then I slid my finger across the screen to answer the call. "Yello," I said.

"Russell Benjamin. It's so good to talk to you. Welcome home, little brother."

"Hello, sis. It's so great to hear from you at last. One might think you didn't know I've been home for weeks now."

"You don't get to sass me. I will come down there and whoop you."

"I'd love to see you try." I really would. Abby hadn't been home in over a year at this point.

"You'd better watch your mouth, Big Talker, because we're coming for Christmas."

"I'll believe it when I see it." I looked down at all my new junk from the mall, and Birdie came to mind. With one arm, I swiped everything out of the way and dropped myself down onto the bed.

"Well, you will be soon. Just see that you stay out of trouble long enough to enjoy this visit."

Pfft. "Yes, Mother."

"I mean it. I'm trying to convince Miguel that we should visit more often, so I want everything to be perfect. You know how much he hates this drive."

Yeah, I did, which was dumb. Six hours was nothing. That was barely across the state. "He's still a tool, but I love you. I'll be on my best behavior. More or less." Absentmindedly, I lightly traced the skin around my tattoo. It was nearly completely healed, the itching long gone.

Abby chuckled. "You punk."

"You love me."

"I sure do. So, how have you been?"

"Fine. Mom and Dad are the worst, as usual. I'm sure they've told you everything."

"They have, and you'd do well to fall in line. They're doing the right thing. They love you."

"Are you kidding me right now?"

"No, sir. Just mind yourself and things will go your way. That's really not so difficult, is it?"

"It's annoying. I'm too old for them to have this much control over me still."

"You really aren't."

"Whatever."

"Even after everything, you still have such a chip on your shoulder." She sighed. "Russell, you think you know it all, and you know nothing. Trust me, I have five years on you and I'm still figuring it out. You won't have your crap together until you've lived out in the real world for longer than even I have, so just stop acting like you do."

"You think I don't know the real world? I was in prison, or did you forget?"

"Even in prison, you're taken care of. And despite feeling like Mom and Dad are strangling you, you have it made at home. They're doing so much to help you get your life on track. Seriously, you don't know what it's like to fend for yourself, and you're lucky you don't because you're not ready. Take advantage of the comfort and support while you have it, because it won't always be there. One day, you're not going to be number one in your world, and you will see what self-sacrifice is really like."

"Wow, when did you get so pessimistic?"

Abby growled, "I'm not, I'm just hoping to warn you. The real world is hard, so don't alienate your family and try to live it all alone."

"Whatever you say, Mother."

"In one ear and out the other," she grumbled, but quickly moved on. "Anyway, what else is new? You meet anyone interesting lately?"

Anyone interesting, like Birdie Jo MacLean? Adorable, sweet Birdie Jo with her jingling bracelet and her cowboy boots and her lacy dresses? With her curly blonde hair and obscenely beautiful blue eyes? "No."

"You hesitated, you little liar! Tell me everything right now!"

"There's nothing to tell."

"But there is a girl?"

"No. There's nobody and there's nothing."

"I know you're holding out on me." There was a crash of something and then the shrill cry of a toddler. "For the love..." She sighed. "I gotta go. You've lucked out this time, twerp, but I will expect a full report, and soon."

"Have fun with that. Bye, bye, Mommy Dearest."

Just then, like a bat out of a cave, my mom stuck her head into my room. "Did you call me?"

"No."

"Oh. Well, I actually wanted to see if you'd come with us to church this Sunday. We're going to try out the one your friend recommended."

My friend. "Why do you even want to go?"

"Because we should. It feels right. Plus, our family has a lot to be thankful for lately, don't you think? It's been a long time since we've given God praise, and your dad and I feel we ought to."

"Have fun."

Her disappointment didn't absolutely annoy and crush me. "We won't make you go, but we do hope you change your mind."

"Maybe." I said it only to get her out of my hair, but as the word came out, I began to imagine the possibility of seeing Birdie. She would be there. But so would tons of others, all praying and talking about God. I didn't understand. Our family only believed in God enough to say a couple of words at Thanksgiving or Christmas. We weren't church-going people. We weren't like Birdie.

With the idea rejected, I lay back down and let the flowers and flames on my arm darken my vision. *'Maybe'* didn't put us on the same level. Maybe it wouldn't actually make sense to do just about anything to spend time with her.

Even if I wanted to.

RUSSELL

23

"You know," I said suddenly, breaking from the formulas Birdie was forcing me to copy. "There's an Amish community up in Beeville." I don't know why I hadn't thought to tell her sooner.

Her eyes went alive with fascination. "No way."

That was exactly the reaction I was hoping for. "Way."

"I never knew that. There's a STLR campus located up there that I've gone to for meetings a couple of times. Was never able to explore though."

Her voice dipped at the end, making me curious. "Why not?"

She used her pencil to scratch the side of her head. "I wasn't driving." She avoided my gaze, but it didn't help. There was definitely much more to all that.

"Just tell me what I'm missing, so I can finish telling you about the Amish thing."

She laughed, just a little bit. "Fine, you win. At the time, I had only just barely gotten my license, and I was afraid to make that long of a drive myself."

"Well, I saw the Amish once while visiting a friend up that

way. We were heading somewhere in town and, as we drove by, there they were, trotting along in their buggy. Someone told me they'd seen them shopping at H-E-B before, and they even have a hitching post in the parking lot."

"That sounds so awesome." She beamed.

"They actually have a cool shop with random stuff and baked goods."

"What kind of baked goods?"

"Pecan pies, breads, things like that. There's honey and jams and fresh produce, too."

She was practically drooling. I think I stared a little too long at her lips.

"That sounds so cool. I'd *love* to go."

Her look of enrapture took me by the heart strings. I surprised myself with my next words. "As soon as I get my car back, I'll take you."

"Really? You'd do that?"

"Sure, why not?"

"That's very kind of you. When do you get your car back?"

"As soon as I pass this test."

She smiled 100-watts of pure excitement. "Then let's get back to work!"

I bit my cheek again, suppressing my amusement, but this was different. Seeing her that happy, even over something so dumb, made me… also kinda happy. I couldn't remember the last time I'd caused actual joy, or any emotion resembling a positive one, in someone else. The feeling seemed to reverberate off of her and hit me square in the chest. It was infectious.

A small bead of warning suddenly welled up inside me and told me to be cautious, to not get used to it. But it might've been too late to give up on making that girl smile, as I was already wondering how to do it again.

We were packing up for the day when Birdie suddenly stopped. "Hey, Russ?"

"Hey, Bird?"

She flicked a wild strand of curls to the side. "Are you busy on Saturday?"

"Depends who's asking and what for," I said, keeping my complete cool, despite my undivided attention.

"Well, I have to go car shopping this weekend, and I know you're a car-guy. I'm sure you probably have awesome plans, but I could really use your expertise so I don't get swindled," she pleaded. "You know, if, by some chance, you're free."

"Swindled, huh?"

"Yeah." She put on a sad, pitiful expression, which made her bold eyes even bigger and more beautiful. Fake though it was, how could I say no to that?

I released a dramatic sigh. "I could probably reschedule my awesome plans and go with you. I can't have you getting taken advantage of." Hanging out with Birdie Jo this weekend was the last thing I thought I'd be doing, but I found myself looking forward to it.

"Wouldn't want that." She held my stare.

I held hers back. "Not at all."

"RUSSELL?" my dad shouted from upstairs.

"What?" I responded, staring at Birdie's conversation on my phone. She would be at my house at any minute to pick me up.

"Is that Birdie I see in the driveway?"

I peeked through my blinds. A second later, a text from her vibrated my phone in my hand. "Yep, it is." I grabbed my jacket from the edge of the bed and jogged down the stairs.

My dad stood at the door, blocking my exit. "Where are you going?"

"Just around to a couple of used dealerships. Birdie is trying to buy a car."

"I see. It's very generous of you to give up your free time. She's been a great help to you as a tutor. It's only natural to offer your own knowledge in return."

"I aim to please."

"Your mom had charmed things to say about her. From the sound of it, this Birdie Jo is a great girl."

"Yep. Great." *This better not be a lecture in the making.*

"Helping a friend find a car is a worthwhile endeavor. No doubt she'll appreciate it."

"Warning received, Dad. I've got it."

"I'm just saying, Birdie Jo is a really nice girl, and she's doing you a lot of good. Be sure to stay mindful of that."

"Can I go now?"

He stepped aside. "Sure, you can. Have fun. Be careful."

"Will do," I called out as I breezed by him and out the door.

Birdie was unbuckling from the car when I reached the passenger door. "I was actually going to get out and go knock. I wanted to say hi to your parents."

"Don't worry about it."

With a worried glance toward the house, her brows scrunched together. "But it's proper."

But I'm not. Neither is whatever is happening between us, if anything actually is. "Nah, they're fine." I buckled in, and the click of my belt signaled an end to the discussion. "Do you have a place in mind to check out first?"

In the next instant, she was all smiles. "I have one I know of, but I figured I'd let you direct us."

"Sounds good. Head to your place first, and we'll go from there."

A destination in mind, Birdie pulled her borrowed car out onto the access road. "Hey, thank you so much for doing this for me. I really appreciate it. I know there are better things one could be doing on a beautiful Saturday afternoon than spending this rinky-dink time with me."

I couldn't think of any. "It's all good. I'm happy to help."

And help I did. At our first stop, I popped the hood of the first "adorable" car Birdie saw, and with incredible skepticism, dove right in. When the salesman came up beside me, talking a lot of standard issue nonsense about the horsepower and comfort features, I ignored him, simply looking at what quality of life this car had left. Her budget wasn't very big, which wasn't necessarily an issue, but it meant I had my work cut out for me in bestowing my approval on something.

I was just getting tired of the sound of his voice when Birdie's question made me do a double-take. My head whipped up at the same time the sales guy asked, "What was that?"

"I said," she asserted with naive seriousness, "what's the output rating of the flux capacitor?" She vaguely waved toward the Kia's hood from under which I was looking.

Did she really just ask him about a fictitious car part?

Is she serious?

The sales guy nearly floundered in confusion, but he fought back with the bald-faced determination that got him his monthly commissions. "Uh, well, that's a very good question. I'm not too sure about that, but I'll do a little research and let you know."

"That's very kind. Thank you so much."

"Oh, sure. No problem." He cleared his throat and began yapping again, and that's when Birdie stole me a wink.

I couldn't believe the golden little fiend had just made a funny joke. An actual funny one. I had to bite the inside of my cheek to keep from smiling. It didn't work for long, and I had to bury my face behind my arm to hide it when I couldn't stop.

"You two sure know your stuff," the salesman later said, giving each of our hands a sturdy parting shake. "I hope to see you again soon. Please give me a call if there's anything more I can do to earn your business."

"Thank you, sir. We'll let you know."

Back in the car, I had assumed the driver's seat. As we headed toward dealership number two, I shook my head. I didn't even need to turn to face her directly to see her amusement. "You are diabolical."

"Do you mean it?" Her voice was bright with possibility.

"Truly. This one is going to stick with him. He's over there thinking he knows his stuff, until Birdie Jo Rene Lewis MacLean walked in. As soon as he can, he'll make one internet search and then forever remember the golden-haired goddess who tricked him. You may have shot every ounce of his confidence."

She stopped laughing. "I didn't think of it that way. Do you think we should go back so I can apologize?"

"What? No."

"I think we should turn around. I feel so bad now." She pouted.

"Don't, I'm only teasing you. Adding to the fun. This will not derail anything, and I'm sure he's already working on the next customer by now. He may find out you tricked him, but there's no reason to think he won't just laugh about it."

"Yeah?"

"Yes." I couldn't help a little laugh. "Don't worry." This girl was sweet enough to rot teeth. On impulse, I reached out and squeezed her hand, before forcing myself to let go. I had no right to think she welcomed such a thing, and would be better off remembering my place.

BIRDIE

24

WHAT A WHIRLWIND. FIRST, I BROKE CHARACTER AND TEASED A grown man at his place of employment, and was proud of myself for it. Then, when the novelty wore off, I'd felt terrible. But then, Russell made me feel better by being logical, reasonable, and surprisingly sweet. He'd taken hold of my hand to give me comfort, and it had required everything in me not to freak out. It was short-lived, however, because he quickly pulled away. Obviously, he had not meant for me to read much into that, which I understood. We were only there as acquaintances. Maybe buddies. But definitely not anything more.

On the way to the next lot, there was a large banner draped over the entrance of the Honda dealership. My jaw dropped as we drove past it. "Did you see that?"

"See what?"

"Turn around. We gotta go to Honda."

"I thought you were only looking at used cars. Like, really used ones…" he tried to put delicately.

"No, I am. But trust me. We need to go there." My smirk was

so intense it probably scared him. The day was about to get a whole lot more exciting.

"Why?" he asked skeptically, even as he moved to make a U-turn.

"Do you really want me to tell you, or do you want to keep the suspense for a few minutes longer?"

He glanced at me sideways. "Go ahead and tell me."

"Okay!" I adjusted so I could see everything about his reaction. "They're giving out free passes to the aquarium to anyone who test drives the new CR-V."

He scrunched his nose. "That's such a lame car."

"It doesn't matter about the car!"

"What if they think we're only there to scam them out of the tickets?"

"There's no scam, it's their own advertisement. Free tickets for a test drive. We test drive, we get tickets. Sounds simple as fallin' off a log."

Laughing, he shook his head. "I guess the Golden Goddess is at it again," he said, matching my revelry.

That was twice now he'd called me that, and I wanted to preen in response to his amusement. I felt like a cat that had just brought its owner the largest rat on the farm, all puffed up and ready to luxuriate in a job well done.

Smiling to myself, I wondered what Russell would think about his Golden Goddess when she started providing the dealership with our totally made-up but adorably entertaining backstory.

RUSSELL

25

I COULDN'T BELIEVE WE WERE DOING THIS, AND HONESTLY, I couldn't wait. "This might actually be fun."

"Of course it will, unless I fall in love with the CR-V and then get depressed that I can't afford it."

"Nah, it's a wannabe mom-mobile with sluggish acceleration. You won't enjoy the ride."

"The funniest part is you don't realize that you're actually talking it up. Those are reasons why I *would* want that car."

I supposed that would be true, considering the way she'd spoken about being a nervous driver, though I hadn't seen any of that with her behind the wheel today. I bit my tongue, rather than making a comment about how awesome speed was, and that she was missing out.

"Whatever the case, we don't have to stop in and do this if you don't want to. We can move along."

She was already unclipping her seatbelt. "Yeah right, dude. Let's go get those tickets!"

Birdie did really like the CR-V, though I couldn't for the life of me figure out why. It was a slow, clunky thing, and aside from the interesting color, it had very little going for it. Especially at the price point, but whatever. Suffice it to say I wasn't a fan, but after the test-drive, we were halfway to getting our aquarium tickets. Our last order of business was to sit down and take a survey.

She raised her hand. "Excuse me, sir? We're all done."

The salesman looked up with a smile and received tickets from his finance manager before heading our way. "Wonderful," he said as he took the empty chair across from us. Birdie handed him the clipboard.

"Looks great," he said, looking it over. "Just a few more items here at the bottom on our end. Are you guys married?"

My mouth was halfway open to protest when I felt Birdie's arm slink through mine.

"Well, not yet, but we did just close on our first house. It is the most charming little single story with a wrap around porch that is just perfect for watchin' the sunset. Russy's great-grandfather built it with his own two hands after comin' home from the war. That's actually where we first met. Ya see, Russy's mother sold fresh milk from the family cow, and well, one thing led to another and the rest is history." She tittered, putting her free hand down over mine. I didn't dare contradict her, and was too stunned to try. I just gave a small, nervous laugh and nodded in support.

"Congratulations." The salesman gave me an offbeat smile and continued his final assessment. "How did you hear about this promotion?"

"We drove by and saw the banner," I said, equipped to handle that one.

"Great. Well, thank you both for stopping in today. Here is my card, for when you're ready to take home that new car. And here are your tickets."

I took them. "Thank you, sir," I said, emulating Birdie's snow-white demeanor.

On the way out, I elbowed her, snickering. "Your accent gets so thick when you're being completely ridiculous, did you know that?"

"Was it too much? I couldn't help myself."

"No, it was great. I'm impressed. But the idea of my mother selling fresh milk or even touching a cow?" I shook my head. "Insane."

We laughed the whole way back to the car. I opened the door for Birdie Jo, handing her the tickets. Then once I'd buckled myself in to the driver's seat, she held them up.

"So, who actually gets those?" she asked.

"What do you mean? There're two tickets and two of us. Obviously, we each get one."

"Do you mean we would go together? It might look like a date."

"Just a few minutes ago, we were getting a house together, and now you're questioning a trip to the aquarium?" A small laugh slipped out. "Who cares what it looks like. We're just two people hanging out. I want to see the flamingos."

She sat in thought for a moment. "I like flamingos."

I couldn't let her back out now. "How about I meet you there at, what, eleven tomorrow?"

"I have church in the morning."

"After that then? How about one o'clock?"

"Okay. Sounds like a plan. Pink flamingos, here we come!"

Victory. *First date, here we come.*

RUSSELL

26

Traffic at the aquarium was starting to pick up. I watched people enter in small crowds as I waited for Birdie by the ticket counter. One family reminded me of mine, from a time long ago. I could remember visiting this place a few times over the years, but they wouldn't have gone on a Sunday. They hadn't always gone to church, but they did tout *'The Lord's Day'* all the time. Mostly I figured they used it as an excuse to not do anything once a week.

They asked me to go with them again this morning. I told them I had plans, and indeed I did. I wouldn't have missed this date for the world, even if it was only a date for me.

Besides, what a joke that they wanted to be proper Christians now. They didn't *'love their neighbor'* when they didn't even give a proper crap about their own son.

Birdie's entrance snagged all of my attention, and for a moment, I felt struck by something otherworldly. She wore a white dress with lace accents, a straw cowboy hat, and tall, decorative leather boots. Her ensemble was topped with a jean jacket, and she glittered with silver jewelry. Her charm bracelet twinkled in the sunlight as she adjusted the strap of her purse over her shoulder. She looked like the perfect example of being too good for me, and yet, I thought I might be ready to admit I wanted her more than anything I'd ever wanted before.

On her approach, I figured I was giving too much away.

"Hey," she said. "You okay?"

"I'm fine." *You're perfect.* "You look great."

"Thank you," she replied, tone soft and sweet.

"Shall we?" Clearing my mind, I stepped forward and held the door open for her. After handing over our tickets, we walked inside and began our self-guided tour, and were transported into a world of tropical nature and discovery.

"Look who it is! Aren't they so awesome?" Birdie called out, pointing to the flamingoes like a little kid, her glee absolutely fascinating me.

She snapped so many pictures. I had to get one of her, too. It just so happened at the moment I snapped the photo, she had one leg bent up like the birds we were looking at.

"Your turn! Come stand here like they do."

I stuffed my phone in my pocket so fast and shook my head. "Nope."

She tilted her head and put her arms on her hips. "You have to. I did."

"No way."

"Please?" She pouted.

I wondered if I even possessed a spine anymore. My whole body felt gelatinous. I was stepping forward before I could stop myself. There I stood, perched like a flamingo, for the silly joy of a girl. One girl that I couldn't help but like making happy.

Standing there, feeling absurd, I found I didn't care as much about being embarrassed as I did about the smile on her face as she took her picture. I almost didn't even notice when one of those oh-so-adorable pink birds reached across the boulder ledge and bit me on the shoulder.

She rushed over, pulling me a safe distance away. "Ouch. Are you okay?"

"I'm fine. Didn't even feel it."

"I guess they put those signs here for a reason. Flamingos really will bite if you get too close!" One exhibit down and we were already having this much fun. It was a little mind-blowing.

We rounded the corner, moving on from the birds, and she came to a stop. With a sigh of solemnness, she turned to me. "Do you know what they used to have here?" Looking around, I shrugged. "Xena, the sloth. Did you ever see her?"

"Don't think so."

"Aw, she was so cute. She's the only one I've ever seen in person."

I made a face. "Sloths are ugly."

Her jaw unhinged. "Who doesn't like sloths? They're so precious."

The only precious thing I've ever seen is you. "I'll take your word for it."

We moved on, making our way through the place. When we made it to the fresh water area, I thought Birdie would have a heart-attack over the penguins.

"Ugh, this is torture," she soon cried out.

I faced her. "What is?"

"Every exhibit is cuter than the last! I could just burst from it all."

"Uh-oh. Then we probably shouldn't stop here. You might actually explode."

"Why? What is it?" She looked around and walked forward

until she saw them. “Awwwww!” she cooed, getting as close to the glass as she could. River otters swam all around, making loop-dee-loops in the water. Once in a while, one would pull itself onto the ledge and roll around in the dirt before diving back in.

I looked over the animal information, reading out loud for her to hear. “Funtastic Facts: Sea otters, a relative of river otters within the *Mustelidae* family, utilize their exceptionally dense fur to float on their backs while sleeping. To prevent drifting away during slumber, they form living rafts by clasping hands together.”

The look on Birdie’s face was indescribable, and so was the feeling it elicited in me. If I had to try, I’d maybe say… warm? Precious? Downright heavenly?

“Wow,” she mused. “How is it possible that these fluffy babies can get even *more* enchanting than they already are?”

Smiling, I said, “I thought you’d like that.”

“I don’t just like it, I love it! God’s creations are all so perfect in their own way.”

At that, I simply continued to follow her from room to room. Our unofficial first date was no place to get into a debate about religion and how amazing God was or wasn’t to some.

BIRDIE

27

THE PHOTO STORAGE ON MY PHONE WAS FILLING UP FAST. WHO knew I could take so many pictures? But there was so much to see and do at the aquarium. I was having so much fun with Russell, and I wanted to document all of it.

He resisted in the beginning when I asked him to take photos, especially if it involved standing behind an exhibit cutout of some kind, but eventually, the resistance stopped. Instead of me having to drag him around, he went willingly. He even started pointing out photo-ops I hadn't caught.

As firmly as I wanted to keep my feet on the ground, this guy had me feeling so high in the clouds. I hated the feeling but craved more of it at the same time.

Next up were the sharks. We entered the darkness with only the giant tank of fish to light the way. It was exciting and beautiful, and when I saw the tunnel, I acted on impulse. Linking our arms together, I could almost feel the flames around his wrist tickle my skin. I tugged him along, descending into the cylindrical walkway. "This is so cool!"

"What if it springs a leak?" he asked, eyeing the whole thing with suspicion.

"It better not. This is my favorite outfit."

Trying to appear as though he weren't looking me up and down, he said, "I think it's my favorite, too."

Smiling at him, I winked. I didn't know where my bravery (or stupidity!) was coming from, but he brought it out of me somehow. As much as I didn't want to get involved with him, actually getting involved with him felt like the most natural thing in the world.

I turned, catching a glimpse of him putting his phone away. "Russ, are you taking my picture?"

"No, I'm taking a picture of the hammerhead."

I looked around, pointing. "He's over there."

"Yep. I was just waiting for him to come back around."

"Uh-huh."

"I mean it."

"Then give me your phone."

"What? No." That flustered him right up. I suppressed a laugh.

"Fine then," I said, walking toward with him determination. I pulled my phone out and turned the camera around, then leaned as close to him as I could, absorbing the heat of him into my side. "Say cheese!" But he didn't. I looked up at him, our faces the closest they'd ever been, his eyes a fathomless blue, deeper than the ocean itself. I elbowed him to distract myself, turning back to the camera. "You have to smile or I won't stop."

He shook his head but finally did what I wanted. With a great big smile, just silly enough to still be real, he even said, "Cheeeeese!" We ended up both laughing as I snapped one picture after another. When I finally stepped away, an unsavory coldness took the place of where his heat used to be.

"Oh, by the way," I said, needing a quick change of subject in my mind. "Today is my last day driving my dad's car. Guess which one I decided to get."

"The Honda."

"A brand new car? Yeah, right. No, I'm getting the Kia, even without the flux capacitor."

"I think it's fair you buy from that guy, since you gave him such a hard time."

"Agreed. I do feel a sense of justice. Plus, I really loved that color."

"That funky baby blue?"

I delivered my hand to my heart. "There's nothing funky about a nice periwinkle. It's beautiful."

"It wouldn't be my first choice, but I guess it does suit you."

The conversation waned as we took in the sights around us. We were surrounded by the curved walls of the tank, delighted by the swimming creatures above us. The more I looked up, craning my neck to follow their travels, the more my neck ached. The tension began to travel up the back right side of my neck, up into my temple, and to the top front of my head. Rubbing my neck with my free hand, I grumbled under my breath, following it with a small prayer.

Russell noticed. "You okay?"

"I'm fine, just getting a headache."

"Do you want to sit down? Do you need food or anything?"

"Well, I'll always take food, but don't worry. I'm fine. Headaches are par for the course for me. I've learned to ignore them for the most part. I just have weak eyes or something."

He looked confused. "Oh, okay."

My attention was then snagged by the most adorable puffer fish I think I'd ever seen. I scurried over and crouched down.

Pressing my finger against the glass—but not tapping, of course—I said hello. "Aren't you just the cutest little guy? Yes, you are."

Russell's throaty chuckle sounded from behind me. From the corner of my eye, I could see his phone was out again, but this time, I pretended not to notice. I smiled at the cute fish in front of me, but really, I was smiling for a different reason.

RUSSELL

28

The aquarium gift shop had that distinct smell of saltwater, sunscreen, and plastic. Flicking my finger through the dangling dolphin-shaped items on a rotating display, I pretended to be fascinated by their price tags. Birdie compared postcards with all the seriousness of someone selecting fine art for a penthouse apartment. Kids darted between shelves with sticky hands and colorful cups of blue and red slushie. Somewhere behind us, a toddler wailed about a broken bubble wand.

I didn't mind. I liked this—the noise, the normalcy. What a calm yet exciting day it had been. The way Birdie had gushed over the otter exhibit had failed to leave my mind.

Sea otters hold hands while they sleep so they don't drift apart.

She had pressed her hand to her chest like she might actually cry. It didn't get more wholesome than her. Could that be a dead give-away that I was barking up the wrong tree? Yeah, probably. But would it stop me from barking? Nope.

Don't drift apart.

"Birdie?"

The voice came from behind us, warm, surprised.

Birdie turned, and her whole face lit up. "Daisy!"

I followed her direction. A woman who didn't look much older than Birdie stood with two little boys orbiting her legs like restless moons. Her hair was pulled into a messy bun, and one hand rested subconsciously over a rounded stomach.

"It's so nice to see you," Birdie said, stepping forward. "Are you on day-leave?"

"Yes." Daisy nodded, smiling in a way that appeared both grateful and exhausted. "I'm here with my sister and her kids. Enjoying getting out while I can."

Birdie introduced me. "This is Russell. He's... a friend."

I tried not to overthink the word, focusing on the woman in front of me. With a nod, I offered a simple, "Nice to meet you."

Daisy's voice was soft but steady. "You too."

The boys began arguing about who got to hold the shark plushie. Daisy crouched slightly, whispering something calm and firm. The storm dissolved almost instantly. Birdie watched her with complete awe.

After a few minutes of small talk—how far along she was, how the women's campus had started a new parenting class, how grateful she was for her sister—Daisy squeezed Birdie's hands. "Thank you," she said quietly.

Birdie shook her head. "You're doing the hard part. Just keep the faith. You're already doing so amazing." They parted on a promise to see each other in the coming week.

I waited until Birdie and I had stepped back out into the humid coastal air before speaking. "So, that girl—Daisy. She's allowed to just leave?" I asked, shoving my hands into my pockets.

Birdie glanced at me, probably catching that edge in my tone. "It's called day-leave," she said, her response gentle.

"She's in rehab, right?" Though I kept my voice neutral, something old and sharp slipped in anyway. "When I was locked up, nobody got to take aquarium field trips."

Birdie stopped walking. Not dramatically. Not angrily. Just… still. "That's because you were incarcerated," she pointed out softly.

I exhaled deeply through my nose. "Yeah, I know."

"When you voluntarily enroll in the program, you can earn certain privileges. Being able to go off-campus for excursions like this is one of them."

I stared out toward the water beyond the parking lot, gulls circling overhead.

"That's why we don't get to see Dan," she added, her voice dipping. "He didn't choose it. The court ordered him there as an alternative to jail. He's going through a stricter program than she is."

"Because he didn't choose it," I repeated, chewing the words over, trying to comprehend.

"Right." She looked at me fully now. "Because restoration works differently when it's forced."

That landed. I didn't like how *much* it landed.

"I just…" I ran a hand over the back of my neck. "I guess I don't get it. You trust them. So fast. It looks like the two of you have been friends for years. How long have you known her?"

"Just a couple of months."

"You're kidding."

Her brow knit slightly. "I'm not. And it's not that I trust them fast; I just believe in them."

"There's a difference?"

"Yes."

We stood in the heat, the distant crash of waves filling the silence.

"She messed up though," I said carefully. "Whatever she did, it was obviously bad."

"Mmhmm," Birdie agreed.

"And now she gets day trips and family and stuffed animals and…" I trailed off.

"And grace?" Birdie offered quickly.

That word. I felt it like a splinter behind my fingernail. "Grace didn't get me out of a cell," I muttered.

Birdie's expression shifted, showing an empathy that somehow made it worse. "You didn't enroll in STLR," she said. "You didn't want it."

"I didn't want religion shoved down my throat," I snapped. "Besides, the judge wasn't very keen on me at sentencing. I don't think I could've gotten a cozy program like STLR even if I'd begged for it."

"The program is not about shoving; it's about choosing."

I let out a short, humorless laugh. "Easy for you to say."

She tilted her head. "Is it?"

I looked at her then, harder than I had before. Birdie spent her free time tutoring a guy fresh out of the slammer for a test he should've passed a year ago. She showed up to court hearings for families she hadn't known long but still treated like best friends. The girl remembered kids' names and lit up at otters holding hands. And she always spoke to *me* like I was worth something.

She was incredible.

"You really think people can just change?"

"I've seen it," she said simply. "Over and over."

I didn't respond. Determined, I turned back toward the gift shop.

"Where are you going?" she asked.

"I'll be right back."

I found it almost instantly, right near the checkout. A small plushie, brown and soft, of two otters floating together on their backs. Their little fabric paws were sewn together across their chests, their bodies forming a heart shape.

Don't drift apart.

I stared at it longer than I meant to, but something about it made my chest ache with awareness rather than pain. Forcing myself into motion, I walked to the counter and paid before I could overthink it. When I stepped back outside, Birdie was leaning against the ramp railing, watching the water in the distance.

Awkwardly, I held the plushie out to her. "For you," I said.

Her eyes widened. "Russell..."

"You liked the exhibit," I shrugged. "Figured you could use a reminder."

She took it carefully, like it was fragile. Like she liked it. "Sea otters hold hands so they don't drift apart," she said silkily, looking up at me.

"Yeah, I remember."

There was a pause. Longer this time than before. Full of something more, but I couldn't dare guess what. I didn't know why I'd bought it. Didn't know why it mattered that she looked at me like that. All I knew was I didn't want to drift anywhere that didn't include her.

"You really do care about people," I said before I could stop myself.

"Are you just now realizing that, or didn't you believe me before?"

I swallowed. The honest answer sat right there between us. "I'm still figuring it out," I admitted. Slowly but surely.

Her smile softened with patience, without a hint of triumph or judgement. How did she always do that? She lived like she wasn't ever afraid of the fire, like she knew some things didn't turn to ash when they burned.

BIRDIE

29

We'd certainly had better days. Today's GED Prep was proving to be a rough one. Russell had missed two fraction questions in a row, and I had explained improper denominators three different ways. I circled the latest mistake with more force than necessary, the pen tip digging into the paper.

Hey, I was patient by nature, but everyone had their limits.

"It's not that I don't get it," he muttered, tapping his pencil against the workbook. "It's that my brain just refuses to cooperate."

"Your brain cooperates just fine when you're arguing with me," I replied, putting my pen down beside the problem I'd just circled. "You just don't like slowing down."

He gave a faint smirk. "You say that like it's a flaw."

"It is a flaw."

"I feel personally attacked."

"You should," I quipped back at him, looking up. *Uh-oh.* That proved to be a big mistake. I tried not to smile. Tried and failed. All joking aside, he'd been trying harder lately. Actually trying. Showing up on time, bringing a pencil, reading the explanations instead of just waiting for me to talk. Despite his tattoos and general pessimistic demeanor, he looked less like a delinquent and more like... Russell. It did something for me.

"That's enough for now," I said, closing the workbook. "Five-minute break before my brain explodes."

"Thank you. I couldn't take much more right now." He leaned back in his chair, stretching his arms overhead. His T-shirt lifted slightly at the hem. I noticed, then got after myself for noticing.

I looked away, meeting his gaze instead. That was another mistake. "Don't worry. You're going to pass this thing," I stated.

He looked at me like it was a revolutionary thought. "You really believe that." A statement, not a question.

"Yes."

He didn't look away. The air felt thicker. That was the moment it shifted. It wasn't dramatic. No music swelled, no lightning struck. Just his eyes holding mine a second too long, and my pulse deciding to betray me.

He leaned, and I tracked his every move, our eyes locked together, as he grabbed the bottom of my chair and pulled me close. He wasn't cocky, but nor was he careless. Oh, this was very, very intentional. I felt it before I understood it, and by then, my heart was hammering in my chest so hard it almost hurt. My pulse was so intense it practically rattled my neck.

He leaned closer, searching my face like he was trying to solve something more difficult than fractions. "I've been wanting to do this," came his quiet confession. My breath caught. He lifted his hand, hesitated, then hovered it near my waist like he was asking permission without words. I didn't stop him. The place where his hand came to rest was ablaze.

And for one dizzy second—just one—I wanted him to. That

was the worst part. I didn't freeze because I didn't want him. I froze because I *did.* And if I didn't say something soon, I…

"Russ—"

He went for the kill, and at the last second, I turned my head. His kiss landed against my cheek. He went still, creating more of that nervous silence. Then he pulled back, dropping his hand as if I'd burned him.

"Sorry." The word came out rough. "I thought—"

"No, you didn't do anything wrong," I rushed out, but the damage was already done, I could hear it in his voice.

Standing up and shaking his head, he reached for his jacket, lifting it from the back of his chair. "I misread it. That's on me."

Something inside me panicked. I didn't want him to leave. We needed to process this. Quick decision made, I reached for his wrist, my hand enveloping the flames that enveloped him. "Russell, wait," I pleaded, worried he might pull away, then feeling relieved when he didn't. "Please don't leave like this."

He looked down at my hand then back at my face. He was already halfway shut down, fortifying himself. "I don't want to pressure you. If you don't want that, I'm not going to make you."

"I know." That's what made it worse. I let go of his wrist, taking a deep breath. "But I want you to understand something about me. I made a decision after my ex. He proposed, and it was a huge surprise," I explained.

His jaw shifted slightly.

"But I told him no."

"Why?"

"Because the second he asked, I knew that I didn't want to marry him."

"Sounds like you were honest."

"It felt like I was cruel. He's a good guy, Russ. He had every good quality anyone could want, and I still couldn't say yes."

He frowned. "So, you broke up."

"Right."

"Well, that sounds brutal for him, but not you."

"It was for me, too." My throat narrowed. "I've spent my whole life watching love fall apart. My parents' divorce was a slow-motion explosion. It was years of pretending, and tension that lived in the walls, festering unseen until it could no longer be hidden. After that, I promised myself I would never drag someone into a future I wasn't sure about. I couldn't say forever until I was absolutely ready to give it."

He watched, listening very carefully now.

"So, after Nick," I continued, "I decided that was it. No more dating. No more physical anything. No kissing, no blurred lines. I don't want to wake up one day and realize I'm halfway down a road I shouldn't have taken. So, the idea of love or relationships and all that, it just makes me kind of… irrational now."

His brow lifted slightly. "Kissing makes you irrational?"

"That's not quite what I meant."

"Then what did you mean?"

"It makes me attached." The honesty burned on the way out.

"And attachment scares you," he stated.

"Yes." *Ignore the silence. Ignore the silence. Oh, Lord, what is he thinking about me now?*

"You think kissing me would attach you?" he asked with care.

I hesitated, but ultimately could not lie. I just wouldn't tell him the whole truth. "Yes."

Something soft flickered in his eyes. "And that's bad?"

"Yes, because I don't trust myself," I whispered. "I don't trust that I won't start caring too much, too fast. And I don't trust that caring won't end the same way it always has."

"By someone leaving," he finished my thoughts for me.

"Exactly. Attachments are dangerous. For both of us."

He studied me for a long second. "Birdie, I think you're overthinking things, because I've been the dangerous one my whole life. I know what it looks like."

"That's not true."

"I was a thief. A criminal," he said flatly. "I dragged my best friend into it. I spent time behind bars. I don't exactly scream *'stable future'*."

"You made a mistake."

"I made choices." His voice was laced with a sad heaviness. "And I thought if I kissed you, it meant maybe I wasn't just the guy who ruins things anymore. But when you turned away, it felt like confirmation that *is* who I am." His admission was heartbreaking. My chest tightened.

"That's not what that was. And you don't ruin things," I was quick to say.

He let out a humorless breath. "That's not what my record says."

"I don't care. I don't see your record. I see you." That one struck a nerve, I could tell.

He stepped back then, creating deliberate space between us. "I won't try again. Not unless you want me to." He was clear, respectful. My heart twisted harder than it had when he leaned in to begin with.

"I don't know what I want yet," I admitted defeatedly.

He nodded once. "It's okay."

"But I don't want you thinking I rejected you."

"You literally turned your head away."

"Because I'm afraid," I corrected. "Not because I don't feel anything." The words hung between us, fragile and bright. I couldn't believe I'd said that much, but there was no taking it back. Honesty was the best policy, right?

"You feel something?"

"Yes, I do."

He swallowed. "That's all I need to know."

The air shifted again, less fragile now and more aware. I glanced at the clock. "We should probably call it."

"Yeah." Neither of us moved toward the door. Then Russell reached for his jacket again, tossing it over his shoulder. "See you tomorrow?"

I smiled. "See you tomorrow."

He paused at the edge of a bookshelf, just before disappearing. "Birdie?"

"Yes?"

"I'm glad you stopped me."

My pulse skipped. And then he left.

I sank back into my chair, pressing my fingers to my cheek where his almost-kiss had landed. My vow was still intact. My heart, however, was no longer untouched. I could deny it no more. And for the first time since Nick proposed, I wondered if maybe the problem wasn't who I was dating, or even physical intimacy. Maybe the problem was that, along the way, I'd confused fear with wisdom.

And I wasn't entirely sure which one had just taken over me.

So much for having limits. Russell hadn't just tested most of them; he'd blown each one to bits.

~

THROWING my backpack into the passenger seat, I leaned back and closed my eyes with a deep, heavy sigh. The library doors shut behind Russell ten minutes ago, but the moment kept replaying in my head on a loop.

His hand at my waist. His voice.

'I've been wanting to do this.'

The assurance in his eyes right before I turned away. I shivered.

I called up Jenna, waiting to hear her voice over the speaker in my car. I held my breath until she answered.

"Hello?"

"Girl, you busy?"

"Not after hearing that tone. What's up?"

"I just made a total fool of myself at the library with Russell."

"Well, this sure sounds juicy. Do go on."

"He tried to kiss me."

"Shut up! What happened?"

"I turned away, of course. And I told him I don't kiss or date and why." For the most part.

"You told him? What did he say?"

"He didn't say anything bad. I'm just so paranoid now. I told him that I was into him, but I didn't trust myself with those feelings. What does a guy like him think of something like that? I can't tell if he thinks I'm a challenge now or if he *really* likes me, and I just hurt his feelings big time. Or what if he thinks I'm a freak and that was his way of being nice about it? I just don't know anything, and I really wish I didn't care."

"Wow."

"I know." The headache building behind my eyes pulsed harder.

"You know," Jenna started carefully, "just because you decided not to date anymore doesn't mean you can't change your mind. I mean, if you like him…"

"Don't go there. I drew a line, and I'm sticking to it. Besides, he's got his own stuff going on. He doesn't need me adding drama to the life he's working so hard to recover. This is for the best for both of us."

Wasn't it?

"Hm. If you say so."

"Plus, I can guess all I want, but I don't even know if he likes me. Not truly. Sometimes it seems like he does, but then others, I worry he might just want a good time, which is the last thing he'd get from me."

Russell was gorgeous and confident in a rough-edged way. Worldly. Experienced. He'd lived a life far beyond tutoring sessions and volunteer work. He was far and away out of my league. What guy like him would appreciate a girl who froze pre-kiss because she was scared of attachment?

"I doubt it's like all that. It'll be okay, Birdie. Just finish the tutoring and then forget about him if that's what will make you feel better."

I let my face fall against the steering wheel. Was that the trick to making myself feel better? Ignoring the way Russell actually made me feel? I could keep denying it if I wanted, and I very much *did* want, but the truth was—yes, I had developed feelings beyond professional, beyond friendship for him. And I didn't know how to stop it.

Worse yet, I wasn't sure I still wanted to anymore. This afternoon had crossed us into something unfamiliar, something vulnerable yet honest. It was deeper than I had even gone with Nick. He had been safe and predictable. I'd never told him about my attachment issues, because I worked so hard to suppress them. I didn't think I'd even put it into words for myself before today. I'd never admitted that I always kept one emotional foot near the exit, even with him.

But with Russell, I'd just shown him the messy, unfiltered version of my heart. And what if, now that he'd seen it, he decided he didn't want it?

"I guess I'll try. I'll pray about it, too," I finally said. Could I really just fake my way through the rest of our time together? I supposed if God wanted me to, I could. But would I get a clear-cut answer like that? A Heavenly memo that read: *Proceed* or *Abort mission?*

Guess I'll find out.

"Yeah, sure, if you think you need to," Jenna said.

"I definitely do. And *you* should be in prayer every day, girl." I could do with a subject change. "You still haven't told your mom about Birdie Junior."

She chuckled. "It's a miracle she hasn't figured it out yet."

"It really is." I rubbed my forehead and looked at the time on my phone. "I better get. I've got to turn some stuff in tonight. I want to be perfectly deadline-free by Friendsgiving so I have nothing to worry about." Besides the obvious.

"Oh, yeah, I can't wait! Do we know yet if Sammy is going to make it?"

"Last I heard, she's still trying. I think her flight was set for the same day, and she's hoping to change it."

"That sounds like a headache, but I hope it works out. It won't be the same without her there."

"Agreed. And speaking of headache, I'm getting one, so I'm going for real now. Time to drive before I keel over."

"Okay. Are you still sleeping over tonight?"

"Yep, I'll be there. Just need to go home and decompress a bit first. Should I bring anything in particular?"

"Um, would you be okay with smuggling in some snacks? Or like, a lot of snacks?"

Laughing, I nodded, even though she couldn't see me. "I'll bring my heating pad, too, just in case your back starts hurting again."

"You are literally the best."

When we finally got off the phone, the silence in the car felt heavier than before. I started the engine, but I couldn't pull out right away. Russell and I really had stepped into something tonight, hadn't we? Not a relationship. We hadn't even asked any questions about the future, but something about the territory was new and terrifying.

With Nick, I'd known the rules because I'd set them. With Russell, I didn't even know the language. What if he walked away now that he knew how cautious I was and how tangled up my fears were? What if he wanted someone freer, easier, and less complicated?

The thought tightened around my chest. I didn't want to be left again, not after choosing honesty. Not after feeling for him...

You'd only have yourself to blame, Birdie Jo. You knew better.

I pulled out of the parking lot, my head throbbing steadily now. By the time I made it home, all I wanted was a cold pillow and a dark room, but I had assignments to turn in, snacks to gather, and I needed a heaping dose of prayer.

As I lay back on my bed, the otter Russell gave me bounced beside the pillow. I clutched it in one arm. Then, pressing my palms over my aching eyes, I started with the prayer.

God... we really need to talk about Russell...

RUSSELL

30

I WAITED FOR MY DAD IN THE PARKING LOT, SITTING ON THE CURB off to the side with my elbows on my knees, replaying the look on Birdie's face when I leaned in. It already haunted me.

I really hadn't expected to spook Birdie like that. After she explained the way she felt about things, I felt like a real jerk. Not about attempting to kiss her, because every fiber of my being had demanded it, but I hadn't realized how deep her fear ran. From the moment I met her, she appeared to be hiding something below the surface. Who was always that kind, happy, and full of joy, after all? But I hadn't meant to intimidate or upset her, and I was afraid I'd managed to do both.

I wouldn't have believed I had the power to chase her off, but that defeated look on her face told me I did, at least in some way.

The library doors slid open and footsteps sounded. A car door shut nearby, then a few minutes later I heard my name and I froze.

A pair of voices rang out from none other than Birdie's car. Her speaker volume was so loud the entire library could probably hear it, but not everybody had a personal stake in this phone call.

And it was only me in the parking lot listening to it. I wouldn't have, but it was my name that flew out of her mouth.

I told myself to ignore her conversation, to respect her privacy. But then she spoke about the kiss. She obviously couldn't see me from where I sat, tucked near the edge of the building. Guilt slid through me, sharp and immediate. I knew I should've walked away, but instead, I inclined my head.

"You told him? What did he say?" asked a feminine voice.

"He didn't say anything bad. I'm just so paranoid now. I told him that I was into him, but I didn't trust myself with those feelings. What does a guy like him think of something like that? I can't tell if he thinks I'm a challenge now or if he *really* likes me, and I just hurt his feelings big time. Or what if he thinks I'm a freak and that was his way of being nice about it? I just don't know anything, and I really wish I didn't care."

Each word landed with a fresh hit.

A challenge.

A freak.

She expected me to think those things about her? I swallowed hard. Was that what she thought of me? Was it… true?

"You know, just because you decided not to date anymore doesn't mean you can't change your mind," the friend said. "I mean, if you like him…"

"Don't go there. I drew a line, and I'm sticking to it. Besides, he's got his own stuff going on. He doesn't need me adding drama to the life he's working so hard to recover. This is for the best for both of us."

For the best.

I stared at the asphalt. She was trying to protect me? Or push me away?

"Hm. If you say so."

"Plus, I can guess all I want, but I don't even know if he likes me. Not truly. Sometimes it seems like he does, but then others, I worry he might just want a good time, which is the last thing he'd get from me."

That one stung. I'd worked so hard not to be that guy with her, or at least I thought I had. Maybe I was wrong and would never be right.

"I doubt it's like all that. It'll be okay, Birdie. Just finish the tutoring and then forget about him if that's what will make you feel better."

Forget about him.

My chest tightened. I strained to hear Birdie's response, but she took her time answering. That's when my dad rolled into the parking lot.

Of course. *Now* he decided to be punctual.

I stood quickly, trying to look like I hadn't just been eavesdropping on a phone call I had no right to hear. Birdie was still in her car, still talking. She hadn't noticed us, and I hoped she wouldn't.

"Hey, kid," Dad called as I slid into the passenger seat. "How was it today?"

I glanced once more toward Birdie's car before we pulled away. "Fine."

"Come on, don't give me that automated teenager response. How did it go? What did you learn? Was it fun?"

I gave him a dry look. "It was school, so no. Not really fun."

"I thought you liked—what's her name?"

"Birdie," I muttered.

"Right. Birdie. That's a very old, southern name."

"She's a very southern girl."

He side-eyed me. "Is she now?"

"Don't read into it."

"What? I'm just curious about the girl tutoring my son, that's all."

"There's nothing to be curious about, so drop it."

He hummed, clearly not convinced. "Uh-huh. Whatever you say, buddy." He flipped through radio stations, never settling on one. I stared out the window, Birdie's voice still echoing in my head.

'I just don't know anything, and I really wish I didn't care.'

But she *did* care. That part cut through everything else.

She cared.

But she thought I might be treating her like a game. Or worse, like a temporary distraction.

"By the way," Dad casually chimed in, "I need you to find out when your test will be and let me know. See if you can get a date on the books."

"How do I find that out?" I didn't even know where the test would be yet.

He gave me a look like the answer was obvious. "Probably start by asking your tutor."

I almost rolled my eyes hard enough to sprain something. As if I didn't know what he was doing. "I don't want to. And I don't know why you're pushing for her so hard."

He sighed, patient but firm. "Russell, all I need to know is your test date. You let me know when you find that out, okay?"

"Okay, Dad. You got it." He let it drop after that, but I didn't.

The rest of the drive home, everything I'd heard played on a loop in my head. She thought I might be the kind of guy who'd flirt with her boundaries just to win. She thought I might only want something temporary and fun.

She had no idea how right on the money she would've been,

but things were different this time. I didn't know how, or why her, but I didn't want a conquest. I wanted… I didn't know, but something more than I'd ever had before, and I didn't mean physically.

And now I had a reason to text her. A legitimate one. We could talk about testing dates, not feelings. Not almost-kisses, and definitely not the fact that hearing her say she might *'forget about'* me made something go *snap* inside my chest.

As my dad and I pulled into the driveway, I had uncomfortable clarity about something. Birdie may start drifting before I even got a chance with her, and I was determined not to let that happen. If she thought I was only after a good time, I was going to have to prove her wrong.

BIRDIE

31

JENNA INSISTED WE KEEP TO OUR NORMAL SLEEPOVER TRADITIONS, even if we had to modify them for swollen ankles and a third-trimester waddle. So, we were cross-legged on her bed, backs propped against a mountain of pillows, green clay masks cracking on our faces, while a pint of cookie dough ice cream sweated between us on the comforter. Tiny folded onesies sat in neat pastel stacks at the foot of the bed, ready to be hidden away, evidence of our earlier productivity. Now we were rewarding ourselves.

"Okay. Let me know when—ah!" Her voice pitched and she clutched her stomach.

I shot to my feet so fast the spoon flew out of my hand. "What's happening?"

"Oh, sorry. It's nothing." She winced, pressing her palm to the side of her belly. "I just got jabbed."

My shoulder slumped but my heart was still racing. "Don't do that! You scared me."

With a slight laugh, she rubbed her stomach. "My bad. It still takes me by surprise. And man, sometimes it really hurts. Feels like she's trying to rearrange my organs."

I exhaled and sat back down. "She's redoing her room is all. She's definitely going to be a princess like her Auntie Birdie."

Jenna laughed until she sniffled.

"Hey. You okay?"

She wiped beneath her eyes, mindful of the drying mask. "I wish we could have another Treetop Confessional."

The memories came back, some recent and some so far away now. Us at twelve years old, whispering secrets in Sammy's backyard treehouse like the world couldn't touch us up there.

"We can pretend we're in the treehouse now," I offered. "Seriously, Jen. You can tell me anything at any time."

"I'm just..."

I reached for her hand. "It's okay."

She nodded, chin trembling. "I'm starting to get scared. My due date is really coming up fast." Her tears fell without warning, like a sudden summer rain.

My heart wrenched for her. She was in such a tough situation, and it was only going to get tougher. I wrapped my arms around her, rubbing her shoulders and back until her breathing steadied. There was nothing more I could do except be with her. *Mourn with those who mourn.*

When she pulled away, her eyes were red and shining. I looked at her growing bump, and the reality of it all hit hard. "Tell your mama, Jenna. She needs to know, and you need her."

Her voice was so torn down. "She's gonna hate me."

"You can't know until you tell her. But I, honest to God, doubt it."

"I wish I had your confidence."

"Pray for it! I'm serious."

She huffed. "Praying is just a fluff practice for people who *already* have it all together."

"You don't pray because you have it all together. You pray because you don't. Well, there's many other reasons, too, but this is just a small point I'm trying to make. Besides, I pray on the daily, thank you very much."

Jenna waved her hand up and down at me. "No kidding. Have you seen yourself? I rest my case."

I blinked. "Wait. What?"

"You have everything, Birdie. The grades, the job, the family, the pageants, the face, the body. Even your breakup with Nick was neat and tidy. You land on your feet every single time."

Wow, that… hurt. It wasn't true, but I was desperate enough to wish it all was. "I could go back and refute everything you said, but there is no point. Why are you picking on me all of a sudden?"

"I'm not trying to." Her face puckered as much as the green clay would allow. She hiked her shoulders then threw her arms down. "I'm just so—I don't even know! Nothing makes sense. Everything in my body aches and hurts, and my mind is a literal omelet of craziness. I'm sorry that I suck, Birdie."

"You do not suck." I reached over the side of the bed and grabbed the heating pad I'd brought. Plugging it in and firing it up, I nestled it behind her, settling it low on her back. Then I pulled her close again. "Everything will be okay."

"I'm really sorry."

"I know." And that was *not* a word Jenna ever said, so I knew she had to mean it.

She sniffed. "We need a new topic so I can stop crying. Tell me about this new guy of yours."

"I don't have a new guy."

"Oh, *pleeeease* spare us both your denial. You've spent nearly every day with him for a while now, and let's not forget the whole storm thing and today's little incident. There's no way you don't like him even just a little bit."

"Jenna..."

"Please just humor me? I'm too hormonal to drag it out of you slowly."

I groaned. "Fine. You know what? Yes. I do like him *'even just a little bit.'"*

"Ha! Yes! Now, do tell."

"I really don't know yet, but the obvious? He's beautiful, super flirty, and he has... history. But aside from being stubborn about studying and loving to tease me relentlessly, I don't know a whole lot about him as a person."

"Sounds like plenty to start with."

"He does make little suggestive comments here and there, but..." I shrugged. "I know that I'm not his usual type."

"That's crap. You're too beautiful and sweet not to be everyone's type."

I couldn't absorb the compliment. "I get on people's nerves. Did you know I've been told I'm too happy before? Nobody is everybody's cup of tea."

"Girl, whatever. Just be bold and say something. Some guys are just dense."

"He's not dense. He's just out of my league." I called upon my previous thoughts. Boy, the truth stung when voiced out loud.

Jenna rolled her eyes so dramatically I'm surprised they didn't get stuck.

I ran to my own defense. "He's had time and ample opportunity to ask me out now that we've gotten to know each other better, and hasn't. I think he likes me or he wouldn't have tried to kiss me, but it could've been impulsive and not meant anything else for him." He'd asked to take me to lunch early on, but that was to repay me for tutoring. The aquarium thing didn't actually count, did it? He didn't ask me anything, and stopping for the tickets was my idea. "There's no reason to think that'll change."

"He could be waiting for you to flirt back. It's possible he thinks you don't like him, you know."

"Even still, a guy like Russell doesn't get intimidated. He's too busy doing the intimidating."

She leered at me. "I think you're underestimating your appeal, but okay."

"Aren't you just the sweetest." I pinched her cheek, and she swatted my hand away.

"I'm not sweet, I'm sour. And I think you should go for it."

"I don't know about that. I'll think on it."

The truth was, I had yet to *stop* thinking about it, and I wasn't any closer to a sensible conclusion. That's who I was, right? Sensible. Calculating and reasonable, but kind. But the way our last encounter had shifted into something deeper had shaken me to my core and would not let up. Was that a sign that things were right, or things were wrong? It had to be one or the other.

And again, what if he decided I wasn't worth it? What if he learned more than he cared to know? At this point, I'd need a miracle to sort out my feelings.

You hear that, God? Do you have a small miracle up Your sleeve for me and my confused heart?

RUSSELL

32

It was probably too late. Birdie was probably asleep by now, but I texted her on the off chance that she wasn't. And not because my dad had been circling me like a shark all evening, asking about test dates and future plans and whether I'd considered my *'options.'*

Nope. This was purely my own idea. Totally.

RUSSELL

> My dad keeps grilling me about finding out my test date. Do you know anything about that yet?

And yeah, maybe I was shamelessly using my dad's nagging as my excuse to extend my reach beyond the library, and even beyond dealerships and aquariums. I wanted to get into her texts, to spend more time with her, to remind her I was still here.

I could admit that Birdie Jo was nothing like my usual type. She was slow where I liked them fast. Serious where I liked casual. Blonde where I usually went for brunettes. She quoted Scripture and used color-coded planners. I preferred spontaneity and a little chaos, and certainly preferred to leave God out of, well, everything.

Everything about us was in contrast, and yet it was her I kept thinking about, her I kept looking forward to seeing, *her* laugh that I held on to like it was something I'd earned.

Her I secretly hoped would be awake right now so she would text me back. *Sigh.*

How did this happen at all, let alone so fast? I just wanted my life to return to normal. Keep my head down, pass my tests, and avoid a second round with the judicial system. I did not expect to get hung up on a girl, but she had this way about her. Something that made her shine brighter than the rest without even trying. Something incredible.

On the surface, I wondered if it was only because she rejected me. Maybe I wanted what I couldn't have. But the hours and days spent with her proved otherwise. I'd never really looked forward to seeing a girl before. The last thing I'd anticipated with that much eagerness was being released from that miserable sentencing.

Maybe I was just desperate. That could be it. Female attention had dried up the minute the handcuffs clicked, but before that, you could've called me popular, at least within certain circles. Money flowing, wheels rolling—that was my life.

Things were different now. Even knowing I was basically a nobody these days, Birdie Jo made me feel like a somebody. If I had to chase her to keep that feeling, I would. When she finally admitted to feeling something for me, she'd said it like someone with regret, not joy. I didn't like that at all. Even the girls who only wanted one thing from me never looked at me the way Birdie did.

My phone dinged. She *was* awake.

BIRDIE

Unfortes not. I'll have to get back to you on that.

I stared at the screen. *'Unfortes?' Who says that?* Birdie didn't even use contractions half the time. She was the type to say *'unfortunately'* like it was a moral obligation.

RUSSELL

That's okay, I'll let him know. Thanks.

There. That was casual enough. Except she didn't respond again right away. The conversation felt off.

Then:

BIRDIE

You suuure that's all you texted me for?

I leaned back in my chair. What was this? Miss Birdie Jo was teasing me? That was new. Suspiciously new.

RUSSELL

You feeling okay? Do I need to call 9-1-1? Use the safe word if you need police assistance.

We didn't have a safe word, but I figured she'd improvise. Three dots appeared. Paused. Disappeared. Reappeared.

BIRDIE

Don't mind me, I just think it's time we stopped beating around the bush.

Okay. This was so not normal Birdie behavior. I rubbed my jaw, half amused, half wary.

RUSSELL

Agreed. Let's do that.

A beat passed.

BIRDIE

You can go first.

I huffed out a laugh. Cheeky little thing. For a second, I debated playing this. Flirting around it. Tossing out something vague and seeing how she handled it, but that was probably my problem right there. Birdie didn't want someone playing anything. She said it herself—no drama, no games. If I wanted a real shot, I'd have to be real.

Was that seriously what I wanted? Something real with Birdie Jo? And if she gave me an actual chance, what would that look like? Would she let me close enough to see what she was like when she wasn't holding it all together?

Could I even take that?

Couldn't know unless I tried, so I typed before I could overthink it.

RUSSELL

I can't stop thinking about you.

I released a pent-up breath. There—simple. Honesty at its finest.

The response came quicker this time.

BIRDIE

I figured as much.

Ha. Confident tonight, aren't we? But that didn't tell me anything.

RUSSELL

It's your turn now.

This was it, the moment of truth. There was a long pause, much longer than seemed fair, until:

BIRDIE

Ask me tomorrow ;)

I stared at the winking face.

This girl.

For a second, I didn't know whether to be impressed or irritated. She had just flipped the entire thing on me. I laid it all out, and she sidestepped with an emoji.

I think I just got played.

I studied the exchange again. Something about it still felt off. I knew I didn't have a lot of experience with it, but Birdie wasn't a winky-face kind of texter. She was a period-at-the-end-of-every-sentence kind of texter.

But fine. If she wanted to do this in person, I could do it in person.

RUSSELL

Oh, I will. Count on it.

I set my phone down and leaned back once more, staring at the ceiling. Tomorrow then. If she thought she could feed me a taste of my own medicine and walk away unscathed, she had another thing coming.

Because if Birdie wanted honesty face-to-face? I was going to give it to her. And I was going to get to the bottom of whatever her weird personality shift was, one way or another.

Tomorrow, I was going after her. Full speed ahead.

BIRDIE

33

I HAD NO WORDS. NOTHING COULD ADEQUATELY EXPRESS HOW utterly horrified I felt when I woke up and Jenna casually confessed what she'd done while I was asleep. We were still in pajamas. I was still half in dreamland. And she dropped it like she was announcing the weather.

"I had an interesting chat with Russell last night."

Instantly, my stomach dropped, and I had no appetite for my Fruity Pebbles. "What? How?"

"It's really not a big deal," she stated, carrying her buttered toast. I eagerly followed her back to her room as she continued. "Your phone went off. I saw it was Mr. Beautiful, and I took the liberty of responding a little."

My brain stalled. "You what?"

"You were sound asleep! And it was just sitting there. And I knew you would only overthink it to death if you handled it yourself."

If we'd been in a cartoon, steam would've shot out of my ears. "You impersonated me."

"I prefer the word assisted."

I lunged for my phone and scrolled. There it all was, in bold, undeletable text.

Unfortes. Winky faces. Stupid, brazen confidence that did not belong to me.

"Oh my word, Jenna."

"What?" She turned, unfazed. "Russell *likes* you. Now you know. This is a good thing."

"But he thinks that was me!" I hissed. "He thinks I—I—"

"That you what? Like him? You do."

"That's not the point!"

"It's exactly the point."

I paced across her bedroom, running my hands through my hair. "That was a blatant betrayal of trust. You had no right to interfere in my business like that."

"All I did was send a few texts, all of them were honest, right?"

"You pretended to be me. That is a big problem."

Jenna crossed her arms. "You have become far too scared of everything for no good reason. *Somebody* had to do something if you couldn't do it for yourself."

I almost couldn't even respond. "You don't get to decide that."

"Someday you'll thank me."

"I highly doubt that."

She stepped forward, eyes locked on me. "Russell likes you. You like Russell. And now you both know for sure. That's more important than how you found out."

"But you've put me in a position I didn't ask to be in," I argued, my voice cracking. "And now I have to have an uncomfortable confrontation with him today that I don't want any part of! I don't even know enough about how I feel to explain anything to him!" It was hard enough telling him as much as I did yesterday.

"Yes, you do."

"No, I don't!"

"Birdie, look at me and tell me you feel absolutely nothing for him."

I opened my mouth and choked. Nothing came out, because I couldn't lie. Yes, I'd already told him that I care for him, but admitting to stronger, romantic feelings, especially after yesterday's conversation, was a whole other thing.

But I still couldn't lie.

Her expression softened. A little. "That's what I thought."

I hated that she was right. Her means of proving it were wrong, and we would have to deal with that separately, but still.

"I've created the perfect opportunity for you to be bold about your feelings. That's all it has to be. Tell him it was me all along if you want, I don't care. Just don't back down. You both deserve the truth."

At that, I gave her a look. "Just like your mom does, too."

Her lips pursed. "Don't start with me."

"I'm not starting. I'm finishing."

"Just go," she said, turning away. "Go talk to him."

"We're not done talking about what you did though," I warned her.

She mumbled an acknowledgment and I headed out.

The worry was already pounding through my head like a drum line. I couldn't possibly entertain a relationship right now. My health had only just stabilized, more or less. I was finally finding my footing at work. School needed my focus, too. My life needed to stay predictable and controlled for the time being.

Unfortunately, (*not unfortes,*) Russell was none of those things.

~

So, I did take Jenna's advice. I left for the library an hour earlier than necessary because sitting around waiting felt like psychological torture. I packed and unpacked supplies that didn't need organizing. Wandered and wiped down tables that were already clean with sanitizing wipes I kept in my backpack.

This would be our last study day before Russell's tests began tomorrow, one each day for the next four days, and I needed everything as organized and ready as possible to make sure he was ready.

Eventually, I settled on opening my book and staring at the same paragraph until the letters went fuzzy. Every two seconds, I looked up toward the entrance, my heart in my throat, anxiety swelling. This was easily the most intolerable hour of my life, except for the one I spent in that tiny courthouse waiting room during my parents' divorce.

And honestly? I preferred that one. At least then I knew what to expect about the ending.

Fifteen minutes early—a miracle in itself—Russell walked through the stacks. His gaze was already honed in on me.

I defaulted to my brightest smile. "Welcome to another day of learning, soldier. How are we feeling today?" *You can do this, Birdie.*

He gave me that sideways grin, the sultry one that should've been illegal. "I'm feeling fantastic, and yourself?" He dropped his backpack into the chair across from me. Then, to my utter dismay, he walked around the table and pulled out the chair beside me.

Right beside me!

How had I not seen that coming?

When he sat down, he took up entirely too much space. One

arm rested on the table, the other draped over the back of my chair like he owned the place.

Like he owned me and every ounce of my oxygen.

"I'm doing great," I said, praying my voice didn't betray me.

He studied me for a second, with too much concentration. "You sure about that?"

"Yep."

Another moment passed.

"So." He leaned closer, similar to yesterday, only he reached a point where he stopped and didn't come further. "I believe you owe me an answer."

There it was. My heartbeat roared in my ears. He reached over and casually twisted the end of my hair around his finger. The gesture was slow. Intentional.

"And," he added, cool as a hot cucumber, "I believe I already know what you're going to say."

Oh, Lord, help me. Because I think he's right.

RUSSELL

34

I held her gaze for a long moment, giving her time without letting up.

"Fine," she said, exhaling. "You want answers, and I think you should have them. Everyone deserves the truth."

"Sounds great. Lay it on me. I can take it."

She hesitated, which told me this was not going to be light. "First of all, you know those text messages from last night?"

My lips twitched. "The ones where you suddenly developed a personality transplant?"

Her eyes narrowed. "Yeah, those. Well, surprise, that wasn't me."

"That's no surprise at all."

She folded her arms. "It was Jenna."

"Jenna." I tilted my head, scanning through memories. "She's the little Mexican girl, right?"

"She's a lot more than that," Birdie shot back, protective fire flashing in her eyes. "But yes. You must remember her."

"Barely. But that explains a lot. I wondered what was up. The texts didn't seem like you."

Her shoulders lowered a fraction. "So, you knew it wasn't me talking to you about… that stuff?"

"I suspected. I've picked up enough about the way you speak to know you aren't the emoji and abbreviation type."

Despite herself, she smiled.

But…" I continued, leaning just a little bit closer, but not too close. "What about the part where you didn't deny… that stuff?"

Her expression sobered. "That part was real." She drew in a steadying breath.

I could see this was difficult for her. I almost wanted to get up and leave right then so she didn't have to admit anything else. But I had to know everything for certain.

"I might care about you as more than a friend," came her words.

Might.

"But nothing has changed," she rushed on. "I don't date anymore. That's strike one."

Hey, wait. "There are strikes?"

"Yes. Here's the thing… I scratched the surface of this topic yesterday, but I didn't fully explain, and I just want you to understand."

Dang. Everything she'd said about attachments and emotions was only the surface?

She continued. "After my last relationship, I decided it's in my best interest to focus on school and work. I don't need distractions."

Distractions, huh? Nice. That's what I am.

"Keep going," I prompted. Might as well hear it all now, all at once.

"Even if I did date—which I don't and won't—I don't kiss."

"Right. Because of forming attachments and all that?"

"Uh-huh."

I thought about it. "So, that means you don't kiss casually?"

"More than that." She met my eyes without flinching. "It means I've never kissed anyone, ever. Not once."

For a second, my brain misfired. Birdie Jo Rene Lewis MacLean had never been kissed. Never? How was that possible? She was unapologetically herself. The kind of girl boybands wrote ballads for.

My first instinct was disbelief. My second was something dangerously close to reverence.

"Not even once?" I clarified.

"A little peck on the cheek once in a while, but that's it."

I relaxed—sorta—into my chair. Part of me thought it was tragic. Another part thought what a privilege it would be for someone in her future. And then, far too quickly, I wanted to be that person.

"I understand now," I said, keeping my tone as even as I could. "What I don't understand is why."

"It's just a personal vow. I'm saving my first kiss for marriage." I let slip a small laugh before I could stop myself. Her eyes hardened instantly. "I don't expect you to get it. You don't have to. This is between me and my future husband."

Future husband. I rolled the words over in my mind. That phrase should've sent me running. Any sensible guy would hear that and bolt. But instead of feeling deterred, I felt challenged. If I'd had half a brain, I would've dropped it. Maybe I should've even been offended. Instead, I sat up straight, putting on an air of seriousness.

"I'm sorry I laughed. It's just not something you hear every day. What made you decide that?"

She was considerate of her words. "If you seal a marriage

bond with a kiss, then to me, kissing really counts for something. Holding hands, hugging—that stuff isn't as big of a deal. But a first kiss? You only get one."

It seemed like such a dramatized outlook to me. "Kissing isn't that big of a deal either."

"It is to me." Her voice sharpened. "I'm not sharing something intimate with just anyone. I've always wanted my first kiss to be special. What could be more special than saving it for the man I'll spend the rest of my life with, someone who will always be there?"

Her logic didn't line up for me, but who was I to judge? "You won't have any stories to tell him. No experience."

Birdie smiled awkwardly. "Who wants to hear stories about their husband or wife being physically intimate with other people? I don't love the idea of my husband having experience with anyone but me."

I had to pretend that didn't sting. She wasn't talking about me, of course, but still. That already meant she would never consider me as anything more than—

Stop. That's following the fantasy too far down the rabbit hole.

"What if he's terrible at kissing?" I countered. "But then you're married and stuck."

She shrugged. "If I don't know any better, why would I care? I won't be comparing him to anyone."

"He probably won't give you that same courtesy, you know. The odds just aren't there."

"Maybe not. But that doesn't change what I choose. I know he'll appreciate the gift of my loyalty. There aren't many firsts to give, and I want him to have as many as possible."

It wasn't her fault, but she had me suddenly aware of my own past, of who I'd been and the girls I hadn't thought twice about.

She wasn't rejecting me out of cruelty, but she was drawing a line, and I was standing on the wrong side of it.

Birdie turned back toward her books like the conversation was over. Like she'd laid down her terms and that was that—but I wasn't finished.

"I don't want to be your husband," I said, probably a little too bluntly.

Her head snapped toward me.

I probably sound crazy to her right now. "I'm not saying I don't respect what you're saying, because I do. I just don't understand it. And I'm not pretending to be marriage material, but whatever is happening between us is real. I don't know what that means we should do about it, but that's *my* honesty."

Her fingers tightened around her pen. She could live in denial if she wanted to, and pretend this tension didn't exist. She could act like I didn't make her nervous in the best way all she wanted. But that wasn't something I could do anymore.

Our familiar silence returned and it was okay. I would give her the space and time she needed to digest my feelings. I could be patient. I wasn't giving up on the idea of her and me together. Even if it wasn't the right time to ask yet, I knew what I wanted. If she could act in the name of a personal vow, so could I, and right in that very moment, I vowed that Birdie Jo would one day be my girl. I just had to deserve her first.

So, how in the heck do I do that?

And before then, I had GED tests to pass.

RUSSELL

35

THREE TESTS DOWN. ONE TEST TO GO. TWO SCORES: PASSED. ONE score: pending. Anxiety: through the roof. Up next: math.

I'd always said math was pointless. Numbers didn't care about you. They didn't bend or bluff or back down. Either you were right, or you were wrong. Turns out that's exactly why I used to skip out on it.

But this GED? It wasn't optional. It was the difference between moving forward and staying where I'd been stuck since the garage got shut down and life as we knew it came to an end. Thank God for Birdie though. She'd made sure I wouldn't walk into the test blind.

Whatever. If I got through science, I could get through this.

She insisted on driving me to the school each morning for testing. I told her my dad could do it, but she insisted anyway. I didn't argue too hard, but I still hated that she was the one doing the driving. I should've been the one picking her up.

Soon though. Better late than never.

As we pulled into the parking lot, she squeezed the steering wheel so tight one would think she was about to go take the test herself.

"You can stop white-knuckling it," I teased her.

"I'm not." But her hands loosened. "Only one subject left," she said. "Do you feel ready? I mean, of course you do. I know you know this stuff. You've studied so hard. You'll do amazing. You always—well, you've been doing amazing."

She was spiraling. I reached over and lightly pinched her cheek. "You did your best, Sweetie Bird. Stop worrying. It'll be fine. I've passed everything so far."

"We don't have the science score yet," she reminded me.

"I still think I passed it."

The science test had sucked. I just did not have a mind for the STEM subjects. But if I survived the monster that is genome sequencing and mitosis, I could survive slopes and equations.

"Remember, we might not get results for a few hours, or even a few days. Don't get discouraged."

Was she telling me or herself? "Got it, boss."

"I wish you would stop calling me that."

"But I like you being in charge."

She rolled her eyes, but she was smiling. She hated that she liked it, too. "What are you going to do when you don't have me forcing you to memorize all this junk anymore?"

"Maybe I'll fail today so I need more tutoring."

She looked horrified, like she believed I just might. "Don't you dare."

I laughed. "Then I guess we'll have to come up with another reason to hang out."

"If you pass, we'll work on that."

Oh, really?

"Why wait?"

Her eyebrows drew together. "What do you mean?"

I turned to face her fully. "If I pass this test, you let me take you out on a real date, without tutoring or errands. And I don't mean spending hours together almost every afternoon while we study, but a date. A real one."

"And if you fail?" she asked.

"Then *you* can take *me* out on a date." I let her laugh. "I'm kidding. I won't fail. You're giving me that look. I know what you're thinking, but it's not arrogant to trust what you taught me."

She took a deep breath. "All right then, Mister Confident. You have a deal."

For half a second, I thought I'd imagined it, then I realized she was serious. I opened the door before she could take it back. "Deal. I'll text you later. Thanks for the ride."

"Of course."

I hesitated. There were about a dozen other things I wanted to say, about how she'd changed everything for me. About how I wouldn't even be standing here, almost a GED graduate, if she hadn't decided I was worth investing in.

Instead, I settled for, "Hey, Birdie? Thanks for everything else, too."

"You're more than welcome."

Her smile had me grinning like a fool the entire way into the building, until the weight of what was at stake hit me like a tire-iron.

If I passed this test, I would not only have my GED, but my car would belong to me again. I wouldn't have to depend on anyone to take me anywhere. I would be one relieving step closer to not feeling like a charity case or dead weight.

I would have something that was mine.

And I'd have a date with Birdie Jo.

I slowed near the sidewalk and looked up at the sky, feeling all sorts of ridiculous. "Okay, God," I muttered. "I know I haven't exactly been Your star student." *Big understatement.* "But I've been trying. You know I have."

A couple kids walked past me, and I dropped my voice.

"I need this. Not just for the car or to satisfy probation. I need to prove I can finish something." I rubbed my head. Was I seriously talking to God right now? "And… if you wouldn't mind… I really would like to take her out."

I sighed. "I should've made her pinky promise."

The doors to the school loomed ahead of me, smelling faintly of disinfectant and teenage regret. I squared my shoulders. Maybe Abby was right. Maybe people really could change. If that was true, then this was the moment I proved it—to the court, to my parents, to Kevin… and to Birdie.

I pushed open the heavy door and stepped inside. Math and I had unfinished business.

BIRDIE

36

Leaving Russell at the school for his final exam this morning was unexpectedly difficult.

Over the course of the last four weeks, I'd grown to like him. Possibly too much for my own good. But how could I *not* fall hard into like for him? His incredibly good looks aside, his presence had turned into a friendship I realized I was happier for. I looked forward to seeing him nearly every day. I adored watching his skills improve and his confidence grow.

And then, over the course of these last few days, I'd grown desperate for him to pass. That desire hadn't begun with Russell's little challenge to take me out either, but it was ending that way.

Every day had been fresh misery as I waited for his texts, to hear how he'd scored on the latest subject. So far, so good. Everything had been a passing score. His worst subject, science, had given him some difficulty yesterday, and much to my torment, that score still had not populated. If he passed science yesterday, I knew he would pass math today. He was marginally better at it.

I had to stay positive. I had to ignore the risk. It was either ignorance or dwell on it completely, and I couldn't do that. I had to be in the office today, which meant I needed to get my mind on the task at hand.

How exactly did I go from being decidedly anti-boy to all-out boy-crazy? And for just one boy in particular.

By the time I pulled into the STLR parking lot, I gave myself a firm internal lecture. *You are here to work, so don't be staring at your phone.* Walking inside, I hoped to leave those thoughts behind.

It became a lot easier when I opened the door and saw Stephanie already there, hunched over her desk, rubbing a worried crease in her forehead that hadn't been there yesterday.

I stepped to the edge of her desk. "What's wrong?"

She startled. "Oh, Birdie. You snuck in like a ninja."

"I'll have to add stealth to my resume." I laughed.

Her lips curved faintly, but her eyes didn't follow through. A thin file folder sat open in front of her, turned just enough that I didn't catch the contents.

"Are you ready to do a bit of the boring stuff? It's just filing today," she asked, briskly closing the folder up.

"Yep. But is everything okay? You looked pretty serious when I came in."

Her chest rose and fell. Then she gave me an easy smile that I didn't quite believe. "It's nothing for you to worry about right now."

Right now?

"You sure?" I pressed.

"Absolutely sure." She slid the file into her desk drawer. "Let's dig into those reports."

I could tell she'd given me less of an answer and more of a boundary, but it was all I had to go on. I got to work stacking progress reports into neat piles, each depicting drug screens passed, parenting classes completed and consistent counseling attendance. They were all milestones achieved that we highlighted in bright yellow. Redemption, right here, measured in bullet points and neon ink. It was beautiful. It was the fruits of so much labor.

My eyes skimmed one familiar name from earlier in the year —the brave mother from the court hearing who had fought so fiercely for custody of her kids. I remembered the way they'd all cried after the judge ruled in her favor. The way her son and daughter had clung to her.

I smiled at the still-fresh memory. That's why I loved my job. That right there was the hard evidence of why I believed so strongly and did everything I did, because people were worth it. They surprised you.

"Steph," I called. "Have you heard anything new from Gia—"

"No," she answered much too quickly. I glanced up. When she caught my gaze, she eased her tone. "Sorry, I'm just overwhelmed with all these updates we've got going on. But no, I haven't heard much. She's… working her plan."

O-Kay…

Something about the way Stephanie said that made my stomach twist, but it was clear she didn't want to talk about it. Regardless, it sounded above my pay grade. Maybe Gia's ex was back in the picture and making things difficult.

We worked quietly for a while. The hum of the printer filled the office, and soon, my mind returned to normal function. A resident called about rescheduling a counseling session. It was all so hum-drum I was able to forget my earlier suspicions and focus again on operations as normal.

By mid-afternoon, however, my focus was shot. Every time my phone buzzed, my heart leapt. Every time it didn't buzz, I imagined worst-case scenarios: failed scores, silent disappointment, Russell pretending it didn't matter when it absolutely did.

Unable to stand it any longer, I grabbed my phone and sent him a text. There's no way he wasn't done by now, and I had to know how it went.

BIRDIE

Did y'all hear anything about science yet? How did you do today with math?

RUSSELL

If you're that anxious to go out with me, why don't you just say so?

Ugh. Very funny!

But seriously, that's what I get after all my concern?

I typed and deleted three different responses before settling on none at all. He'd tell me when he knew something. Pestering him wouldn't make the results portal refresh any faster.

"Everything okay?" Stephanie asked from across the room.

"Yeah," I said, quickly locking my phone and setting it down. "Just waiting on some news."

Her nod had a somber quality to it. "Waiting is hard."

"That's an understatement."

"Sometimes we have to let people finish their own process. Even when we can and want to intervene, we can't always make a difference for everyone."

I frowned, not following. "Intervene how?"

"By trying to control the outcome."

I nodded, though I wasn't sure which outcome she meant anymore, but I realized I could apply it to Russell's test. I just had to be patient.

When I left the office, the sky had darkened to a dusky blue.

My head ached faintly, a combination of tension and far too much overthinking.

And we apparently *still* had no test scores.

That night, sprawled across my bed, I stared at the spinning ceiling fan for a whole five minutes before giving in and texting him again. Hours had passed. I needed *something.* Maybe simply reaching out would be enough to prompt him to fill me in, although I couldn't imagine he would leave me hanging when he had insisted on so steep a prize for passing.

Our official first date hung in the balance.

RUSSELL

37

"So, how do you think you did?" my dad asked when he picked me up after the test.

"Aced it." I was already smiling at the thought, willing that passing score into existence.

"What has you so sure?"

"I had a really good teacher." The words slipped out before I could filter them.

Dad shook his head with humor. "I knew it! I can't wait to tell your mom."

"There are no results yet. There's nothing to tell her."

"Not that." He chuckled, merging into traffic. "Your mom told me about your little run-in with Birdie Jo at the mall recently. We've been debating how long it would take you two to become an item. She said you'd be too stubborn and it wouldn't happen. I said it would within the month."

Wow. "Dad, as much as I'd love to help you win a bet about my personal life, Birdie and I are not an item."

"No?"

"No."

He actually looked disappointed. For me? Seriously?

Go ahead. Tell him. Why not?

"But she did agree to go out with me if I pass all four sections of the test." Two scores were good. Two were still dangling in the universe somewhere.

Dad slapped his hand on the steering wheel, radiating satisfaction. "There it is. You see? I knew it."

I laughed, unable to help it. I couldn't remember the last time I'd voluntarily offered my dad information about a girl.

"Your mom had nothing but glowing things to say about her. I'd love the chance to meet her for myself."

"She's pretty incredible."

He glanced at me. "That's probably the most enthusiastic review you've ever given any girl you've ever been interested in."

"I hardly said anything."

"Exactly, and yet you said plenty."

I stared out the window again, watching houses blur past. She really *was* incredible. She was kind and pretty, for sure, but she was also gracious enough to re-teach me algebra like I wasn't a complete idiot. She believed in me when I hadn't exactly earned it.

We hit the driveway and the engine cut off. Dad didn't move to get out right away. "I just want you to know something," he said.

Great. Lecture incoming? Does he think I don't know about the birds and the bees or something?

"Whatever the outcome of this test, your mom and I are proud of you."

Not what I expected. I swallowed, eyes still forward.

"You really put effort in. You showed up. You studied. You didn't quit when it got frustrating." He nudged my shoulder. "Even if part of the motivation was to impress a girl, you stuck with it."

"It wasn't only about a girl."

"I know," he smiled. "It was also about a car."

I huffed a quiet laugh.

Then his expression went from teasing to something more anchored. "Russ, I've been praying for this shift in your life for a long time. Not the test or the car, but your heart." He tapped his chest. "God's been working on you. I can see it."

That comment hit hard and strange. "I messed up. A lot."

"Yes, you did, no sugar-coating there. But you owned it, you paid for it, and you're rebuilding. Fixing things matters more than messing up." He rested his hand on my shoulder. "You've made strides lately, son. I can't tell you what that means to me and your mom, and even Matt and Abby. And probably to Miss Birdie Jo, too." His mouth curved. "I pray you start seeing yourself the way God does, and the way we do. You are not your worst mistake, and you have a very bright future ahead of you."

My throat tightened. What did I even say to that? No doubt he was giving me more credit than I deserved, but something inside me warmed at the words, and I could feel that warmth take root. But what did that feeling mean?

And would it last?

"Thanks, Dad," I managed. "I appreciate it."

He gave my shoulder one last squeeze before opening his door. "Your mom and I will be watching your portal, waiting for those final results."

"Sounds good."

Inside, I headed straight for the shower, letting the hot water pound against the back of my neck. The confidence I'd felt walking out of that testing room was still there, but now it was layered with something heavier. Expectations. Things had been a lot easier when I thought my parents were just nagging me. Realizing they actually cared? That they were praying for *me?* That carried a weight.

After changing into sweats, my phone buzzed on the dresser.

BIRDIE

Anything?

I grinned. She probably spent all day pretending she wasn't invested, and she was failing miserably. I liked it a little too much.

RUSSELL

Nothing yet. But you don't need excuses to talk to me, you know.

I could practically hear her exasperated sigh through the screen.

A few minutes later:

BIRDIE

Goodnight, Russell Sprout.

I laughed out loud. Mom had revealed that precious nugget of information at the mall food court like I was five years old, and Birdie had nearly choked trying not to laugh. I'd tried to be mad about it but I couldn't. She wielded it so well. She could call me anything she wanted.

RUSSELL

Goodnight, Sweetie Bird.

After plugging my phone in for the night, I tossed myself into bed, laying my hands under my head. Even I couldn't believe the scores weren't in yet. But I was no longer panicking about what I didn't know or about what would happen if I failed. I'd done the work. My family was proud of me. God was apparently still working on me. And a girl I really cared about had said yes to a date. Things might actually be turning around, and I may even be turning with them for once.

MONDAY ARRIVED, and with it came my parents knocking on my empty doorjamb bright and early.

"Russell, get up," Dad's stern voice called.

What did I do now?

I rolled over, tangling in my standard-issue bedsheet as I went. I cracked my eyes open just in time to see them both striding in. It was too early for me to discern their expressions, but they clearly had something to say.

Good news or bad?

"What is it?" I asked, lifting onto my elbow.

Mom sat on the edge of my bed. Dad stood beside her, hands in his pockets, looking too composed for my liking. Mom's hand emerged from her tucked arms, death-gripping a piece of folded paper.

"What is this?" I dared ask.

"The rest of your test results."

Oh... Oh!

I shot upright so far that I nearly head-butted her. My gaze flicked to Dad. His face was unreadable.

Crap... No GED, no car. And no Birdie.

No. I couldn't accept that.

From the tension in the room, I was sure they'd brought bad news. I'd failed. I knew it. Math and science had always been my weak spots. It's not like I guessed every answer, but what if I'd missed just enough?

"I tried my best. I really did."

"All those hours you put in with the tutor, Russell," Mom said.

"I know." My stomach dropped. I already dreaded the look on Birdie's face. She'd worked so hard with me. How could I have let her down? Maybe I could delay telling her. Or pretend I hadn't checked yet. But eventually, I'd have to retake the stupid thing. There was no dodging any of this forever.

"Good thing you did," Mom said, mouth curving. "You passed."

I blinked. "What?"

She opened the paper when I didn't take it. There they were. All four sections, all with passing scores.

I'd passed! Really and truly?

Finally, I grabbed the page from her hands, scanning it closely. Not only had I passed, some of these scores were actually good! Science, the one I'd been most worried about—solid. Math? Better than solid. I could barely believe it.

"Wow," I breathed.

Mom radiated with pride. "With scores like that, I have no doubt you can get yourself through college. Maybe you could take some local credits to start with."

College? Let's not get crazy.

But still...

The thought of possibilities was a temptation I couldn't have imagined I'd ever feel.

"Good job, Russ. I'm real proud of you." She wrapped her arms around my neck and squeezed.

"So am I," Dad added. "Birdie will be, too."

That made me grin.

"Thanks, guys," I said, awkwardly patting Mom's back because I wasn't used to this much affection before noon. Or ever.

She stepped away, still smiling, and nudged Dad.

"A deal's a deal," he said, pulling something from his pocket.

My keys!

I didn't even give him a chance to finish the sentence before I snatched them midair. "Yes!" The weight of them in my palm felt unreal yet familiar. I had *earned* this.

"You still have a curfew," Dad said, his firm, all-business tone in full effect. "And if at any point your location turns off, we'll do more than take your keys. Your GED is a fantastic accomplishment, and we want to make sure you continue down this path. We've always known you're capable of great things. We hope you're seeing it now, too. Keep it up. Understand?"

"Sure, Dad."

"I really hope so." He smiled in his half-cocked fatherly way and then turned toward the door. Mom lingered, her eyes suspiciously misty.

"Good grief," I muttered at her.

"I'm really so proud of you. My boy."

"I think I liked it better when you hated me." I sighed, falling back against my pillows.

"I have never hated you. Being justifiably angry does not equal hatred, but that's all in the past now. Congratulations, Russell Sprout. I love you. Why don't you go show off your results?"

I shot her a look. She was right, I totally should. But then something else caught my attention. "Wait. When do I get my door back?"

"Ask again after you get a job!" Dad shouted from down the hall. Mom gave me a sympathetic shrug, then finally disappeared.

Alone at last, I held my hand out, just staring at my keys. They were just keys, but they stood for so much more. Best of all, I wouldn't have to hurt Birdie with my failure, and these small metal things were tangible proof.

In fact, I was about to make her day.

I sat up suddenly. "Dad!" I called, jumping off the bed and jogging down the hall.

He was just at the bottom of the stairs and turned back to look at me. "What's up?"

"Can I borrow some cash?"

"Is it for what I think it is?"

"Dad. Please."

He sighed, putting on a show of thinking about it. "How much?"

"Enough to not look like I picked flowering weeds from the side of the road."

He laughed, reaching for his wallet. Pulling out a few bills, he handed them over. "This is a loan. And next time, you fund your dates yourself."

"Fair."

"And Russell? Take her somewhere that shows effort. Not just money."

"I will." I already had the best idea in mind.

"And remember, God's been generous with you this week. Don't waste what He's doing."

I swallowed. Nodded.

Back in my room, I got ready in record time. Clean jeans.

Decent shirt. Keys tucked securely in my pocket so they couldn't vanish again. Then I paused, looking at myself in the mirror. Glancing at my tattoos, I smiled, not realizing when I reached over and thumbed the roses with my other hand.

Oh, yeah, things were actually turning around. GED—*check.* Car—*check.* Date—*secured.*

Still grinning, I took off with only one destination in mind.

Ready or not, here I come, Birdie Jo.

BIRDIE

38

Russell passed. Not barely, not by a miracle of mercy. He *passed*-passed, and with good scores. The kind that made an honest woman out of me because now I had to keep my word and go on a real date with him. I couldn't have refused even if I'd wanted to. And I didn't want to because I liked him.

There. I admitted it again. Fully, plainly. No more hiding behind tutoring sessions or friend-zone technicalities. In fact, I liked him a *lot,* but embracing the truth didn't make it a good idea. It didn't mean things wouldn't end in emotional disaster.

But truth was truth, and I was *stupid* into Russell Grandy.

"Tell me where we're going," I begged as we merged onto yet another unfamiliar highway. We'd been on the road for nearly an hour and nothing looked familiar. Granted, I hadn't paid much attention to road signs, being far too distracted by the radio and the smell of his cologne.

"You'll find out soon enough."

"So mysterious."

"You're still afraid of driving, aren't you?"

The question caught me off guard. "Pardon me?"

"You keep looking at my speedometer. Does my speed worry you?"

I hadn't realized I'd been doing that. "I'm not a fan of freeways," I admitted. "Too many lanes with too many stupid people, and I don't like speed unless it's on a horse."

"You're missing out. Riding horses sounds way more dangerous than driving a car. There's so much fun to be had behind the wheel. Why don't you let me show you?"

"How?"

That smirk of his should have warned me. "You'll just have to be patient and wait for our first stop."

"We have more than one stop?"

"I only had two planned, but there will now be three."

"My, my." I wiggled my shoulders dramatically, hair bouncing. "How exciting."

And I meant that. Until we pulled into what appeared to be a small airport.

I straightened. "What in the world are we doing here? Oh! Do you have a private jet? Are we going to Mexico on a luxurious day trip?"

He snorted. "You read too many romance novels."

Moving slowly enough for me to have ample time to freak out, Russell drove to the far end of the complex and eased his car into a sort of starting position. Behind us and all around was an open field. In front of us, where I could not pry my eyes from, laid a long, grey ribbon of runway.

Dread settled like a bowling ball in my gut.

"How do you know about this place?"

"They do drag races out here sometimes."

My eyes widened. "But it's an airport. Won't we get in trouble for being here?"

"It'll be fine. We won't stay long."

"But—"

He reached over and gently took my face in his hand. My thoughts froze solid.

"Hey. Do you trust me?"

"Yes," came the immediate and silly truth. "But that question automatically makes me nervous."

He chuckled, then reached over and tightened my seatbelt. "Is that still comfortable?" I nodded. "Good." As he pulled back, he stole a quick kiss and my cheek burned. My heart raced. And *he* grinned. "You ready?"

"Yes." I could do this. Totally. I could ignore that innocent little kiss and be brave. Russell was smart, and he loved his car. He wouldn't hurt it. And, surely, he valued human life above horsepower.

Right?

"It'll be fun, I promise. If you don't love it, just tell me to stop and I will. Okay? Pick a safe word."

"Donuts."

Laughing, he squeezed my knee. "You got it. And if you're good on our field trip, we'll stop through town and get you some."

"Just drive before I lose my nerve."

"Think of the donuts, Birdie."

"Right. Let's roll." Readying myself, I gripped the door and armrest as tightly as I could. If the seatbelt didn't keep me in, maybe my kung-fu death grip would.

Russell gripped the wheel firmly with his left hand, right hand on the gear-shifter. The engine roared. The car launched.

Every sensation hit at once—the rumble beneath my feet, the violent push of acceleration forcing me into the seat, the wind screaming past the windows.

And my own voice screaming louder than all of it.

Russell didn't laugh at my reaction. He didn't even look rattled. He was laser-focused, hands steady, controlling the car with the precision of second nature. Changing gears felt so buttery smooth like he knew how to drive better than he could walk, to the point where the only jarring I felt was from the raw power of our speed. He knew exactly what he was doing.

By the time we reached the end of the strip, my shrieks had downgraded to breathless gasps. Then we came up on the turn.

We spun, tries gripping, body tilting, and I squeezed my eyes shut and flattened my palms against the glass. We accelerated again. Faster. And this time, I wasn't screaming at all. I was purely exhilarated. Even flying at 20 miles per hour on horseback had never had this much power.

The open pavement stretched forever ahead of us. There was no possibility of traffic getting in our way out here. Just one car, two people, and the sense of endless freedom.

On our second pass, I actually laughed.

Russell glanced at me, grin spreading. "Still alive?"

"You could say that!" I shouted back.

Then, as we reached the middle of the strip, he began to slow down. Doing something with his foot and the emergency break, Russell put us into a tight spin. I shrieked again. "Are you doing a donut?"

The spinning stopped abruptly and we rocked back and forth before everything went silent. He turned to me, serious. "You okay?"

I blinked, panting. My body felt charged with pure adrenaline. "What?"

"You said donut."

It took a moment. Then two. Then I burst into laughter. "I did, didn't I?" I gasped, laughing harder. "I'm sorry, Russell, I wasn't using the safe word! I was asking if that spinny-thing was called a donut!"

He dropped his forehead to the steering wheel, shoulders shaking. "Oh, man," he said between laughs. "You had me scared."

"Accidentally! I'm so sorry!"

"It's okay." He reached for my hand and laced our fingers together. "Were you having even a little fun?"

I paused, trying to focus on the question and not the way our hands fit together. I wondered about him stealing another kiss. "I think so. But I'm not really sure. Why don't you start her back up and try again?"

His face lit up. "Your wish is my command, Princess."

Princess. I tried not to melt.

He revved the engine again, and this time when we launched forward, I didn't brace, I trusted, in Russell, in the seatbelt, in the fun of it all. I lifted my hands, and I lived.

When he finally slowed and rolled us toward the exit, my hair was wild, my heart pounded, and my cheeks ached from pure joy.

He parked and turned to me. "So?"

I shook my head, a breathless wonder. "I can't believe I liked that."

"I told you."

"But still, don't do that on the freeway, please."

"That's fine," he said, his eyes warm. "We'll make new roads."

My heart did that dangerous little flip thing again.

"Now, are you ready for stop number two?"

"I'm ready, but unless we're actually going to Mexico, I don't see how you can top this."

He grinned, taking us in the direction of somewhere new. "Oh, Sweetie Bird. We're just getting started."

BIRDIE

39

Surrounded by cotton and corn fields, and long stretches of lonely highway, our second stop turned out to be a genuine Amish store tucked into the middle of the small town of Beeville, not too far from my new favorite airstrip-slash-racetrack.

I squealed when we passed the first yellow sign with a black buggy silhouette. Wild! "Amish crossing!" I clapped my hands. "Russ, this is not real life."

He smiled like he'd been waiting for that exact reaction. "Told you I'd bring you."

How much could a girl smile in one day?

I hadn't necessarily believed him at the time he said it, but I'd learned since then that Russell didn't throw words around lightly.

We turned off the main road and onto narrower country lanes. The pavement grew rougher. The houses grew simpler and the sky felt wider.

"We're definitely not in Corpus anymore," I said, pressing my forehead to the window like a child hunting for reindeer on Christmas Eve.

"Observation skills on point."

"Look!" I pointed at the road. "Hoof prints! And those are wagon wheel ruts. You can literally see them."

We came to a T in the road. The GPS instructed us to turn left, but I was still staring straight ahead when Russell squeezed my hand.

"Birdie. Check it out."

I turned and behold—a horse and buggy rolled down the road toward us. "No way. That is the coolest thing I've ever seen."

Russell eased the car closer to the brush and overreaching huisache so they'd have plenty of room. The Amish gentleman gave a polite nod as he passed by. Russell lifted two fingers in a casual wave. I, on the other hand, could barely contain myself. It was probably a silly thing to be so excited about, but how cool was it to see something I'd only read about come to life right in front of me?

Russell had done this for me.

"Look at the pretty horse. I wonder what breed they raise."

"Horses are… intense."

"Have you ever been riding before?"

"Nope."

Oh, boy. Challenge so accepted. But I'd bring that up later.

"The buggy is so beautiful, too."

"They make and sell them at the shop we're going to."

My jaw dropped. "You are so lucky we can't fit one in your car."

"I think your wallet is lucky. They're not cheap."

Russell resumed the short drive the rest of the way. The shop was just at the top of the small hill where the buggy had come from. There was another car parked there so we settled in beside it. To our left was a greenhouse, which I could see was spilling over with various plants. I wanted to go in there first. To our right was the combination shop itself.

We were surrounded by a couple of dirt roads leading to various properties, and houses stood all around. Straight ahead was the nearest one, and it fascinated me to see it so close. Simple white paneling, two story, with a cozy front porch and rocking furniture. A clothesline had been strung out front, and a woman, complete with navy blue dress and sunbonnet, hoisted up and hung her damp laundry.

"Oh, wow. Do you see her?" Looking straight ahead, it was my turn to squeeze Russell's hand. "She's wearing a bonnet and everything. I wish I could see what the inside of her house looks like. I bet it's homey and wonderful."

He followed my gaze. "You're romanticizing. Not everything is like you read in books."

"But sometimes it is." Suppressing the desire to keep holding his hand, I released it so I could unbuckle and reach for the door handle. "Let's go!"

Russell stopped me. "Hold up." He got out of the car and jogged around the hood. He opened my door with a small bow. "You have to let me do all the date things. I passed my GED, remember? I earned this."

"Oh, you're right. By all means, good sir, proceed."

He walked me through the greenhouse, and by the time we emerged, I had two already flowering tomato plants and the most beautiful multi-colored lantana.

"Where are you putting all this?" Russell asked, loading them carefully into the back seat.

I waved my hand. "Details," I answered with disinterest. One did not ask where new plant babies were going; one simply made the room.

On our way toward the front door of the main shop, I got distracted by two fledgling turkeys pecking through the grass and dirt, cheeping away.

"Aww, Russ!"

He didn't even look. "No."

"But look at them!" I crouched down, and one of them tilted its head at me. I tilted mine back.

"They're plotting," he accused.

"They are not."

"They absolutely are. Don't even think about putting those things in my car."

"They're hot out here, and don't they look super lonely?"

Russell came and put his arm around my shoulder, gently steering me onward. "Let's go inside. You haven't even seen the pies yet."

I did want pies, but the fight for those turkeys was not over.

Inside, I lost what little restraint I had. There was fresh bread, homemade jam, and honey in thick glass jars. Shelves of canned vegetables and cartons of fruit. Hand-stitched dish towels and quilts. Two pies somehow found their way into Russell's arms. Three jars of jam and a pint of honey found their way into mine.

When we stepped back outside, we had enough delicious preserves to survive a minor apocalypse. Then, we passed by the turkeys again. Despite my full arms, I slowed. "You know, that's a pretty good price," I said casually, reading the sign above them.

Russell rubbed his chin. "It's a little late for Thanksgiving. Don't think they'll get big enough in time."

I gasped. "Russell Benjamin."

"What?"

"You stop that right now."

He shrugged. "Mmm I can imagine it now. Roasted turkey.

Mashed potatoes. Green bean casserole. Sweet rolls… Very festive."

"That is it." I shoved my items into his arms. "Put these in the car. I'll be right back."

"Birdie—"

Too late.

A few minutes later, I emerged triumphantly with a cardboard box, breathing holes punched neatly in the sides, and a kind Amish teenager who'd unlocked the cage for me.

Russell stared at the box. "You did not."

"I did." Birds loaded in, the box wiggled. From inside came a chorus of indignant peeping. "I had to. They're all alone, Russ. They need a home. Can't you see it in their eyes?"

He shut his own eyes briefly, pinching the bridge of his nose. "Tell your new pets if they don't stop all that ruckus, they're going on our Christmas menu next year."

Our. The word wrapped around me, warm and unexpected.

I crossed my arms. As much as I liked the implication that we would be making future Christmas plans together, I had to protest his idea. Full stop. "We are *not* eating Lucy and Ethel."

"You named them?"

"Yes, I did, and they're going to live long, happy lives far away from gravy boats and cranberry sauce."

"You can't tell me you don't like a good roasted turkey leg," he hmphed. That was irrelevant. "What if they're not females?"

"Then I'll reevaluate their names as needed. Maybe I'll end up with a Henry and Henrietta. Wouldn't that be precious?"

He laughed, shaking his head. "You're unbelievable."

"You drove the getaway car," I said sweetly.

"Yeah, I did." His eye contact was nearly too much, making my chest feel full in a way it never had before.

The turkeys chirped. The car rolled back onto the road, and I realized this might be the happiest I'd felt in a very long time. I ignored the faint ache in my neck, knowing what was coming. It must've been the extreme car-ride. And I ignored the subtle nagging in my heart that something was amiss at work. Those things could wait. For now, I had plants, pies, and turkeys.

And I had Russell.

RUSSELL

40

BIRDIE'S JOY FROM THE DAY WAS GOING TO STICK WITH ME FOREVER. I'd never forget the way she'd screamed on the runway, or how she'd gasped about a buggy and a simple woman in a bonnet. I could hardly believe it when she'd marched back inside for two doomed turkeys like that, either. I'd never seen someone love the world the way she did.

The turkeys, however, did not return the favor. They chirped and clucked and scratched the entire drive back toward town, and it wasn't until we pulled into the dirt parking lot beside Taqueria Chapala that a certain reality hit me.

"Is this stop number three?" Birdie asked, peering over at the building.

I cracked the windows then cut the engine. "It is, but I just realized we have two poultry pests in the backseat."

"They are not pests."

"They're loud."

"They are adjusting."

"Well, we can try to be quick?" I offered.

"No way. It's much too hot. They'll die in here. It doesn't look like quick is an option anyway. This place is packed."

"You're right." I would just have to go inside and get our food to go. "What do you want to eat?"

"Let me pull up a menu real quick."

It wasn't real quick, but I was in no hurry. The sooner we ate, the sooner I'd have to take her home, and our date would be over. That meant my first day of real and true freedom would be over, too.

Finally, she found something. "Ooh, I will take the cheese enchilada plate, please. With a lemonade."

"Done. Stay here. You and the chickens keep cool." I turned the car back on, closed the windows up, and let the AC flow.

"Turkeys," she corrected.

"They all taste the same," I teased. She gasped like I'd committed a felony, reaching protectively toward the birds. Laughing, I headed inside to order.

I came back out balancing two Styrofoam containers and drinks. She opened the door to take them from me, and I was taken aback. My car had been transformed.

The sunshade was up, blocking the worst of the late-afternoon glare. The seats were pushed back so we had extra legroom. The radio softly played some worship song I didn't recognize. And something sparkled from my rearview mirror, clinking and catching the light as it swayed from our motion.

It took me a second to process. She'd turned my car into a little restaurant.

"Here is yours," Birdie said, placing my drink into the top cup holder. She handed me my food.

"Thank you," I said, receiving it all and still taking in our surroundings. "What did you do in here?"

"Do you like it?" she asked, eyes hopeful. "I thought we could decorate a little."

I glanced around again. It felt comforting and adorable, just like her. She'd built a tiny world out of nothing. "It looks nice." I nodded toward the thing hanging from my mirror, finally taking a good look at it and realizing what it was.

"It's my James Avery bracelet. It shines like a disco ball, don't you think?"

I let the silver charms slide between my fingers. Crosses, hearts, tiny symbols of moments I didn't know yet. "So it does," I agreed quietly.

We started eating, turned slightly in our seats to better face each other. She sang under her breath between bites, completely unbothered by the fact that I did not share her enthusiasm for what she called *'Jesus music.'*

I didn't mind though. I minded even less that she had already programmed her favorite station into my radio. When, I wasn't sure. I didn't want to listen, but I didn't want to change it, either.

"Do we have napkins?" she asked.

"In the bag."

She reached in. "Got 'em. But there's more in here." Pulling out another white container she held it out. "What's this?"

"Desert."

"Ooh." She opened the lid and peeked inside. She looked at me like she either wanted to cry or laugh and couldn't decide. "Donuts?"

I nodded once, winked. "Donuts."

"You are nailing this date thing, I'm just sayin'."

A little bit later, a commercial cut in after the latest song, and she froze. "Hey. Did you hear that?"

"No?"

"Listen." She turned the volume dial.

The ad was for a nonprofit that repaired cars and donated them to single moms and women trying to rebuild their lives.

"Isn't that so cool? You could totally do something like that, too."

"What makes you think so?"

"You love cars. Maybe you could partner with them or even start your own program at home. I know that STLR is always looking for affordable transportation for their graduates. Can you imagine how many women you could help? It would be such a great use of your skills!"

The more she talked, the more animated she became. She was so sure, treating it all like a real possibility. If only I wasn't a guy with a fresh record and a recently obtained GED, and a habit of messing up everything he touched.

I forced a smile. "You're cute when you're excited."

"So, you think I'm cute all the time?"

"And then some."

"Thank you, by the way. Not just for dinner. For all of it, and for putting up with all my new babies. I hope we didn't ruin the evening by requiring adjustments."

"Nothing's ruined. This has been the best day ever. Turkeys or no turkeys."

Her smile went shy at the edges. "Yeah. Agreed."

We finished eating while Lucy and Ethel provided background commentary. When I started the car and pulled back onto the road, I reached over and laced my fingers through hers.

She startled. I glanced over. "What?"

She looked down at our hands like they'd appeared out of nowhere.

I smirked. "It's allowed."

"What is?"

"Hand holding. We're on a date, remember?"

"Oh. Right." She blushed, a hint of a smile coming through.

She slid her hand back into mine. She fit there. It felt like she'd always belonged.

The sun dipped lower and the road stretched ahead. The turkeys rustled in their box. And for the first time in a long time, or maybe ever, I let myself think something dangerous. Maybe one date wouldn't be enough. Maybe I didn't want it to be.

If nothing else, I prayed it wasn't our last.

BIRDIE

41

We lingered on the final trip, walking to my door with our hands still threaded together and swinging between us like it was the most natural thing in the world. Kinda felt like it was. That didn't make it any less terrifying.

All my loot from the day was already delivered inside the house, except for the turkeys. Lucy and Ethel chortled softly in their box as Russell placed them down at my feet. He leaned back against the recessed wall framing my entryway with one shoulder propped, the image of casual perfection. "So… How much fun did you have today? Driving fast was the best part, I bet. Admit it."

I did. I loved it, each and every minute of it, from his steady focus when he drove us around that airstrip to the Amish store and everything that came with it. And then dinner and donuts? It was truly the best date I'd ever had.

This man had completely enraptured me. He seemed happy when I was happy. He held my hand like it was meant to be. It was all as scary as it was thrilling, leaving me with more questions than answers and more feelings than fear, which surprised me.

"I admit it. I did have fun. After the initial shock wore off, even the drive was amazing." I rubbed at the back of my neck where the tension had begun as a dull creeping and was now a mild migraine. At least it had graciously waited until the end of the night to appear. "No wonder you love cars so much."

"I knew it. I'm glad I could change your mind."

His tone and the satisfied way he held tightly to my gaze gave the impression he wasn't only talking about impressing me with his speed skills.

Choose your next words very carefully. "Me too." *Not careful at all. Fail. Why not just hand him your heart on a silver platter?*

Russell pushed off the wall and stepped toward me, eating the space in a single stride. My pulse thudded hard in my ears, radiating pain from the back of my neck, but when he looked at me like that, I nearly forgot about it. "I had a lot of fun, too, Birdie. Thanks for coming out with me."

He got within a breath's reach, and all I could do was stare. I was afraid to open my mouth to speak in case… in case…

The more he leaned in, I didn't pull away. I didn't think about my rule at all. I didn't think about wisdom or restraint or being sensible.

I wanted him to kiss me.

And I wanted to know if he would stay. If he knew how I kissed, would he see something worth keeping?

His breath brushed my cheek, but then he stopped. He pulled back, scrubbing a hand down his face. "I'm sorry. I forgot."

So had I.

Reality flooded back in, loud and humbling. My rule. No

kissing unless you're certain. No kissing unless you're safe. No kissing unless you're sure he's staying.

Which means no kissing until you both say 'I do.'

But the deeper I fell for Russ, the less that rule seemed to matter, which was exactly why it had to.

Get it together, Birdie Jo. You don't know him well enough. Temptation is not confirmation, and butterflies are not promises. You have this rule for a reason.

I bent and picked up my two new feathered friends before my resolve could wobble again. "Goodnight, Russ."

"Wait." Russell stepped forward again and gently cradled the back of my head with his hands, fingers slipping through my hair. Then, he leaned in, pressing a kiss to my forehead before pulling back.

Having left me breathless, he reached around me to push the door open. Familiar spiced cinnamon washed over me in the most tortuous way. "Goodnight."

I slipped inside and nudged the door closed behind me, pressing my back against it for one steadying breath before moving on. The house was quiet. My head was not.

I carried the turkeys through to the back, settled them into a tote I found to use as a brooder, and let the rhythm of care steady me.

By the time I straightened up, my migraine had fully bloomed and the pressure thrummed through my brain from one end to the other. My body always demanded payment for too much excitement sooner or later. I would have to shower and sleep it off.

But first…

BIRDIE

You make it home yet?

RUSSELL

Just now. Everything okay?

BIRDIE

Yep. Just looking after you.

RUSSELL

Oh, okay.

I like you looking after me.

BIRDIE

Did you really have fun with me today?

RUSSELL

Do my eyes deceive me or is Birdie Jo being insecure?

BIRDIE

Don't piddle around, just answer.

RUSSELL

lol

Did I have fun with you today? Yes. One hundred percent. Five stars. Do recommend.

Actually, scratch the last part. I do not recommend.

BIRDIE

What??

RUSSELL

Nobody else better go near you.

BIRDIE

Do my eyes deceive me or is Russell being jealous?

RUSSELL

Ummm, I believe you're the one piddling now, ma'am.

BIRDIE

lol. I have one more question to ask you.

RUSSELL

What is it?

BIRDIE

What do you think about spending more time with me?

RUSSELL

Are you asking me out now?

BIRDIE

Yes, I am. I'd like you to be my date to our annual Friendsgiving dinner this weekend.

RUSSELL

Sounds like fun. Are you bringing Lucy and Ethel?

BIRDIE

I warned you about that, Russell Sprout...

RUSSELL

lol sorry. I'll be good.

BIRDIE

See that you do...

I'm going to bring a pasta salad.

RUSSELL

Sounds good. What should I bring?

I smiled like an idiot. Tonight had made us braver. Laying my head delicately onto my pillow, my migraine pulsed on, but my heart was full, too. Maybe I didn't know if he was staying, but he wasn't leaving either. And tonight, that felt like enough.

RUSSELL

42

FRIENDSGIVING WITH BIRDIE'S FRIENDS, IN FACT, DID *NOT* SOUND fun, but I was going with gratitude for the invitation to spend more time with her.

"Remind me again what's so special about this get-together?"

She smiled. "Don't sound so intimidated."

"I'm not."

"Mmhmm."

"Seriously though, what are we going to be doing?"

"Eating too much. Catching up. Being grateful." She shot me a look. "Very scandalous."

"Simply wild."

She laughed. "It's just our people hanging out. You'll like them."

Our people? I didn't say anything to that.

We pulled farther down the street, and things started to look familiar. I knew these trees and that mailbox. The driveway sloped the same as it always had. The old house had gotten a major facelift, but I recognized it just the same. I'd spent too much time here not to.

Then she slowed. Parked. I stared at the house in front of us with new eyes, shocked at what I hadn't noticed the day of the storm, when I'd been here last. It had fresh siding and repaired windows. No more blackened boards. I couldn't believe I'd been too preoccupied and self-absorbed to realize before. Had I seriously *not seen* any of this?

Kevin's place. More specifically, Kevin's place without the evil stepfather and his chaos. And if I could see all that from the road, what else was had changed without me?

My jaw tightened before I could stop it.

Birdie was already unbuckling. "Come on. I think we're some of the last ones here." I didn't move. She looked over. "What?"

"Why are we at Kevin's house?"

She blinked like it was obvious. "He's the host this year."

Music drifted from the backyard, followed by hearty laughter. It sounded easy and normal. Like nothing untoward had ever happened here.

"You okay?" she asked.

I opened my door slowly and stepped out, scanning the place like I was back in another lifetime. An irksome thought crept in and took hold. Why was it that Kevin got released from his sentence first, and had time and money and energy to do all this to his house, and yet he never once called me? I had yet to hear a peep from him. Why? How did he end up better friends with Birdie and *her* people than me?

Birdie came around the front of the car and grabbed my hand. "It'll be good," she said, mistaking my silence for nerves. "You and Kevin will probably disappear and talk cars for an hour. It'll be like old times, only better."

Her optimism was darn near infectious, even if she were just a smidge off the mark. "You think so?"

"Of course. Y'all have been friends forever. I'm sure he's excited to see you."

I doubted that, but what else was there to do but walk in? I mean, I could try at least. We were already here, and Birdie was counting on me.

Heading toward the side gate, each step felt heavier than it should have, and I stopped, turning toward her. "Birdie?"

"Hmm?"

"Kevin and I haven't talked."

She maintained her grip on my hand. "What do you mean?"

"I mean we haven't talked. At all. Not since before." I shrugged, suddenly feeling stupid over nothing that felt like something.

Her forehead creased. "I didn't know that." She studied me more closely now, reading something there she hadn't seen before. "Did you try?"

The question scraped my consciousness. "Sort of. I went by his house, after that storm actually, and I guess he wasn't home. But he got out first. He's had all this time to reach out to me and hasn't."

She absorbed that. For a second, her positivity didn't have a ready answer. Then she stepped closer. "Okay. So maybe tonight is just, like, a reset."

"Or it's awkward."

"Or it's healing."

I sighed.

She squeezed my hand. "I didn't bring you here to blindside you, but I didn't know there was something going on below the surface. If you want to leave, we can."

The offer surprised me. She would really leave her special

Friendsgiving event for me? I searched, looking for any reason to doubt her, and came up empty. She really meant it.

My heart flipped.

I looked past her toward the glow of firelight and the shadows of figures moving beyond the fence. Then I looked back at her. She remained unmoved and sure, leaving the decision to stay or not up to me.

I tightened my own grip on her hand, sharing what assurance I could. "No. We're already here."

"Are you sure? Don't make this decision because of me. I want you to feel completely comfortable."

I wasn't sure complete comfort was a possibility, but I was sure I was willing to endure the night. The idea of making her happy outweighed my break in confidence. I gave her a smile and said, "Let's go in," before we finally stepped through the gate together.

Tables loaded with casseroles and desserts, steam rising from them in smoky tendrils, took up one corner of the yard. String lights hung overhead, anchored to a newly built pergola that extended off the back door. Just beneath it, bathed in its soft light, was a large banquet table already arranged with plates and utensils and decorations. Across the yard, a small crowd gathered around the fire pit, turning to see who had just arrived.

I felt every eye on me and became hyper-aware of everything. The tattoos on my arms, the scars on my knuckles, the unpleasant history I carried in my back pocket. I wasn't dressed to impress whatsoever. Even my boots against the stone pathway seemed to single me out.

Then I looked at the girl beside me, the one who was brave and confident enough to walk in here with me hand-in-hand.

The lights caught in her hair, making her appear more angelic than she already was.

We were a contradiction. She fit in here. I didn't. They would all see it. Kevin was going to see it first. And because I had no luck, eventually, Birdie would see it, too.

Whatever this night would be—awkward, tense, healing, humiliating—we were walking into it together. *Here goes nothing.*

SOMEONE TURNED down the music when they saw us coming.

"Birdie! Finally!"

My hand became want for her warmth as Birdie threw her arms out wide. A girl with dark skin bounced across the yard, her high ponytail swinging behind her. They collided in a squealing hug like they hadn't seen each other in years rather than weeks.

I realized I recognized her from that infamous party at Daniel Schellers' house forever ago, but didn't know her name. A tall, athletic blond guy followed behind her with an easy smile and relaxed posture.

I scanned the yard again, taking in more details. The string lights that hung this way and that were the only illumination in the yard aside from the fire pit. There was polished patio furniture filled with friends that weren't mine. The landscaping was fresh, and even the back of the house had no broken shutters. No sagging gutters or broken, dead trees, or rusting metal objects. Most notably of all, there was no Craig stumbling through the screen door yelling at someone, ready to throw down.

It was Kevin's house all right, only it didn't feel like it to me anymore.

"Hey, I'm Jared Tomlin," said the blond guy, with a friendly extension of his hand.

"Russell Grandy."

He nodded, grip firm. "Good to meet you." He gestured toward the girl now clinging to Birdie. "This is Sammy Ballard."

Sammy pulled back from Birdie and narrowed her eyes at me. "I kinda remember you."

"From Dan's party," I confirmed.

"Yeah. That's it."

Birdie hooked her arm through mine like she was presenting me as something special. "You've gotta meet everyone else." She practically dragged me toward the fire where more of them were sitting. "Jenna! Come and meet Russell."

A Mexican girl with shoulder-length hair in a half ponytail rose with groaning effort from a lawn chair. My eyes dropped of their own accord. Her stomach was round and undeniable. I tried and failed not to stare.

She snapped her fingers in front of my face. "Hey, buddy. Eyes up here."

Heat crawled up my neck. "Sorry."

"Uh-huh."

"Jenna Rodriguez, this is Russell Grandy," Birdie said. The way she gave my name to everyone she cared about made me feel like I meant something. I could really get used to that.

"Do you remember him?" Birdie asked.

Jenna squinted in thought. "Maybe?"

Before I could respond, the screen door squeaked open, and there she was... Sarah Stevenson. Still put together and looking like she belonged in magazines instead of this town.

Birdie launched herself into another intense hug.

Watching Birdie light up like that did something strange to

my chest. It made me want to be better. How did I become something worthy of hugs like that?

But just as quickly as the feeling came, doubt chased it away, leaving me hollow instead of hopeful. Birdie Jo might enjoy spending time with me right now, but how long would that last? She already had people like this. What did she need with someone like me long term?

The two of them turned toward me. "Sarah, I know you remember Russell," Birdie said buoyantly.

"Of course I do." Sarah stepped forward without hesitation and wrapped her arms around my shoulders, and I cringed instinctively.

When she pulled back, she had a smile on her face. "It's really good to see you, Russell. How are you doing?"

"Fine."

"Glad to hear it. Kevin will be out in a second."

Birdie beamed. "I bet he can't wait to have his best friend back."

"Former best friend," I corrected on angry impulse. But a best friend would've called or written. The Kevin I knew would've shown up.

I just couldn't get over it. He got out first. He had freedom first. If he'd even tried, my parents would've handed him every detail about where I was. They always did like him, always saw something good, probably something better than me, in Kevin.

"Dang," a voice said from behind me. "Didn't know I'd been demoted."

Kevin. Every muscle in my body went rigid.

When I turned around, he looked surprisingly good. Healthy and filled out, like life had been feeding him rather than starving him. It annoyed me in the most intrusive way.

"Long time no see, Russ." Kevin held out his hand.

I looked at it. Didn't take it. His hand hovered there a second too long before dropping.

"How you been, man?"

"Great," I said flatly. "Haven't my parents told you? The accommodations at home are almost as good as they were in prison."

A couple people shifted uncomfortably.

Kevin let out a short, unconvincing laugh. "Still dramatic, I see."

I glanced past him at the house. The windows had been replaced on this side as well. Even the siding was new. The porch light didn't flicker anymore. The yard was growing instead of patchy and dead.

I remembered this place when Craig lived here. He left beer bottles just about everywhere, and the walls were so thin they did nothing to buffer all the shouting, inside or out. Kevin would sleep on the couch when his mom locked herself in their room because he wanted to be close by in case he heard her struggling.

Back then, we were in it together. Back then, he needed me.

But now?

I stood there feeling like the only version of me that ever mattered was the one who suffered alongside him. Why did Kevin's life have to be in shambles for him to seem like my friend? If he wasn't broken anymore, how did I fit into his life?

Were we ever really friends? Or were we just two drowning people who grabbed onto each other and didn't know how to let go? Maybe he learned how, but I still didn't.

Birdie squeezed my arm, unaware of the war raging inside my head.

Kevin noticed. His eyes dropped to where her hand rested on

me, then back up. "I'm glad you came," he finally said. I couldn't tell if he meant it.

"Yeah," I answered. "Birdie invited me. Wouldn't miss it."

But as laughter picked back up around us and someone turned the music up again, I couldn't shake the feeling that I didn't belong here now. It wasn't just the home improvements, or the change of company. It was reality.

Kevin fit this life. Birdie fit this life. I was just visiting it. And sooner or later, visitors always went home.

BIRDIE

43

Being as excited as I was, perhaps I failed to notice the night wasn't off to a great start.

From the moment Russell agreed to join me tonight, I couldn't wait to see what the others would think of him. Really think of him, without relying on their past impressions. I'd talked about him here and there since we started working together, sharing all of his praises with my friends, and I assumed Kevin had been excited to see him again, but Russ wasn't like the rest of us. I knew my friends to be accepting of people, that was no issue whatsoever, but I couldn't help feeling like not only would Russell stand out like a sore thumb, but *we* would.

It wasn't that standing out was a problem for me. I was proud to be here with him tonight. But just what sort of *we* were we? How did I field the questions, comments and suspicious glances?

Ever since we'd parted ways after our first date the other night, I'd been wondering if we were making a mistake. By agreeing to his proposal, had I agreed to *date* him, like for real? Was it a one-time deal or did he want something regular with me? Were we exclusive or was I not-so-simply testing the waters

while I lied to myself? I couldn't figure it out. When it came to Russell, I knew nothing, not even my own intentions.

After I reunited with two of my girls, Kevin and Sarah finally came out of the house. Russell and Kevin had a super tense encounter, and I almost regretted inviting him. Putting him into an uncomfortable situation had not been my plan at all. I just thought this was the perfect opportunity to get to the heart of things again.

It was called Friendsgiving, wasn't it?

Russ and I made our way toward the fire where the girls and Jared were now sitting, and that's when I took in the long, beautiful table under the arbor. Candles flickered between dishes and cloth napkins. Beside it all, on its own table, steam rose from casseroles and pies and things that smelled like butter and sage and a little bit of Heaven. Kevin and Sarah had gone all out. I couldn't wait to dig in.

Then it hit me. "Oh my gosh, we forgot our food in the car."

"I've got it," Russell said, then spun on his heel and headed back the way we came. Was it a convenient excuse to get away from us so soon?

"I'll give you a hand," Jared called, jumping up to follow.

Russell glanced at him with a look that said he would rather him not, but he nodded anyway.

The second they were out of earshot, Sammy tilted her head thoughtfully. "Not bad, Birdie. I never thought I'd see the day you show up with a bad boy on your arm. And you've got him running around doing you favors, no less."

"Seriously," Jenna chimed in. "I nearly choked on my cheese."

I looked down at her hands, struggling to hold in my laughter. "You're just munching on a bag of cheese cubes? You really brought that to Friendsgiving dinner?"

"Don't judge me. The fetus wants what the fetus wants."

"And don't try to change the subject either." Sammy honed back in on me. "Let's talk about what *you* brought to Friendsgiving, Birdie Jo. Tell us about your new guy."

"He's not… we're not…"

"Uh-huh. Save all that. Tell us about him. More than just how he sucks at fractions or any other vanilla tutoring stuff."

"I'd like to hear more, too," agreed Sarah, smiling like she already knew my heart.

I twisted around, half-expecting to see him already. "He's going to be back any minute."

"Oh, I'm sure Jared is talking him to death by now," said Sammy.

Sarah nudged me with her shoulder. "You never did tell us how your date went."

"Yeah, come on," Jenna pleaded. "Give us something."

"You guys are the worst," I said, but I couldn't stop smiling. "He's kind of wonderful."

"Dang. She's smitten already," Sammy observed.

Yes, girl, I am.

My face felt flushed. "Our date was pretty great. He took me up north to see a real Amish neighborhood and let me buy turkeys, drove really, really fast, and got me Mexican food and donuts."

"Turkeys?" Sammy asked, sharing everyone else's confusion.

Laughing, I said, "I'll have to tell you more about that later."

Sarah looped an arm around my shoulders. "He indulges your love for donuts and your soft spot for animals. That sounds pretty serious."

"He a good kisser?" Jenna asked bluntly, taking a long gulp of strawberry milk. Where was she even holding these things? "He looks like he would be."

My nerves fried. Lord, forgive me, but I wished I could tell them.

"You know I can't answer that. We haven't kissed."

"Wow. So, he's that gorgeous *and* patient? You hit the lottery." Jenna's tone was one part jealousy and two parts bewilderment. She must've already forgotten about Nick.

With as red as my face felt and the fact that all I could do was smile like a weirdo, the girls took that and ran with it. They shrieked. Sammy clapped, and Jenna nearly spilled her milk. Sarah squeezed me tighter. And it was all mortifying, yet wonderful. Somewhere between their teasing and cheering, one fact settled quietly inside me: I more than liked Russell Grandy.

I could not say I was testing the waters or trying to figure out my feelings. I really liked him in a immoveable but growing kind of way. Saying he was *'kind of wonderful'* hadn't been an exaggeration, it had been restraint. And despite my track record, I wasn't second-guessing that feeling. I was excited about it. Even if I had no idea what we were or where we were going.

For once, that didn't scare me.

EVENTUALLY, the boys returned with food in hand. As they delivered our contributions to the table, Russell's shoulders were bouncing as Jared slapped him on the back. If I didn't know any better, I would say they were actually enjoying each other's company. *How cute.* I just knew Russell would find a way to fit in.

Not long after they both sat back down, Kevin announced

that the rest of dinner—fajitas, sausages, and roasted elote—wouldn't be much longer.

"Good, because I'm starving," Jared said, rubbing his hands together before throwing his arm around Sammy.

It made me smile how in love they were. He'd gone just as long as the rest of us without seeing her in person, and she had only just flown home days ago from her first mission trip to Mexico. We were all so happy to have her back, especially in time for this special occasion.

And Sarah had recently returned from college for Thanksgiving break, though she'd be leaving again soon until winter break hit.

I knew that life was taking us all places, but it never got easier saying goodbye to my friends.

The conversations were going strong—even Russell was participating—when I caught a newcomer approaching from the corner of my eye. I froze.

Nick had just shown up.

He strode through the little gate, laser-focused on not dropping a large container of something balanced in his hands. He hadn't looked up yet.

Russell, thankfully none the wiser yet, remained engaged with the others.

Seizing the moment, I jumped to my feet, yanking Sarah aside. "What is Nick doing here?" I whispered harshly.

Her eyes widened when she spotted him. "Birdie, I'm so sorry. I didn't even know he was coming after, well, everything."

"He seriously cannot be here. I brought a date," I hissed.

I suppose that answers the debate. Russell and I were dating. Officially.

Lord, help me.

"I get that," she said, trying very hard not to smile as she glanced toward said date. "But I can't just kick him out now. He's already here. Technically, he's been invited for months. Nobody knew y'all would break up."

"Why didn't you call and tell him not to come once we did?"

"I really didn't know it would be a problem. You didn't even tell me you were going to bring anyone."

"I didn't know," I admitted softly. "But someone is here, and I can't imagine how this is going to make them both feel. What am I supposed to do?"

"Stay calm. It's just dinner. Everyone here is civilized enough to get through one meal without incident, don't you think?"

That might be debatable, but... "Well, yeah, but I recently told Russell about why Nick and I broke up. I don't want there to be any more tension here tonight. I mean, look at him, he's doing so well." I tilted my head slightly, observing another laugh from Russell, and my heart warmed.

"You mean, you told Russell about Nick's proposal?"

"Yes."

"Ah. Well... Look at it this way. Russell is here with you because you wanted him here. Nick sitting across from you at the table won't change that."

I wasn't so sure. "I guess if Jared and Kevin can stand each other after what they've been through, anything is possible."

Sarah laughed. "Exactly. Besides, he's still our friend, Birdie. Now come on. It'll all be okay."

"I'm going to grab a cold water first." I was going to need it. My head was already starting to make threats, my throat felt dry, and the backyard suddenly seemed ten times smaller.

Hang in there. Sarah's right. It's just a dinner.

Kevin helped Nick set his Dutch oven on the food table, and

they exchanged easy pleasantries. I realized too late that I lingered too long. When Nick finally turned around and saw me, I could not escape.

"Hey," he said, with a vivid smile, as though we hadn't walked through the wreckage of a broken relationship.

I stepped forward, stopping short of immediate personal space. More for Russell's benefit than Nick's. "Hey." I treaded carefully. "How are you?"

His response came without hesitation. "Better now. It's so good to see you."

Before I could brace myself, he wrapped his arms around me, lifting me clean off the ground. A toe-lifting hug, the kind he'd always given me. The kind that used to mean safety and now meant nothing.

All I could think about was whether Russell was watching. And if he was… how angry was he going to be?

RUSSELL

44

I think I'd endured pretty well tonight, all things considered, but watching that guy put his paws all over my girl made my blood boil.

Whoa. My *girl?*

Get a grip, Grandy. You don't have a girl. And if you did, it wouldn't be this delicate flower, Birdie Jo.

So, why did the sight of him lifting her off the ground both disgust and infuriate me? My stomach flipped while my hands balled into white-knuckled fists. If that guy didn't back off soon…

No. He needed to back off *immediately*.

Before reason could overtake reaction, I was already moving toward them. Blood whooshed in my ears. I couldn't hear what they were saying, could only see her shoulders now bounced with generous laughter.

Beautiful, sweet laughter like she'd been giving *me* lately.

Mine, my mind chanted, inebriated with an intense, foreign feeling. Nobody should've made her laugh like that but me.

So, I swooped right into their conversation. "What are we

talking about?" I asked, sliding my arm around the small of Birdie's back, pulling her against me. A new sensation unlocked. We'd never touched like this before. I was feeling very territorial about it.

And I loved it.

My tone hadn't come across as friendly, because the guy's jaw tightened. Good. I wanted him uncomfortable.

"Hi," he said after clearing his throat. "My name's Nick."

When he held out his hand, I looked at it for a long second before meeting his eyes instead. After a beat, he slowly tucked his hand into his pocket like nothing had happened.

Birdie looked nervously between us. "Nick, this is Russell Grandy, my—"

"Boyfriend," I cut in, shocking even myself. Birdie stiffened beneath my arm. Her breath caught just enough for me to feel it.

And I smiled.

Nick, for all his efforts to keep calm, paled a solid shade or two. "Boyfriend?" he asked her, not me.

"That's what I said," I replied evenly.

"It's very new," Birdie squeaked out.

"But very exciting, wouldn't you say?" I gave her hip a light squeeze—maybe too familiar, maybe too much—but I didn't back off. "Well, it's been nice meeting you, Rick, but Birdie and I were just about to go grab an appetizer. Catch you around."

"It's Nick," he quietly corrected me, but I didn't care. I was already steering her away.

But instead of letting me lead her toward the table to pick at the edibles, Birdie grabbed my hand and dragged me through the back door, through the kitchen, and down the dim hallway.

When she stopped and turned, her cheeks and neck were flushed. With anger? Embarrassment?

Something else?

"What was that?" her adorable twang demanded.

"What was what?"

"That display, whatever it was! You totally humiliated Nick, not to mention me!"

"Are you sure you brought me to this dark, secluded hallway to lecture me?" I took a step closer, letting the tease tug at my mouth.

She planted her hand against my chest. "Russell. Don't."

Russell. Not Russ. So, I was making backward progress. Great. Never before had anyone using my actual name grated my nerves so much. *And I used to detest nicknames.*

I put my hand over hers. "Fine. I'm listening. Tell me what you're really upset about. Is it the boyfriend part?"

"Not only that—and yes, we will be discussing that—but…" She went silent.

"Hey." I moved my hands to her shoulders, gently caressing. "What is it?"

She sighed, a deep and loaded sound. "Promise me you won't get mad at what I'm about to tell you."

My spine straightened and my hands fell to my sides. That sentence never led anywhere good. "Probably not," I admitted. "But I'll try." *For you, Birdie. Only for you.*

She exhaled slowly. "Nick is the ex I told you about. The one I broke up with recently."

The serious, long-term one who'd mattered enough to propose to her? "That guy out there asked you to marry him?"

"Yes."

"The one who wanted forever." It was a question, but not. I was processing slowly.

A strange heaviness moved into my chest and took over. Nick

was Mr. *Stable*. Mr. *Good Reputation*. Mr. *Approved-by-the-Parents,* I was sure.

Mr. *Would-Never-Embarrass-You-At-Friendsgiving.*

And here I was, the guy who just claimed her like property and called her ex by the wrong name just to make him squirm.

"If he hadn't proposed..." I started, then stopped. I didn't know if I could stand to confirm my worst thought, but I had to. "If he hadn't proposed, you might still be with him. Am I right?"

Her lips parted. No words came out.

"And I would be... what? Just the guy your conscience had you helping to pass a test." In essence, I would be nothing.

The hallway suddenly felt too small and too honest for comfort, but still I continued.

"You said no, but you were close enough for him to ask." I ran my hand through my hair. "I can't compete with that, Birdie." With guys who offered rings instead of attitudes and didn't have criminal records.

My bravado had been completely drained. Defeated by something I didn't even know I was fighting against, I turned to leave.

Birdie's hand wrapped around my shoulder before I made it three steps. "Russ, stop."

When I turned around, her eyes were glistening with sadness. "I didn't want to break up, but he said he couldn't be with me if we weren't moving forward. So, he left."

Somehow, her words weren't helping. He left her because it would mean more pain to be with her. That didn't make me angry like I thought it would. Instead, it caused a horrible sinking feeling inside my chest.

He hadn't been a jerk. He'd been a good guy who had wanted forever with Birdie. He probably couldn't have been more perfect for her, and yet, she'd told him no. She hadn't chosen him. Which raised an uncomfortable question I really didn't want to ask.

If a stable, decent guy like him hadn't made the cut, what chance did I have?

"Say something," she prompted with a quiet urgency.

"I'm thinking."

"About?"

"About how I don't know where I fit into all this."

"You fit differently," she said, matter-of-fact. But what did different mean? It didn't mean better, or safer. I felt like I was already losing the ground I'd been so proud and careful to gain and I didn't know what to think anymore.

Birdie took one nervous step into my space. "You called me your girlfriend." As she looked up at me, I didn't know how her eyes could contain that level of vulnerability.

"Yes," I said, steadier than I felt. "I did." And now I didn't know where it had gotten me.

"Was it all for show?"

"No."

"So how did you mean it?"

I released a pent up breath. She asked a fair question. It was time to pony-up and give her a real answer. "I meant I don't want to stand halfway in anymore. Pretending this is casual when it hasn't felt casual for a long time is ridiculous. I don't like the idea of you with someone else, and tonight made me realize I don't want to keep acting like I'm not already invested."

"Is this because Nick showed up?"

"Yes," I said with certainty. "Seeing him didn't make me want to fight him, like I would have thought. It made me realize I could lose you. I feel like we've already started something and I want to see it through properly."

It couldn't get any more truthful than that.

"And that scares you?" she guessed, echoing the question I'd asked her not too long ago.

"Yeah."

"I understand being scared." She swallowed hard. "But if I thought he was my future, I would've said yes when he asked."

"But instead, you said no, and then he left."

Her eyes flickered, like something old and bruised had just been touched. "He did. And I survived."

So, her actions weren't defensive. Something clicked for me then. This wasn't about Nick. This was a pattern, a response to what she expected out of life. Men leave. And her decision was her way of ensuring she didn't need them when they did.

"Birdie." I gently combed one of her curls behind her ear. "I'm not him."

She leaned into my touch. "I know."

I closed the remaining space she hadn't moved to close herself. "Then let's stop hovering," I said, plain and simple. "Let's choose it. You and me. Nothing about this is guaranteed and it won't be perfect, but it's what we want. It's something real."

Her voice wavered. "And if *you* leave?" The question was barely audible, and I didn't rush to answer.

"I'm here right now, and I'm choosing to stay." And that was all I could promise her.

Her eyes searched mine for something, maybe certainty, maybe proof. But finally, "Yes," she breathed. And then, with more confidence, "Yes. Let's do this."

To my surprise, relief didn't rush in like a wild circus performance. It settled in slow, heavy waves. Still, like the desperate man I had become, I held my pinky out. "Then let's make it official."

She stared at it for half a second like it was the most serious covenant in the world. Then, she hooked her pinky around mine, returning the gesture that locked us together. Her smile was brighter than ever as she nervously bit her lip, unintentionally drawing my hungry gaze.

Without thinking, I leaned down. When I realized she wasn't pulling away, reason returned, and I stopped, but she was leaning in, too. She *wanted* to kiss me, or was she simply swept up?

Then in that moment, I remembered every boundary she'd drawn, and every reason she'd given. I wanted kissing her to be something she decided on with an open, willing heart, not something I took in the heat of the moment.

I was just about to pause and ask how she felt about that when the back door creaked open.

"Hey, Russ? Birdie? Were did you guys go?" Kevin called out.

We jumped apart like a spring, and I moved in front of her without thinking.

"Everything okay?" Kevin asked, eyeing me as he approached.

"We're good. We'll be right out."

He lingered too long, out of concern maybe. Or as a warning? Irritation threatened to surface, but I had to choke it down. The truth was, I didn't really know him anymore, and he didn't know me. His judgment didn't stand for much.

Birdie's forehead rested briefly against my shoulder blade once he left. "You okay?"

She nodded. "I'm just caught off guard. This is all very new."

"Yeah." I couldn't disagree. It was new alright. And risky, and without guarantee. But it was decided. We were together now.

We walked back out together as something defined—as an *us*. For someone who always rejected the idea of a steady girlfriend, I'd managed to find myself with one. I'd chosen her, and she'd chosen me back. It was possible that should have terrified me, but as we sat down around all her friends, and her pinky brushed mine under the table, I concluded that nothing else mattered but this.

Just like Birdie, I didn't feel like I was waiting to be left. I felt like I was standing still, and in that strange stillness, I felt hope.

BIRDIE

45

SOMEHOW, AND I WASN'T QUITE SURE HOW, RUSSELL'S JEALOUSY had been enough to make him forget his pledge of bachelorhood. Somehow Beauty had managed to win over the Beast. Not that I had any idea what I was doing. Not long ago, I had declared myself retired from dating, a voluntary spinster, if you will. Bottom line, I had become a girl who had learned her lesson and would not be making any silly attachment mistakes ever again.

And now…

I was somebody's girlfriend. I was *Russell's* girlfriend. He laid everything bare and said he wanted me. And I wanted him, too.

Russell Grandy—ex-con turned client turned friend turned something much too important—was officially mine.

I pressed my lips together to hide a smile, suddenly aware that I was sitting at a table full of people who had known me long enough to read my face like a devotional. I kept my gaze trained on my plate, terrified someone would see the glow and ask questions I wasn't prepared to answer.

Russell and I had nearly kissed tonight, *really* kissed, and it was nothing like before. The first time, he hadn't known better.

The second time, he'd forgotten. This time, he'd been asking for silent permission, and I'd very nearly given it to him. To *myself.* Heat crept up my neck and warm fuzzies gathered in my chest just thinking about it.

That would've been our first kiss as a couple, and my first real kiss ever. It would have been a kiss of meaning, where we weren't both just fighting the inevitable. It hadn't felt like hormones being in control of us; it felt like the solidification of something special. The look in his eyes when he'd begun to lean in tonight had been intense and laser-focused. I knew it wouldn't have been one of the sweet, chaste kisses Nick used to press to my cheeks.

Russell was all rough edges and fire and barely-contained restraint. I wasn't sure what that meant for me, or how long I could keep pretending I didn't want to find out.

That was something for future Birdie to sort through. Tonight, I luxuriated in the smolder of the man beside me.

But soon, my smile faltered.

Mom.

She dropped into my thoughts like a stone into still water. She had grown to like Nick. It had taken months, but she'd softened toward him. She liked every good and safe quality about him, like any parent would. But Mom's approval came harder than most. She judged against a far more difficult rubric. Beyond anything else, she had to know he wouldn't disappear.

And in the end, he had, and it wasn't even because he was cruel or reckless or aimed to disappoint. He just wanted more than I could give him. It was fair, which was something I hadn't admitted to myself sooner, but I saw it now.

But Mom… She taught me one truth above all others, which was that all men leave eventually. It wasn't something she ever said outright. She didn't have to. It lived in the tension in her shoulders whenever I mentioned a boy's name. Her mouth would tightened as she'd ask me, *'And what does he want from you?'* instead of *'Are you sure you like him?'*

The sad part was that she wasn't always so cold. After my father finally left us, something inside her hardened toward the entire sex. Somewhere along the way, I must have absorbed it. Maybe that was part of why I'd convinced myself to swear off dating after Nick. Or the reason why I convinced myself to hold on to my first kiss like it was a bargaining chip for loyalty.

If you don't invest, you don't lose. If you don't attach, you don't get abandoned. It was wise, really. Being safe was a smart thing.

Sigh. I sounded just like my mother.

I glanced up. Russell was chuckling at something Jenna said, head tipped back slightly, completely unaware that he was about to be evaluated by the harshest critic in the county.

My mother did not do well with rough edges, criminal records, or intensity. She would see his history before his heart, and she would absolutely expect him to leave before he even had the chance to stay. But it was too late. I'd already given in to my heart and accepted the risk. And a small, ugly part of me knew she would be waiting for our demise so she could say, *'I told you so.'*

I squeezed the material of my dress under the table, but then Russell's hand curled over my weary fingers. He flashed me a smile, brief but packing a punch, before returning his attention to the meal and conversation. He'd looked at me with all the adoration of someone who wasn't quite over the fact that we weren't only at this dinner together—we *were* together. His expression said he didn't want to let go. Like he was happy he stayed, and that everything would be worth it.

I didn't want to borrow my mother's fear anymore. As much as I loved her, maybe I could write an entirely different ending for myself. My pinky brushed his again, and he smiled without looking down.

Whatever Mom thought of him, and whatever she said, it didn't matter. Just this one time, if never again, I would allow myself to feel happiness without bracing for a negative impact.

Lord, please protect Russ from the brute force trauma that is Caroline Ruth Lewis.

And maybe, while You're at it, protect me from becoming her.

RUSSELL

46

After dinner, we all sat around the fire. It was something I'd done countless times during my long friendship with Kevin, with very different people. It was such a different experience now. Only six months had separated us, but returning home made it clear it wasn't merely our arrests that drove us apart. Something else had changed in a big way.

Even the familiarity of the inside was a startling difference. It went beyond the repairs from the fire Craig had caused. Even the things that were the same seemed different. The shock was what *wasn't* there anymore more than what had appeared.

Looking around, it wasn't hard to observe the differences. Instead of aluminum cans and bottles and lighters, the yard was full of people and purposeful decorations. Craig's *'Shed of Wonders'* was long gone. Marie and Craig weren't there, messed up, leaving us to dabble in and deal with their leftover trouble. It was a strange feeling to experience such a normal event at this place.

And the people… they were normal. Clean, healthy. Each of

them looked like they belonged in a brochure for small-town redemption stories.

And Kevin… well, he wore it well. His posture was relaxed, like he'd always been this version of himself. He ate it all up and played everything so cool, his arm leisurely around his girl, an easy and confident smile on his face.

Everyone there adored him, and I guess I could see why they would *now*, because look at everything he had to offer them. But where were they all when he was often beaten, and before he became the quintessential Christian or whatever? Nobody here but me saw him take it to the face when Craig gunned for Kevin's jaw, and broke it. Not a single one of them kept Kevin's head above water while he self-medicated every weekend. Where were *they* when I held the position as his best and sometimes only friend?

And where was Kevin recently? Where were all his letters, all the phone calls? Where were his visits once he was released before me? Where was *my* best friend when *I* needed him?

He was right here, apparently, making buddy-buddy with the picture-perfect townsfolk that we used to have nothing to do with. He'd been too busy becoming better than me to care.

I knew it was going to bring change when he started seeing Sarah. I *knew*. But I had no idea the changes would be this drastic. Nearly two decades of loyalty, and for what? What did any of it matter?

"What was it like, Kevin?" I heard Jenna ask.

All eyes were on him, curious about his answer. All but me. I didn't need him to tell me how cozy juvie was when I knew the harsher realities of the state pen.

I drained the rest of my paper cup and tossed it into the fire.

The flames sputtered and jumped, embers snapping loudly. A few people startled. Birdie's hand tightened around mine.

"My bad," I muttered.

They went right back to listening to him, and why wouldn't they? It was nothing but a congregation of disciples following avidly after their master.

I didn't stay to hear what he had to say. The car was more comfortable than his fancy new lawn chairs anyway.

BIRDIE HAD TEXTED me after I'd left, but I'd told her I just needed a minute alone. That minute had turned into the rest of the night, and now we were on our way home.

The silence between us lasted for three turns.

"You ready to tell me what that was about?" Birdie finally asked.

"What?"

"Don't do that. Please just let me in. Remember that I'm not going anywhere."

That should've been a comfort. Should have, but wasn't. "I just wasn't interested in hearing Mr. Wonderful regale his subjects with tales of how much he suffered."

"Isn't he still your friend?"

"That's what I'd like to know."

"You should've stuck around. His *'tales'* might have surprised you."

That got my attention. "Why?"

She folded her hands in her lap. "He shared something after you left. Something he was building up to."

I didn't respond. I didn't nod, or ask. I just stared straight ahead, driving us away.

She sighed. "Nope. I'm not filling the silence for you. If you want to know, then ask and I'll tell you."

"Fine," I said with rigid reluctance. "What did he say?"

"He told us his cellmate was murdered."

I squeezed the steering wheel. "What?"

"They'd traded beds because Kevin was cold. The other guy was killed in Kevin's spot. He woke up and found him, stepped in his blood and everything. He still has nightmares. Sarah says he barely sleeps."

"You believe all that?" I asked, throat tight.

"Why wouldn't I?"

"He could be exaggerating. People love a dramatic story."

She looked at me then. "He's not like that."

"I know he's not," I snapped. "I've known him a lot longer than any of you."

She didn't flinch. "So, again, maybe you should've stayed to hear it from him. Honestly, it sounds like he could use somebody to talk to about it. Maybe you, more than anyone, would be able to understand what it's like to have your own ghosts."

I exhaled sharply. "End of subject." I hadn't intended to be so snippy with her, but I couldn't stand to be lectured about Kevin. Luckily, she let it drop.

Unfortunately, that didn't make it leave.

~

LATER THAT NIGHT, he texted me.

KEVIN

It was good to see you.

Yeah, right.

I tossed the phone onto my nightstand, getting rid of it, but a minute later, it buzzed again.

KEVIN

I mean it.

I didn't open it. Didn't type back. I didn't even know what I'd say if I did.

Then another message came through.

KEVIN

PS… as a peace offering… Birdie's birthday is December 10th. Make it special

I stared at that one longer than the others. I didn't want him giving me tips about my own girlfriend. But the date lodged itself in my brain. I hadn't known it before.

December 10th.

In order to make it special, I needed money. Money meant work. Work meant swallowing pride and turning in the stack of applications sitting on my desk.

I looked around my room. The paint was peeling. Nothing in here belonged to me. My bare-minimum accommodations might've been fair but they were frustrating. This version of my life still looked like I hadn't moved forward at all.

But Kevin had almost died. *He* had changed, and then built something. His house may have burnt, but I was the one left standing in the ashes, feeling cheated and let down by life and the people in it.

My phone buzzed yet again.

KEVIN

Night, man.

I turned the screen face down without answering. But before I went to bed, I pulled those applications into a neat stack and set them by the door. Tomorrow, I'd start somewhere, because Birdie deserved something special from me. The least I could do was expect it from myself, too.

THE AUTOMATIC DOORS slid shut behind me. I made it two steps into the parking lot before it hit. I spoke out loud to no one. "I got it. I actually got it. Just like that." The guy hired me on the spot after my interview, no *'we'll call you,'* no awkward pause while they pretended to care about my application.

The hiring manager, some tired guy with a mustache that had seen better decades, had stuck out his hand and said, "You start Monday."

I stopped between two faded parking lines and looked skyward. My hands came together in front of my face without me thinking about it, fingertips pressed into a steeple. "Thank you," I said under my breath. Then louder. "Thank you, thank you, thank you."

I blinked. Who was I talking to? Since when did I do that?

I dropped my hands and looked around. Had anyone seen me? But there was nothing in the parking lot but shopping carts and the rattling of the wind.

It must've been Birdie. Had to be. She prayed about everything, even parking spots, headaches, and burned toast. Her ways must be creeping into my subconscious. I scoffed at the idea of being desperate enough to actually thank *God* for something.

Anyway, I was officially a grocery store employee. That was my new title. It wasn't glamorous or impressive in any way, but it was a steady paycheck in my empty bank account every month. It was mine. So, I didn't care if I was pushing carts, bagging produce, or unloading trucks at five in the morning. It was legal and steady.

Something I realized I wanted to be.

I glanced back at the storefront. Would a garage have hired me? Doubt it. Not with my record. Didn't matter that I could rebuild a transmission faster than half the guys applying or if engines were the only thing that had ever made sense to me. When all was said and done, paperwork mattered more than skill. History mattered more than potential.

So, fine. It wasn't hard to convince myself not to try because I knew better. And besides, H-E-B wasn't permanent. I didn't know what permanent even looked like. The only thing I knew was that December 10th was coming.

And horses weren't free.

I pulled my phone out and opened the notes app where I'd written it down like a cheesy idiot so I wouldn't forget.

Birdie's Birthday 12/10: Horses + beach.

I'd called and gotten the details from the stable on South Padre Island already, so I knew how much I needed. And if I started work on Monday, I would have just enough to pull it off in time. It was stupid expensive if you asked me, but she deserved something as magical as she was. I wanted to give her something that made a statement.

We're building something, Birdie Jo, and I'm not going anywhere.

That was a lot for horses to say, but my gut told me she'd love it.

I slid into my car and started the engine, feeling light in my spirit, because my future finally felt like a door instead of a wall.

BIRDIE

47

STEPHANIE DIDN'T LOOK UP WHEN I WALKED INTO THE OFFICE. That was the first sign today would be a bad day. Normally, she greeted me before I even got through the door with some bright and cheerful "Welcome in, sunshine." Today, she just sat there, staring at a file with an indiscernible look on her face.

"Morning," I said carefully.

She looked up at me, sadness stirring in her eyes. "Birdie. Sit for a minute?"

Without setting my stuff down at my own desk, I plopped right into the chair across hers. My nerves were firing.

Stephanie folded and unfolded her hands. "I didn't want to tell you until it was confirmed."

My stomach bottomed out. I had known something was wrong around here, but was too afraid to think too much about it. "Tell me what?"

She hesitated just long enough for my mind to run through a dozen terrible scenarios. "It's about Gia."

Instantly, Gia's court hearing was in my mind. The trembling hands and her brave promises. The tearful reunification when her children ran into her arms like she'd come back from the dead. And in a sense, she kind of had. She'd overcome a powerful addiction while enrolled at STLR, and fought so hard to get custody of her sweet babies. I couldn't wait to attend her graduation in January, right around the corner. She was going to speak, in fact. Everyone was so proud of her.

So, what *about* Gia?

"She relapsed," Stephanie said, harsh but gentle at the same time. "I'm so sorry to have to tell you, Birdie."

"No," I breathed.

Stephanie nodded. "CPS removed the kids this morning. She left the program last night. We won't be seeing her at graduation."

The room grew distant, like I was watching this conversation rather than living it. "But she was doing so well. She passed every check-in. She was working. Her kids—"

"I know." Stephanie's words were not dismissive, but tired. She'd wrestled with this for a while then, hoping to not have to tell me until the very last minute. I guess this was that very last minute.

I stared at the wood grain on her desk. Those two kids—Christopher and Corrine. The sweetest little troopers I'd ever met. They'd had so much faith in their mommy. I pictured his Spider-Man sneakers, and her rosy cheeks. All the times Gia cried and promised she wouldn't to lose them again. Everyone believed her. Everyone advocated for her.

"She promised," I choked out.

Stephanie's voice was soft. "Addiction doesn't keep promises."

"So, what does that mean for us?"

"For us?"

"For the program. For the work. For all of it."

She sighed, long and deep. "It means we keep going. Pray for everyone. Help who we can."

"But what if we're not actually helping? What if we just... delay the inevitable?"

Stephanie's eyes met mine fully. "We don't control outcomes, Birdie. We offer support and opportunity. Some people take it. Some people can't."

I shook my head. "That doesn't feel like enough."

"I know it feels that way. Trust me, I feel that way, too. It's just because you care, but you have to know we are not in control."

That almost made it worse. Like caring was actually a problem. I stood too quickly and the blood pulsing through my neck started to throb. "I need a minute."

"Take it. It's going to be okay, Birdie."

THE BATHROOM STALL felt like the only place I could breathe. I locked the door and sat down, pressing my palm to my neck. It ached. My stomach, too. And my heart, all the way to my soul. It all felt so physical, like my grief had a mass of its own, and the weight of it was trying to kill me.

I bowed my head. "Why?" I whispered, the word echoing off metal and tile. "You gave her kids back. You let her win. Why let her fall again?"

No answer came. Just the hum of the vent overhead.

Maybe this was what social work really looked like—failure. Not tidy redemptions and graduation ceremonies, but cycles of relapse and loss and courtrooms, again and again and again.

What if I wasn't strong enough for that? What if I built my

entire future around helping people who would still slip through my fingers?

Corrine's face flashed into my mind. Clutching her mother's waist in celebration, trusting her. Trusting *us,* the people Gia had put her own trust in. My throat burned.

"Are You even listening to me?" I asked the ceiling. The sudden question startled me. I didn't ever question God. Not like that. But today felt unfair in a way I couldn't dress up in positivity. I was certain there were Bible verses I could use even for this situation, but I couldn't recall them.

I stayed in that stall until my breathing steadied. Then, I washed my face, reapplied lip gloss like that could fix anything, and went back to my desk. Work didn't stop. Intake forms still needed filing, phone calls still needed answering. The world didn't pause just because a family had shattered.

By the time I walked through my bedroom door, the ache in my chest had migrated behind my ribs and into my shoulders. I dropped my bag beside the bed, sitting in a heap on the edge. For a long time, I stared at nothing.

I should change. And eat. And probably pray better than I did earlier.

Instead, I picked up my phone.

BIRDIE

One of my moms relapsed. She lost her kids this morning.

At least I didn't have to wait long for a response.

RUSSELL

Oh, wow. I'm so sorry. Are you okay?

I stared at the question. Was I? The honest answer felt dangerous. Too dramatic and needy. So, I swallowed it.

BIRDIE

Yeah. Just part of the job, I guess.

RUSSELL

That still sucks.

BIRDIE

It does. But we can't save everyone.

The words looked mature and wise, like something Stephanie would say. But I hated them. To me they felt false.

RUSSELL

You don't have to be the strong one all the time.

But I do...

My thumb hovered over the screen.

BIRDIE

I'm okay, really. Just tired.

RUSSELL

Call me if you need anything?

Need. The idea scraped something tender in me.

BIRDIE

I will. 🩶

I set my phone down and the room got too quiet. I leaned

back against the wall and pressed my palm to my chest, unable to assuage the aching. It still hurt. The pain had weight all right, and it was pressing more and more inward.

"Part of the job," I murmured to the empty room.

If this was the job, I needed to toughen up. If this was my calling, I needed thicker skin. Or maybe this was God's way of telling me I didn't have what it took. *I* wasn't the Savior. Maybe I'd gotten too attached. Maybe this pain was my own fault. But if it was, then why couldn't I control it and make it go away?

I laid back on my bed and stared at the ceiling. I didn't cry or even pray. I just kept very still, trying to keep the hurt from spreading any further. And somewhere between exhaustion, disappointment, and the mindfully arranged composure, I truthfully admitted that I might not be cut out for this.

BIRDIE

48

When Russell told me to be ready at seven AM on my birthday, I knew something big was coming. He didn't ever get up early for the fun of it.

"You're suspiciously awake," I said, sliding into his car with a prepared smile.

"Well, it's a special occasion."

The way he said it was delightful, warming my chest. Who knew I was even capable of feeling such a thing anymore? The last few weeks had been heavy. Work, finals, the affliction I couldn't quite name but couldn't shake. I'd managed it all. I always managed it.

But today felt like permission to set it down, at least for a little while. For Russell's sake, if nothing else, I had to have fun.

"Where are we going?" I asked.

"Beach," was all he said.

"In December?"

"It's Texas."

"But it's actually cold this year. They're even saying we may see snow."

"Maybe, but not today."

I laughed. "Okay. That's fair."

The coast was bright and the wind breezed over the sand when we pulled in. The water glittered like glass, rippling as the sun caught it. "It's so beautiful." Perhaps joy wasn't as far away as it had felt recently, even despite what had happened the last time I was here.

"First things first," he said, turning off the engine. "I wanted to get here early to give you this."

He handed me a small, red bag, and I knew it immediately. The white script read James Avery. My humble joy had turned into blatant excitement.

"Russell…"

"Just open it."

I did. Inside was a tiny silver rose charm. Simple. Delicate. Lovely. I traced the petals with my thumb. "It's a rose."

"I know you have a thing for them," he replied with a hint of teasing. "And they're tougher than people think. They grow back, even after what looks like death."

He didn't know how badly I needed that to be true. "It's perfect." It really was. For the moment, the painful thrum behind my eyes dulled, and the incessant tension in my neck eased. In this moment, I felt loved and everything else took a backseat to it.

I leaned across the console and kissed his cheek, his nearness a decadent temptation. "Thank you." When I pulled back, slower than I should have, he was watching me intently, the dance of his heartbeat giving him away.

Then the rumbling of a trailer pulling in dragged our gazes apart. I glanced toward the noise just as the ramp slammed onto the sand, and a second later, a horse stepped out.

My jaw fell open. "No way."

Russell grinned like a little boy. "Happy Birthday."

"Seriously?" I grabbed his arm. "Russell!"

A second horse followed, its multi-colored mane whipping in the wind. I got out of the car and laughed, *really* laughed, for the first time in weeks, doing a little hop when I couldn't contain myself.

But then... It couldn't be...

Russell came up beside me. "Are you surprised?"

"Not as much about the horses as I am *that!*" I pointed past the trailer at a familiar sedan pulling up. My stomach catapulted again. "That's my mom's car."

She stepped out, smoothing her coat as for a red carpet appearance rather than squishing her designers in a ton of sand.

I turned toward Russell. "What is my mom doing here?"

"I invited her."

"That was, uh, bold."

His face fell. "Are you upset?"

"It's just..." I searched for a gracious way to put this. "I didn't know we were at the meet-my-mother-on-a-beach stage."

"It's your birthday. Why shouldn't your mom be involved?"

Because she doesn't know how to be nice.

Because she sees everything as a risk assessment.

Because I'm not ready for her to measure you.

But none of that came out. It really wasn't about him, it was all about her.

Russell continued. "Plus, I did have to meet her eventually, right?"

I forced a smile. "Right. It'll be fine, really." It would most definitely *not* be fine, but what choice did I have?

Happy Birthday to me.

RUSSELL

49

I'd made a mistake. I should've asked her first. But that thought didn't form until I saw Birdie's face when she realized her mom had come. She didn't appear angry, but the surprised was probably too much. I didn't know anything about the woman she called Mom. Still, it was Birdie Jo's birthday. Maybe I should have let her decide about this part, but my intentions had been honorable.

My own parents adored her already. My mom knew after having spent less than an hour with her, and my dad knew from only second-hand experience. I'd wanted her to feel the same kind of reassurance from my end. I'd wanted her to know I wasn't hiding, that I was serious.

"Are you sure you're okay? I'm sorry if I did something wrong."

"No, please don't feel bad. It's just, I can't believe you invited my mom on our date."

"Well, this isn't a date for us. It's a birthday celebration for you. It made sense that she'd be here, and felt like a convenient opportunity to meet." And at the time I'd invited her, that had sounded perfectly reasonable. But standing on the sand now, watching Ms. Lewis approach like she was there to inspect a real estate contract, I wasn't so sure.

Maybe there was a reason Birdie seemed so uneasy about it.

"Russell," she said smoothly, extending her hand. "It's so nice to finally meet you."

"Yes, ma'am," I said, suddenly formal. "I'm glad you could join us today."

"While I don't love an opportunity to get dirty," she replied, glancing at the horses. "I couldn't pass up the chance to finally meet you. My daughter seems to think we ought to never cross paths." The polished half-smile on her face was flawless, but her tone was not.

I felt Birdie stiffen beside me. "I never said that," she said.

Was it true? Had Birdie not wanted me to meet her mother for some reason? If she hadn't, I wouldn't have to guess why. There were a dozen reasons she could be ashamed of me.

"No?" Her mother's brow lifted. "Strange. I've only heard small bits about him in passing."

Ouch. This woman was the picture of politeness at first glance, but after taking a deeper look, there was something much too sharp about her.

So yeah. I had *definitely* made a mistake.

"I'm grateful you came," I said quickly, trying to cover the moment with positive vibes. A total Birdie Jo move.

The instructor came over, providing the perfect interruption, and began explaining the route we would be taking. They ran us through all the safety measures, proper usage of the tack, basic stop-and-go functions, and let us meet our horses.

"Mine is named Tara," Birdie cooed, rubbing her nose against the mare's soft red muzzle. "Isn't she the purdiest thang?"

I smiled, reaching over to rub Tara between the eyes, totally enchanted by how strong her accent got when she was carefree and truly happy. A horse may have done that technically, but I could still take credit for it.

Birdie came around to my side, taking in the dappled grey gelding they'd given me. "He's a big boy. What a looker," she commented. "What is his name?"

"Dusty, I think."

"Attentive ears. His eyes are big and sweet, and he's so relaxed. Look at that popped back leg of his. He's going to take very good care of you."

I followed each trait she pointed out to me in wonder. "How do you know all this stuff?"

She held up her bracelet, tugging at the horseshoe charm. "It's not just for show. Didn't I tell you I have three horses out at my dad's property?"

"Ah, I don't think you did. Then you're every bit the cowgirl you look." I smiled, only just now appreciating that her boots looked worn and had traces of work on them. "Well, let's giddy on up, Birdie Jo. It's time to ride."

I walked her to her horse and probably like an idiot stooped to offer her a leg up, because she looked at me and giggled before tucking her foot securely into the stirrup and swinging over effortlessly. The wind billowed strands of hair loose from her pony-tail, while laughter broke free of her like sunlight.

"Dusty is waiting for you, cowboy. See if you boys can keep up." She winked and walked her horse off, taking the lead behind our guides.

I mounted up, definitely not as flawlessly as she had, and seated myself, feeling all kinds of awkward. I knew my rear was going to suffer after this, but it would be so worth it. Look at her. She was enjoying this already. Watching her move along the water with all that radiating joy, I felt proud. At least I'd done *something* right today.

Every time Ms. Lewis spoke, it was like falling into a thorn bush.

"So, Russell," she said, our horses plodding alongside each other. "What are your plans for life?"

I almost laughed. As if I had any plans for anything, but I didn't suppose *'Staying out of jail'* was a suitable response to my girlfriend's mother's question. "Just working for now. Figuring it out as I go." It really wasn't a great thing to say, even I knew that, but it was the only honesty I could get close to.

"Hm." That hum sounded incredibly loaded. "Do you intend to stay in Texas?"

"Yes." I guess.

"That's good. My daughter thrives best near family."

"I can speak for myself, Mom."

"Oh, I know. I'm just sharing."

And that was one of the milder moments when Ms. Lewis *'just shared'* something with me. The rest of our ride passed in careful conversation. I found myself straightening unconsciously, and choosing my words cautiously. Laughing less easily. I had wanted her approval, but had no idea how impossible it would be to get it. I didn't expect to feel like I was on trial, and she were the judge, jury, and executioner all at once.

Even Birdie seemed overwhelmed with her mother throughout everything. She came to my rescue, but I hated that she felt she had to. There was obviously more to this mother-daughter dynamic than I understood.

When we dismounted, Birdie swayed, almost losing her footing.

I was beside her in an instant. "You okay?" I asked in a low voice, keeping my hand splayed steady around her.

"Fine," she said quickly. "It's just windy." But she pressed her fingers to her temple like she was trying to hold something in place. Her mom noticed, too, and her eyes sharpened. My hand fell away as I was moved aside by the sheer force of her mother's presence. Suddenly, I had the uneasy feeling that I'd walked into a story that started long before me. One I didn't understand at all, and possibly wasn't welcome in.

BIRDIE

50

I WAS A FOOL TO THINK I COULD OUTRUN IT.

The ride had been perfect. The wind and salt and hooves cutting through the surf were magical. For a while, the heaviness of the past few weeks had released me from its clutches and I almost felt normal again.

But by the time we'd finished, my head felt like it was splitting open. It was only in the neck at first, then pressure built behind my eyes. Then, light began serrating my nervous system. Sound got louder. Even the ocean, once soothing and beautiful, had started feeling aggressive. All of it caused a nauseous riot in my stomach.

"Birdie?" Russell rubbed my arm but I pulled away. His previously comforting touch now created the opposite effect. "What did I do?"

"Nothing, sorry."

"What are you sorry for?" He looked closer. "You look pale. Are you okay?"

"I'm fine." The words tasted false.

The horses had all gone, and with them went the good day I'd clung to. It was just the four of us left—Me, Russell, my mom, and my best friend the migraine. I took a step toward the car and the ground tilted, nausea churning.

Mom was suddenly in front of me. "Birdie, do you feel okay? Does it feel like last time?"

No. Don't ask that.

Russell looked between us, knowing he wasn't in the know about something. "Last time?"

"No, Mom. I'm fine. Just too much sun."

Her gaze scanned my face. "You're squinting."

"It's bright out."

"You're pressing your neck."

"My muscles are tight."

"You're hunching."

"I'm sore from the ride."

"Birdie."

"Mom." *Stop already. I can't keep this up.*

The pain spiked, protruding through everything else. My tongue felt thick. Even speaking required effort.

Russell moved closer. "We can sit for a minute, then I'll drive you home."

"We'd probably better go now. I will take you." Mom kept her calm, but her words were not lenient.

"Ms. Lewis, if it's all right, I'd really like to drive her home," Russell tried. There was a protective edge in his voice I'd never heard before.

"Don't worry, Russell. She is my daughter and I will take her. Thank you for including me in your plans today." She did a good job of sounding courteous, but I knew better. Russell probably did, too, thanks to her grilling him this afternoon. I owed him such a huge apology later.

If I were feeling up to it, I would protest and remind my mom that I was an adult and could choose who took me home. I wanted to reach for Russell's hand and stay in the good moments of the day. But the pain, sickeningly white-hot, would not let up.

Screw it. Whoever got me home fastest could have me.

"I'm just tired," I assured them. Russell walked me to my mom's car and stood beside the passenger door with me.

He scanned my face with concern, confusion, and something I was too beat up to figure out. "I'll call you later?"

"Okay."

We said goodbye, and I sank into the seat, watching him walk to his car through hooded eyes.

Mom eyed me. "You shouldn't push yourself like this."

I closed my eyes against the blasted sunlight. I was happier not seeing her, either, or the dejected look on Russell's face. "I'm not."

"You are."

I rested my head against the seat and kept my eyes shut, focusing on my breathing. Moving slowly, I rested my hands inside my jacket pockets. There, I felt the rose charm, cold and comforting against my palm.

Why couldn't I be more like a rose? They were a symbol of resilience and strength. Like Russell had said, they grew back after nearly dying every single winter. They were inspiring, and yet, all I could focus on was the worst migraine I'd ever had.

Why did she ask if it felt like last time? If by *'last time'* she meant when I fainted on stage at the last pageant, that was an isolated incident. That was nothing. Ruled as inconsequential by the medical staff who treated me. I had no reason to worry or compare anything to that, or to expect a repeat occurrence.

Right, God?

RUSSELL

51

THE NEXT MORNING, I DIDN'T TEXT HER. I CALLED. I WAS TOO wound up with worry to bother with waiting. It would be harder for her to ignore my concern when she had to answer in real time, too. I just couldn't get over the thought that she was trying to hide something from me.

Or, hide *me* from something.

"Hi," she said, picking up on the third ring. Her voice was thick with sleep.

"Hey. How are you feeling?"

A small pause. "Better." Not convincing.

"Head still hurting?"

"Just… a little fuzzy," she said on a sigh. "It always takes a long sleep to get rid of one of my big headaches. I think yesterday was just too much sun and excitement."

She tried to make it light, but there was something off about the way she spoke, like she had to search for the words.

I sat up straighter. "Did you sleep okay?"

Another pause. "Yeah. I mean, mostly. I kept waking up."

"You sound tired."

"I *am* tired," she said defensively. "Finals. Work. You know."

Yeah, and I knew that wasn't all of it. I hesitated, then hedged, "What did your mom mean yesterday when she asked about *'last time'*?"

"Oh. That."

My grip tightened on the phone.

"I had another bad migraine a while back. They're kind of my thing. She just overreacts."

"How bad?"

"It was just, I don't know. Intense." A faint exhale. "She's dramatic."

That didn't line up with what I'd seen on the beach. Her mom hadn't looked dramatic, she'd looked clinical.

"And yesterday felt like that?"

"No." She answered too quickly. "No. Not like that."

I didn't know what to say, but I knew I wasn't getting the whole truth.

"I'm fine, Russ. Promise."

Uh-huh. I was no dummy. That was girl code for, *'drop it.'* I decided I would. For now.

Her voice brightened a bit. "Hey. Do you want to go with me to the chiropractor today?"

"I told you yesterday I have to work."

Silence.

"Oh." Her voice wasn't playful anymore. "Right. Sorry."

Birdie Jo didn't just forget things. She remembered everything and with vivid detail. Crazy dreams. Anniversaries and deadlines. Conversations from ages ago. Embarrassing nicknames and tattoo choices.

"You okay?" I still wasn't convinced.

"Yeah, I just—" she trailed off. I waited. "Didn't sleep great," she finished on another deep sigh, like she'd pulled a random answer from an imaginary list for the sake of answering my question.

I really did not like that.

"I'll have to go tomorrow anyway, actually," she continued, momentum picking up again. "I forgot I'm helping Kevin wrap gifts for his fundraiser tonight. Too bad you can't go with me."

Kevin at a church for a fundraiser. Couldn't say I was disappointed to miss out on that.

"Yeah, too bad," I said. Then I felt discouraged that she'd somehow spaced her own plans. I was just about to bring it up when—

"Oh, by the way, I'm back in my dad's car. That funky sound I mentioned I'd heard mine make came back, and I'm not risking it."

"You mentioned a funky sound?"

"Didn't I?"

No. She hadn't.

"Maybe you and Kevin can look at it together."

"Are you sure there's a noise, or is this just a ploy to make us reconnect?"

"You doubt my intentions?" she teased, tension easing ever so slightly.

"Yes, I do."

She let out a half-laugh. "Don't worry. I didn't go under the hood and disconnect my own flux capacitor or anything, but it *is* a good excuse to get everyone together. I need all the Sarah time I can get while she's home on break."

She was talking faster now, which looked to me like overcompensating.

"Bird," I said, quiet concern hanging from me.

"Yeah?"

"Are you sure everything's okay?"

The line went quiet so long I thought maybe we'd lost connection.

"Yeah. I'm still just a little fuzzy. It'll clear up. Plus, you did interrupt my beauty sleep." She laughed lightly.

Clear up? Like a fog?

"All right. I'll talk to you after work," I said. I didn't feel better about anything, but what more could I do? She wasn't opening up to me. Best I could do was stay available to her and pretend that didn't hurt.

"Okay."

"Have fun with your wrapping thing."

"I will." There was another small pause. "Hey, Russ?"

"Yes, Birdie?"

"Thanks for yesterday. Minus the sun trying to kill me, it really was the best day I think I've ever had."

"Of course. I'm glad."

When we hung up, I sat staring at my phone for a while. Birdie had told me she was fine, over and over, and yet I struggled to take it at face value. I wasn't the most impressive mind out there, but I would consider myself clever. At the least, I was not an idiot. She paused before answering simple questions and repeated the same odd phrases. And her mom's voice echoed in my mind repeatedly.

'Does it feel like last time?'

I didn't know what last time was, but my gut told me it had been more than just bad. And whatever it was, she was hiding it from me.

BIRDIE

52

I ADMITTED IT. I WAS SCARED. LATER THAT NIGHT, WHEN I PULLED into the parking lot of Sarah's church, I had already prayed the same prayer at least twenty times.

Please let it be nothing.

In front of me, the building glowed warm against the early evening sky. Laughter spilled faintly through the open side doors where the others filed in. This was normal. I could do normal. I *needed* normal right now.

"I'm fine," I told myself under my breath.

Inside, folding tables were covered in wrapping paper, tape, bows, and stacks of donated gifts. Christmas music hummed through a small speaker in the corner.

Sarah was the first to spot me. "Birthday girl!" she called, pulling me into a hug. The pressure made my head pound, but I didn't let it show. "Still riding the high from yesterday?"

"Something like that."

Kevin waved from across the room, elbow-deep in wrapping paper. His face was alighted. "Hey, Birdie."

"Hey, Kev. I heard about your mural."

"Oh, yeah." He rubbed the back of his head. "Well, it's not a mural yet."

"It's going to be wonderful though," Sarah chimed in.

"I'm sure it will." I looked around, noticing Tyler and Cindie over in the kitchen placing something on the counter. *Shoot.* "Was I supposed to bring a dish for a potluck?"

Sarah turned to where I was looking. "Oh, no. Erin and Glen are bringing the meal tonight. Cindie just decided to throw a pie into the mix."

My shoulders slumped in relief.

Sarah stepped toward me. "Everything okay, Birdie?"

Not her, too... "Everything is fine, I'm just a little burnt out still from yesterday. It wouldn't have surprised me if I'd totally spaced a potluck." I laughed, probably not super convincingly.

"If you need anything, you'll let me know, right?"

"For sure. Thanks, girl," I said, slinging my arm around her shoulder to move the conversation on.

We sat down as everyone else arrived, and I already wasn't sure how long I'd last. The lights overhead felt brighter than usual. I kept blinking and rubbing at the pain to no avail.

You're fine.

You're fine.

God, please. Just let this be one of my regular headaches. I don't have time for anything else.

The only response I got was the steady ache that surged from the back of my neck and kept on going.

~

SAMMY DROPPED into the seat beside me upon her arrival. Jenna wasn't coming because her morning sickness was relentless lately, but not everyone coming tonight knew that.

"Good, you're finally here," Sarah said with a devious smile. "I've been dying to ask how things are with Jared."

Sammy groaned. "Why is that the topic of conversation?"

"Because we're invested," I told her.

She smiled despite herself. "Things are good with Jared. Great, actually."

We gushed, laughing girlishly in unison. The guys all turned to look at us and just chuckled amongst themselves, returning to their own wrapping tasks.

"Speaking of relationships..." Cindie said, holding her hand out, fingers wiggling. "Some of you have not seen this yet."

My hands stilled mid-fold. "It's so beautiful! Congratulations!"

"Any thoughts on setting a date yet?" asked Sammy.

"We aren't sure yet, but I might want a spring wedding. We shall see."

Even though I had no regrets, I couldn't help but think of Nick. We would be engaged right now, too, if I had said yes.

Nick's image faded from my mind, and then there was Russell, and I smiled to myself. Despite the war inside my head, my heart was totally at peace. I really cared a lot about him.

I looked up from my wrapping and watched Kevin for a moment. He was a testimony in and of himself. He didn't grow up a believer, and that was putting it lightly. From what I'd gathered of Russell's feelings on the subject, he believed in God, only sort of. God, to him, was not to be fully trusted. What Russ needed was fire, like what Kevin had now.

Give it time, Birdie. Pray for him. Live out Jesus for him. That's all you can do.

I knew better than to compare the spiritual walks of two different people like that, but I so badly wanted faithful certainty for Russell. He was so worthy, and sometimes, it was obvious he didn't think so.

I just wanted everything aligned at the same time for once. Faith. Future. Health. Peace. Couldn't a girl have it all?

"Birdie?" Sarah's voice cut into my thoughts. "You've been spacing out for a while. You okay?"

"Yeah, just tired. Thinking." It was all true, just not the whole truth.

"Is there anything you need?"

I pressed my fingers lightly against the base of my skull, and my pulse answered back.

God, You heal people. You move all kinds of mountains. You restore families. So why is this still here? Why won't it go away?

"I'm sure it's nothing the chiropractor can't fix," I said, forcing brightness back into my voice. "I'm going first thing tomorrow."

Sammy's brow scrunched. "You sure that's a good idea with neck pain?"

"I go all the time. Neck pain is a perfect reason to go."

Sarah regarded me for longer than was comfortable. "Just don't ignore it if it gets worse. Do something about it tonight if you need to. We can help."

Was she speaking from worry caused by events of the past? She didn't confide in us when she was having issues with her Type 1. She didn't even tell us she *had* Type 1 until after disaster struck her at Dan's party.

"I'll be fine. Thanks, girl." But I didn't even believe myself. I was ignoring it.

I continued smiling and wrapping gifts and laughing at the

right moments with my friends. All the while, my migraine bloomed fully into something dark and inescapable.

It's okay. I will make it to the chiropractor tomorrow and get relief. It's just one more day. It'll be fine.

RUSSELL

53

HAVING MY CAR BACK WAS GLORIOUS. EVERYTHING WAS SO familiar. The steering wheel felt good in my hands. The gear shifter was like giving an old friend a handshake. From the pedals to the tailpipe, driving was just second nature. And now that I had a job, little by little, I had the world at my fingertips. My keys and I were going places. Where were we going for the long-term? I couldn't say. But the thoughts and possibilities of freedom were better than just dreaming about it.

With my latest paycheck, I had my parents removed from the title. Now, she was all mine, now and forever.

Earlier, I'd stopped to check in with Harold. He was happy with all my recent progress, and I was, too. I smiled to myself on the way to Kevin's, my last stop of the day before going to see Birdie. Her twinkling silver bracelet still hung off my mirror, and it kept catching my eye. She would want it back soon to attach her new charm.

Just down the street from the parking lot, a shiny old Studebaker I'd noticed from this morning still sat on the side of the road. Only this time, an old man accompanied it. He was bent over under the hood, bundled up in an old wool coat and matching hat, all faded and checkered in plaid.

I kept going, but I had to admit, my attention was snagged.

Birdie's bracelet swung back and forth, reflecting the sun until it darn near blinded me.

If that's not a sign, I don't know what is.

Puffing up my cheeks with a sigh, I took the next U-turn and went back. Pulling up behind the broken-down beauty and its driver, I parked and got out.

Feeling awkward and not entirely sure why I was doing this, I cleared my throat on my approach. "Hey there. You having trouble getting her going?"

Two beady, wrinkly eyes peaked around the hood. "Oh, well, yes. It must be Tuesday." He chuckled.

"It's Thursday," I said simply, not getting his meaning.

"And I'm Roger. And you are?" he asked, coming toward me with his shaking, veiny hand stretched out.

"Russell. Grandy." We shook hands. "This is a very beautiful car, sir."

"She sure is, isn't she? But awful temperamental. She's had a bad attitude since she was new, but my wife so loved this boat of a thing." He spoke of the car with an annoyed love that I found it funny. "I only take her car out once a month to keep it kicking. As you can see, that doesn't always go according to plan. My wife's been gone five years now, but I still do my best."

"Oh. I'm, uh, sorry for your loss."

"Well, thank you, son. It's quite all right. She gets to spend all her time with Jesus while I'm stuck down here in the muck. I reckon she's feeling sorry for me, too." He chuckled again.

He laughed like a young man, so much in contrast to the frail look of his body. And the casual way he talked about Jesus—it was so much like how Birdie did it.

"I fix cars for fun," I told him. "Used to do it for a living. Want me to take a look so you can get rolling again?" The chill had hit, and if I was feeling it, I *knew* he was.

"If you'd be so kind, I'd be much obliged." Roger stepped aside, granting me access to the engine. He continued speaking as I peeked inside. "I thought I knew what I was doing, only because what I'd tried has worked before. Maybe I have done more harm than good this time, seeing as how I'm no mechanic. But it seems that God saw fit to send me one, in any case."

God again. "Well, I don't know about that, but I'm happy to help if I can."

And I could. Fifteen minutes and a quick jog back to my car for some tools I kept in the trunk later, his old car was purring again.

I closed the hood, satisfied. "It'll get you home, but I don't know how long that fix will hold. You'd better get it to a shop before it gets much colder, or you'll end up stranded again."

"I used to take all our vehicles to a little shop over in the Bluff —you know old Marvin? Well, I suppose you probably wouldn't. He retired a while ago now."

No, I hadn't heard of Marvin in the Bluff.

"When you took your rig to him, you knew you were getting good work done. Nothing extra or surprising on your bill when he called you back in. He was a very honest, straight-forward fellow. You don't meet too many honest businessmen anymore these days."

"No, I would say not." Tanner sure wasn't an example of one. "I don't want to get your hopes up, because I'm a little out of practice, but if you want, I could give it a try myself."

His old blue eyes lit up. "You mean, you would work on this car for me?"

I only felt slightly uncomfortable. "Sure."

"Oh, that's wonderful!" He reached out and placed his hand on my arm. "Thank you so much, son. I knew I had a good feeling about you."

I cracked a meager smile. "I will do my best."

"I am certain that's true. Thank you. When should I bring her by?"

When he released me, I rolled my shoulders. "Anytime this weekend should be fine."

"Sounds like a plan."

"Let me just write down my address for you." I reached into my car and flipped open the center console. Grabbing a pen and the notepad, I wrote my name and address, with my phone number for good measure, and tore it off.

"Thank you, kindly." His eyes were on Birdie's bracelet. "I hope I'm not keeping you from your special gal."

"What makes you think I have one?"

"What man would keep a trinket like that hanging from his mirror if it weren't something important to his lady?"

A smile spread across my face. "You've got me there. But no, you didn't keep me."

"Well, I thank you kindly, Russell. See you soon." He climbed into the car, gave me a little salute, and rumbled on his way.

I sat in my car with my keys in my lap. I never thought I'd say such a thing, but Roger was kind of cool for an old man. He had such a fashionable yet casual manner of speaking. His speech really gave him away as being from another era, if his clothes hadn't already. But I found that I was glad I'd turned around and stopped to help him. It felt good and I… liked that.

I wondered if that non-profit garage thing that Birdie and I heard about was anything like this.

Without thinking, I pulled out my phone.

RUSSELL

Hey, Kevin. Have you ever thought of turning cars into a charity?

I stared at the screen… then hit send.

When I finally pulled back out into traffic and then turned back around to head home, a comforting sense of lightness settled over me. Whatever it was, I would've been okay with feeling it again.

54

I GRABBED MY PHONE BEFORE STARTING UP THE CAR TO LEAVE. It was finally chiropractor time.

BIRDIE

Hey, Sarah, wanna get together tomorrow to baby shop for Jenna? It's probably time we start planning a real shower, like, with more than just us. At the very least, she needs more prezzies!

SARAH

Sounds like a great idea! Sammy coming, too?

BIRDIE

I haven't asked her yet. I'm just heading out to see the chiro before going home for class. Do you think you could ask her?

SARAH

Sure will. If she's not already doing something, I'll bring her with me tomorrow.

BIRDIE

Great! Later, then. 

Inside Dr. Jeffreys' office, I greeted Rochelle, the receptionist, and she checked me in. The sleep had done me some good, taking the edge off, but the general pain was still there, especially in my neck. Relief could *not* come fast enough.

There were a few people still waiting, so I sat down and opened my Notes app to jot down a few ideas I had for Jenna. Her favorite color was yellow, and yellow was a happy color, so maybe we could go for a sunshine theme.

"Hi, Birdie," came Dr. Jeffreys' voice, surprising me away from my note-taking. I whipped my head over, wincing at the hurt. "Sore, are we?"

"Yes, very. It doesn't take much." I laughed at myself, standing up and following him through the hall. Within it, there were three open entryways where he and his assistant worked on patients.

A year or two ago, backstage at a pageant, one of the other moms went around recommending a chiropractor to help keep all the girls limber and in good health. After trying it out and seeing how great it made me feel as a whole, how improved my circulation was, how fewer headaches I was getting, the rest was history. I had gotten adjusted at least a few times a month ever since.

To start, I lay back-down on the adjustment table and relaxed. Dr. Jeffreys sat behind my head on his rolling stool. "So, what is bothering you?"

I waved my hand over my head and neck. "All of it. I have been so busy and stressed lately, it's just all kinds of messed up."

"All right then. Let's see what we can do to help." I felt his hands cradle the back of my head. "One, two," he began, then with a calculated flick of his wrist, "three."

Usually, I experienced relief bordering on euphoria. Not this time. "Oh, whoa!" I exclaimed, surprised by a loud pop in my head. Then came a strange, rushing sound, like a giant rain stick being turned over. It poured into my ears, filling them. I had to speak loudly, above the noise. "Do you hear that?"

"Hear what? What's happening?"

"I heard a pop. Now there's a buzzing in my head, like tons of bees. It's so loud," I said, though the words were causing me great difficulty. I didn't want to panic, but I'd heard these bees before.

"Just lie still. Let's give it a few minutes." I could tell he was concerned.

The rain stick sound eventually faded, but other things had set in.

"How are you feeling now?" Dr. Jeffreys asked.

"I can't really tell." But I knew I didn't feel normal. The world felt heavy.

"Can you sit up?"

I made the attempt, trying to hoist myself up, and my body felt like lead and—oh, no. Not good. I was immediately, incredibly, nauseated. "Can't. Feels terrible."

"Can you describe what you're feeling?"

"Nauseous. Body won't move. Talking is hard." I didn't know if he went away, but nobody spoke for a while.

"Birdie? It's been fifteen minutes now, and we're concerned that you're not feeling any better. You're actually worse, so we're not taking any risks. I'm calling an ambulance. Okay?"

Fifteen minutes? That's all it was since this started? Time didn't make sense anymore. Not much did. "Yes," I managed, but I wanted to say so much more, to thank him and ask him to call my parents. To call Russell. It was a terrifying and confusing sensation, trying to will my body to move and my mouth to speak, and being unable to do either.

My entire left side had gone distant, foreign, but I managed to retrieve my phone, nearly dropping it. I tried to use both thumbs to text Russell, but I had to make do one-handed. Why the heck wouldn't my left hand *move?* I could barely use it as a prop to hold my phone, and even then, it wasn't steady at all. Each letter I typed felt like lifting weights with a single finger.

BIRDIE

Something funny happened at the chiro. I don't think I'm okay. Ambulance coming.

The more time passed, the worse everything got inside my head. The heaviness spread. The world was moving at a different speed than me. I lay there with my eyes closed, unable to bear opening them for fear of being sick.

When the EMTs arrived, hands stronger than my dead weight forced me to sit upright. Surely, they were being as careful as they could, but it felt jarring and rough. Lids heavy, my eyes remained sealed shut. The darkness was the only thing that made any sense. Multiple voices surrounded me, asking me questions I could barely comprehend, and my words had to be pushed through molasses to make sound, between one deep breath at a time.

Sitting me up was a mistake. My efforts to keep from getting sick were thwarted, but luckily, somebody had the foresight to hold something out for me. I think I cried, my confusion giving way to fear. What was wrong with me? What was going on around me?

I vaguely made out an EMT telling me I would be okay, that they were going to help make me feel better. At that moment, I tried to believe them but couldn't.

"Call Russell. Want Russell," were the last words I was able to press out before finding myself peeking through the glass window of the ambulance.

God, am I going to die?

RUSSELL

55

BIRDIE

sloiswefbntg fy hagen a. cha i din ok. . . ambblen comig

What in the world?

I'd just parked at Kevin's house when Birdie's weird text came in. I immediately called her back, but there was no answer. I sent her a text. Still nothing.

Confusion swarmed as I tried to decipher what that could possibly mean. Was it a joke? A super long typo? Maybe she accidentally sat on her phone while it was open. Or maybe…

Maybe something was wrong.

I opened my door and called again. This time, she picked up on the last ring. Thank God.

"Birdie? Hello?"

There were sounds in the background I couldn't make out. A low moan that sounded like Birdie, but wrong somehow. Voices that I didn't recognize. Movement. The muffled chaos of something not okay.

"Hello?" I demanded louder, one foot out of the car.

Kevin came down his driveway and rested a casual hand on top of my door. He was smiling until he caught my tone, then his face went serious. “Hey, Russ. Everything okay?”

I glanced at the screen of my phone. The call was still connected, but no one was speaking directly to me. There was only noise. Disjointed sounds that made no sense at all.

“Not really sure. Birdie sent a text full of gibberish, and now she won’t answer, but there’s something happening on the line.”

A new voice broke through, and I snapped the phone back to my ear. “Birdie?” I shouted.

“Hello?” It was a man whose voice I didn’t recognize. It would’ve been easier to be furious in that moment, but something inside me knew to be afraid. And, oh, I was.

“Who is this? Where’s Birdie?”

“Sir, my name is Santos. I’m an emergency medical technician with the Fire Department. Are you related to Birdie Jo MacLean?”

All the air left my lungs. “I’m her boyfriend. What’s going on?”

Kevin’s eyes were still on me, reading my alert, waiting to hear the explanation as much as me.

“She asked me to fill you in. She had an episode while at her chiropractic office. We’re transporting her by ambulance to Mercy Medical South.” Right on cue, sirens ignited in the background.

“Mercy Medical South,” I repeated. Even as I spoke, I returned my key to the ignition and turned it on, mentally mapping out the fastest way to get there. “What kind of episode? Is she okay?”

“We’re not certain yet. We’ll know more once she’s evaluated. If you can safely meet us there, the hospital staff will update you.”

“Has anyone called her parents?”

"I'm not sure. I need to hand the phone back and get her secured."

"Tell her I'm coming." The line went dead, and I threw my phone onto the dash.

Kevin seized my shoulder. "Dude, what is it?"

"Don't know. She's in an ambulance on the way to the hospital." I felt detached from my own voice. "I've got to go."

He said something under his breath. A curse? No, he wouldn't. A prayer, probably. Good for him, but I didn't have time for that. I only needed to get her to her. Now.

I love her.

The realization hit me with urgency. I didn't know when it happened, only that I was suddenly, admittedly, helpless to it.

"Let me go with you."

"No, it's fine," I insisted, but Kevin wasn't listening. He shut my door and ran to the other side, letting himself in. "I know she's your friend, but I said no."

"I'm not just going for her."

I held his determined gaze for two seconds before giving up. There were more important things to deal with than hashing out where Kevin and I stood at the moment. "Whatever." And then I peeled out of his driveway.

As a sharp word slipped past my teeth, I slammed my hand against the wheel. Why hadn't I gone with her when she asked? I thought about how different she'd sounded lately, and how it compared to when her voice was teasing and clear, when her mind was whole...

When she was still okay.

More thoughts came fast and irrational, but I couldn't stop them. I should've gone with her. I should've been there. Maybe I could've done something. What good was I if I couldn't protect her from this?

I almost missed my exit. At the last second, I jerked the wheel and slid into the next lane. A horn blared behind me, snapping me back to attention.

"That was close," Kevin said evenly. "It'll be okay, Russ. Just get us there in one piece."

I forced my grip to loosen and steadied the car. If I wrecked us on the way, I'd be useless to her.

More useless than I already was.

We pulled into the hospital lot minutes later. I barely registered parking before I was out of the car and sprinting toward the emergency entrance, Kevin right beside me.

"Birdie Jo MacLean," I said to the nurse at the desk, breathless. "She just came by ambulance."

"Are you family?"

"I'm her boyfriend. The EMT told me to meet them here."

She took me in before checking her screen. "She's through those doors. One visitor at a time."

"Thank you," I replied, not waiting for anything else.

The hallway beyond was wide and bright, a bathroom on the left, curtained beds lining the right. Monitors beeped steadily behind thin fabric walls, separating patients.

There was Birdie, in the second bed, tucked into a ball on her left side. It was all I could do not to fall to my knees before her. "Birdie?"

Even with as little detail as I had, I knew something had come dangerously close to taking her from me, and I couldn't handle that. Not even a little.

BIRDIE

56

"Russell." I cracked a smile when I noticed him, my voice a soft, meager version of its former self. My eyes opened and closed slowly as it grew harder to keep them pried open. "You're here."

"How are you?"

"The meds are kicking in, so I feel less like throwing up now. So, that's nice."

"Are you sick? Is that what happened?"

If only it were that simple. "Something happened during my neck adjustment. There was a *pop,* a *woosh,* lots of bees, and an insane amount of nausea. Half my body went completely numb and useless. I could barely move. I've never experienced anything like it. I can still hardly feel my left side, and I can't move much on my own even now."

"You're talking really slow, and you keep stumbling over your words like you're drunk." He grabbed my hand and kissed it. "I'm so sorry I wasn't there. I should have been."

"There wouldn't have been anything you could do."

Another tender kiss grazed the top of my hand. "Were you able to call your mom?"

My eyes popped open, and the bright lights assaulted them. I winced, closing them up tightly. "Oh, no, I didn't. She will freak." I reached slowly toward my phone, feeling like a sloth weighed down by iron chains.

"Relax. I'll call her for you."

"Are you sure?"

"Yes, don't worry about a thing." His smile gave me comfort as he spoke, and it might have only been my current distress, but I thought a hint of pink crossed his cheeks.

"Are you okay?"

"That's not even something you should me asking me right now. You're the one lying in a hospital bed."

"Are you totally freaked right now?"

Russell hesitated, but he didn't have time to respond.

"Hello, there, Ms. MacLean," came a new voice. A cursory glance revealed a female nurse in sea foam green scrubs. She appeared young but older than us. "I'm so glad to see you're looking better."

"Had you come by before?" I inquired. I thought her voice might've been slightly familiar, but I hadn't been coherent enough to register much up to now.

"I've been treating you since you came in," she said with genuine empathy.

Oh. "Sorry."

"Don't be. But I'm going to have to ask your friend to step out into the waiting room for a while. We have to take you back for imaging now."

"Not friend. Boyfriend," I corrected, a tendril of nervousness rising to the surface. "Can't he come with me?"

She shook her head. "I'm sorry, love. But I will be back there with you, and you'll be in good hands. We'll have you out before you know it." She smiled at me and Russ.

"It's okay. I'll have your parents here soon and we'll all be waiting for you." Russ leaned down and kissed my forehead before standing up. "Do you want me to call the girls?"

"No, please don't. I don't want anyone telling them anything until this is all over and we actually know what's going on."

"That might be a bit hard, since Kevin is in the waiting room."

I groaned.

"I had just gotten to his house when your text came in…"

"It's okay. Just tell the girls not to come, please. And you be right here when I get back."

He gave me a wink. "You got it, Sweetie Bird. I wouldn't go anywhere."

I shakily held my pinky out just before the nurse wheeled me away. He met me in the air and curled them together, and I knew he wouldn't let me down.

As we rolled off, I couldn't tell where or how far we'd gone. The intravenous meds were good, but the motion didn't make my senses happy, so I reverted to clenching my eyes shut. Things outside of my dark, closed-lidded world were still a bit nonsensical. When I opened my eyes, everything seemed too close and yet blurry at the same time.

When next I ventured to open them, I was in a room with a large, tube-shaped machine. The nurse asked me if I had on any jewelry, and when I told her what I had and that I couldn't move, she helped me remove my necklace and rings. Usually, I also had my charm bracelet, but I had left it hanging from the mirror in Russell's car. Even during my haze, I hoped he was enjoying seeing it there every day, but I suddenly felt desperate to get it back and attach the rose charm he'd given me. I wanted to feel him around my wrist from now on, forever, just like he had me around his.

"We'll have to get you onto this table here. Can you stand?"

"No." There was no way. Though I had some improvement, my body was still virtually useless.

"I'll get you as close as I can, then we can try to roll you over. You ready?"

Not really. But with some effort between the two of us, we made it happen.

"Have you ever had an MRI before?"

"No."

"Oh, okay. Well, we use the same machine, which is this baby right here." She patted the outside of the medicinal white tunnel like a treasured pet. "But we are going to do what's called an MRA. This type of scan focuses on blood vessels, so we can check for damage from your adjustment. Once we see what's going on inside, we'll know more."

They thought this was related to the adjustment? Her explanation didn't help my comprehension, but that wasn't her fault. What was I going to do about it? "'Kay."

"Now, going into the machine can be a little intimidating for some people. I have a nice, soft blindfold here and a pair of headphones to play some music. It should help keep you calm, so you don't feel anxious when you're in there. You'll wanna hold as still as possible so we get good, clear images. We want this to be one-and-done for you, okay?"

The lump in my throat tripled in size. I nodded meagerly.

"You'll do great." She patted my arm, obviously hoping to extend some comfort with her touch. "We're almost ready. Just one more thing." She shuffled around and came back with a syringe. "This is contrast. It's going to feel really warm when it travels through your body. Don't be afraid, but be warned, you might feel like you're peeing yourself." She giggled, and I wish I could, too. "It's totally normal."

"What does that stuff do?"

"Provides improved visibility of the vessels. It helps us get better images." She stuck my IV with the stuff in question. "In it goes. Now in you go next, sweetheart."

The rattling in my ribcage gave me extreme doubts about this. "Wait. I'm scared."

The nurse put her hand over mine. "It's okay. I can tell you're a very brave young lady, and this will be over before you know it. The sooner we get you scanned, the sooner the doctor can help you. These things," she waved to the machine with a shrug, "are no big deal."

"How long will I be in it?"

"The scan itself should take about twenty minutes."

Twenty minutes! There was no way I could lie perfectly still like a burrito inside that thing for that long. But there was no way to avoid it either.

"I'll be right on the other side of the glass. You'll be fine, I promise. Just don't forget to hold very still. Everyone says that's the hardest part." With one last smile and comforting pat of her hand, she put the blindfold and headphones on me and left me in the room alone, lying on my back on a table that would soon deliver me into the tunnel of torture. The only good thing was that I was much too scared to risk any movement.

God help me. Oh, Lord, please. Get me out of this tunnel. Not only the one they've just rolled me into, but the one inside my head. Please, God. I want to see my parents again. I want to kiss Russell, for real. I want to have another sleepover with my best friends. I want to celebrate

Jenna's baby. I want to see Dan get out of rehab. I want to buy a house and dig a pond for a turtle. I want to pet a capybara. I want to get married, eventually. I want to see the rest of my life. Please, please, please.

Beneath the blindfold, I kept my eyes firmly shut, just in case. I didn't want to risk opening them and seeing what the inside of this creepy thing looked like. I had to hold still, or this would all be for nothing and—*ahh!* My body was *hot!*

"You should feel the contrast right about now," came a gentle voice through the headphones. "We are going to begin, so I will play music for you. You may still hear the machine doing its thing, but don't worry. How about a little Beach Boys for some summer vibes?"

The tunes ran one into the other. As she warned, the volume wasn't loud enough to drown out the thunderous shaking-pounding cries of the machine, but I did everything in my power to hold still. My hands were tucked tightly at my sides. The unsteady rise and fall of my breathing, which I tried and failed to control, was the only movement in the entire tube.

RUSSELL

57

When Birdie woke up again, her family and I were still at the hospital, taking turns sitting with her in her small room. For a while, even her little brother and sister were there, but they had quickly grown restless while Birdie slept off what was left of her episode. Eventually, their mother, Nadine, had taken them home. They'd had to settle for a video-call by the time Birdie woke up.

I'd held the phone up for her, although she still wasn't able to talk a whole lot. She sighed a bunch, taking lengthy breaks between every few words, and her eyes weren't very alert. It was a far cry from Birdie's natural state of being, and every second she wasn't herself, my gut twisted into more knots. This person was my Birdie, but also somehow not. I just wanted her to be okay.

The MRA had taken a lot out of her. It took hours after that, but when Birdie's test results came back, they weren't favorable. She'd had a stroke caused by a released blood clot from a right dissected vertebral artery. The trauma to the neck, which was probably the pageant incident, something her mom finally filled me in on, was only the beginning. It got worse. And the overall cause was attributed to a congenital disease she'd never known she had: Ehlers-Danlos Syndrome.

All her life, she had chronic arterial weaknesses and had always been, would always be, susceptible to injuries like she'd just suffered at the chiropractor. She'd had the condition all her life without even knowing it. The right defining triggers just hadn't come along yet. This kind of thing was like a sleeper agent, hovering around the corner of her vitality, just waiting for the moment to finally strike.

At one point during my shift with Birdie, the doctor came to check on her. She was in and out of sleep again at the time. I'd asked him what was special about this neck adjustment when she'd had hundreds of others before. The best he could tell me was that sometimes these things went undetected for a person's whole life; other times, the smallest thing set it off. It wasn't unheard of for someone with these kinds of conditions to *sneeze* themselves into dissections.

"I guess she was lucky all that time then," I'd said.

"Or she got lucky this time, so we could get her properly diagnosed. Now, she can learn the nuances of how to take care of herself going forward. Knowledge is power. And truthfully, there's no such thing as luck."

"You don't think so?"

"The stuff most people credit to luck is the work of God Himself," he'd said with all the confidence in the world. This doctor, this man, who had studied half his life in the name of science and saving people. It struck me. I pondered my brief conversation with him for the rest of the night and then some.

I was still thinking about it when my phone vibrated in my pocket, waking me up from Birdie's bedside. It was just after five in the morning. Was God awake at such an hour, too? God should know, if anyone deserved to be healed, it was Birdie. Surely, He wouldn't let her stay this way. There had to be something someone could do. If no one else, then God Himself. This could be fixed. It had to be.

The door creaked open and her dad, Garrett, slipped inside. He offered me a polite nod. "How are you?"

I stifled a yawn. "Fine." I knew it was my turn to leave, to go rest as everyone insisted, but every time I left this room, I rested a little less. I only wanted to stay with her.

Gently picking it up, I kissed the top of her hand and returned it to her side. She sighed in her sleep but that was it. My gaze lingered on the rise and fall of her chest, and the color that had begun returning slowly to her cheeks. What would I ever do without her?

I quietly pushed back the chair and vacated it. Garrett looked down at Birdie and then looked back to me. "This was an unfortunate way to meet, but I'm really grateful for all the care you're showing my daughter."

I nodded.

"Truly, she's been so happy. I know she's lucky to have you. And you have my thanks for being here for her."

"You're welcome."

He nodded next, before taking up his post in the chair. When I'd cleared the room, I leaned my back against the wall and sighed so deeply, so wearily, my bones almost ached. One foot in front of the other, I made my way, once again, to the lobby to wait. Slumping down into a chair, I hung my head. How had things gotten so crazy?

What if… what if after all this, she wasn't okay?

I tore my fingers through my hair, commanding my thoughts

to change direction. I couldn't allow myself to think things like that. When had I fallen so hard for her?

"Russ."

Looking up, I was surprised. "Kevin?"

I hadn't known he was still there. In his hands were two cafeteria coffees, and when he approached, he handed one to me.

"Thanks. I thought you'd left."

"Nah, I've been out here. Snoozing off and on." He took a long gulp.

"Don't you hate coffee?"

He laughed. "I hate it so much, but I need it. Hospitals are exhausting."

He didn't have to tell me. "How come you haven't left?"

"It didn't feel right to leave you on your own. And my updates are doing just enough to keep the girls from storming the castle."

"I can't believe they listened."

"Well, after I convinced Sarah that Birdie wouldn't have it any other way, she figured that respecting her request right now would probably be best for her health."

That made sense, but… "This really sucks." I leaned back and sighed, draining my coffee.

"Yeah." Kevin reached over and took my cup, sliding it around his own to momentarily dispose of it. "Remember that party?"

Pfft. "Couldn't forget."

"I spent all night in the hospital that night, and nobody would let me in to see Sarah. Her parents had tried to send me away. I had to literally sneak into her room after hours just to see her with my own eyes."

"That sounds like it sucked, too."

"It did, but the wait was worth it. It was the beginning of everything for us."

"How?"

"I told her exactly how I felt. No games or pride getting in the way." He looked at me then. "You love Birdie." It wasn't a question.

How did he already know? How could he tell? Because the truth was, yeah, I did love Birdie, and *wow* that scared me. But feeling like I'd almost lost her—*really* lost her—had scared me more.

So, I admitted it, to my once-closest friend, because hey, he was the only one listening. "Yeah, I do."

Kevin nodded once. "Then don't waste this." He got up and tossed the empty cups into the trash. "I'm gonna head home for a bit, but I'll be back. Text me if you need anything. I'll be praying for her."

As I watched him walk away, I finally felt something other than resentment for him. I'd forgotten what it felt like to be friends with Kevin. Maybe it was this weird, shared understanding of what these women had done to us that allowed us to relate to each other, and that was cool, I guess. At least a little bit, for now.

I knew God heard the prayers of someone like Kevin. I didn't know if God was listening to someone like me, but since I was alone… *I do love her, God. But what does that mean now? Where do I go from here?*

RUSSELL

58

It was my mom's turn to ask me that morning.

"You coming with us?"

I didn't look up from where I stood in the kitchen, staring into the fridge like it would give me answers. "No, thanks."

She paused, I could feel it. Her slight hesitation before the acceptance. Both of them had been asking more often lately, despite my regular refusals.

"You sure?"

"Yep."

"Well, we won't be too long, but there's a luncheon after."

"That's fine." I had plans I refused to miss anyway. I was just killing time until I could go pick up Birdie after her own church service.

Dad clapped a hand on my shoulder, his Sunday best looking sharp and smelling strong. "We'll see you this afternoon, unless you changed your mind?"

"I'm waiting to pick up Birdie."

"I see," he said, adjusting his watch. "How is she doing?"

"Still sore, and still kinda down. She's happiest when she gets to do normal things."

He nodded, empathetic. "We'll be praying for her at church today."

"She'd like that," I said stiffly.

"We'll see you later, Russ." I could tell he wanted to say more but chose not to.

My family left, and I was the only one in the house. I'd expected to feel relieved, but I found the quiet became uncomfortable. The discomfort became guilt. It didn't make sense. I'd skipped church before, plenty of times. I didn't belong there, never really had. People like Birdie and Kevin belonged there. Even my parents.

But me? No so much.

Ever since the hospital though, ever since I'd sent up a desperate little prayer into a fluorescent-lit waiting room ceiling, it felt different. I just didn't know how to figure out how.

Later, I checked the clock—time to head out to meet Birdie. She wasn't supposed to overdo it, but she'd insisted on going this morning. Said she wanted to *'be where people are praying.'* I didn't argue, but I didn't really understand it either.

A knock sounded at the door. I frowned. My parents wouldn't be back this soon, and they wouldn't knock.

When I opened it up, I nearly laughed.

Roger Milton stood there in a slightly wrinkled gray suit, tie crooked, Bible tucked methodically under one arm.

"Well," he said, peering up at me. "I figured I would swing on by. Have I come at a bad time?"

I stepped out beside him. "No, sir. This works."

"Good. I hate to interrupt a man in the middle of something important."

I almost said I wasn't doing anything important, but I just nodded and opened the garage, directing him to where he could park the car for me to work on it. Getting my hands on the hood, it was still warm from the drive over.

"I can't tell you how much I appreciate this," he said as I propped it open for a cursory looksee. "Haven't been able to find a reliable mechanic around here in years. Not since old Marvin passed on."

"Is that the same Marvin in the Bluff you were talking about the other day?"

"Hm? Oh, yes, actually. The very same. Sorry, lad, you'll have to forgive me if I tell the same tale more than once."

"It's no problem." I smiled, still poking around at what was safe to poke at until it cooled down.

"He really was a great person. The man knew his craft, too. But more than that, he cared about people. I get that same kind of feeling about you."

That made me snort. "You're giving me too much credit."

"That's not something I ever do."

I shrugged, tightening something under the hood, mostly to avoid eye contact.

"You can properly judge a tree by its fruit, after all," he added. "And besides, I'm never wrong." A gravelly chuckle followed his comment, but I didn't laugh.

You can judge a tree by its fruit, huh? If that were the case, I wasn't too sure he'd like everything hanging from my branches.

He watched me work in silence for a minute, then started back in with, "You headed somewhere after this?"

"Picking up my girlfriend." I checked my phone. "In fact, I need to head out already. I will dig into this deeper later today or tomorrow." He stepped back and I closed up the hood.

He handed me the keys. "Here you go. And take your time. I can get around without her."

"Sounds good." I pocketed them, then looked around and realized something. "How are you getting home now?"

"With my own two feet. The crisp air is perfect for such a thing."

"Could I give you a lift?" I felt awkward making the offer, but I felt worse about letting an old man walk home in the cold.

"As much as I was looking forward to a good, brisk walk, I won't say no to a ride. My knees thank you, Russell."

I thought Roger might end up regretting his decision because the car ride was quiet at first. He folded his hands over his Bible in his lap and looked out the window like the passing trees were whispering secrets to him.

"How did you and your lady meet?" he asked, breaking the silence.

I smiled at the memory. "During a storm."

"Funny thing about storms. They don't just reveal weak trees, they reveal strong roots."

I nodded, but not with comprehension. "Hmm," I said, avoiding asking for clarification.

The guy really did like trees.

"Where are you picking her up from?"

"Church."

"I see. You ever think about going with her?"

He asked the question I'd been subconsciously circling since my parents left. Birdie had invited me every time, too. None of them were ever pushy about it, and yet it still felt like they were shaming me every time they asked. Could it be that I felt shame because I had something to be ashamed of, and it had nothing to do with the asker or the question?

"I don't really know what I think."

"That's an honest answer," he replied. "God does good work with honesty."

"I'm nothing like Birdie."

"No. You're not." That wasn't what I expected him to say. "But you love her."

"Yeah."

He nodded. "Love has a way of exposing what matters."

We pulled into his driveway. I shifted into park, but neither of us moved right away.

"You're not as far gone as you think," he said in a soft, even tone.

I didn't argue or even say thanks. I just sat there. He opened the door and stepped out, then turned back. "Don't wait too long, Russell."

"For what?"

He smiled. "You'll know." And then he shut the door and walked inside.

I sat there longer than I meant to, the engine idling. The world outside my car kept moving. Judge a tree by its fruit... Storms reveal roots... God does good work with honesty...

It felt like a lot, but it felt like something. Still, I just couldn't understand what.

I exhaled and pulled away. Maybe one of these days I would get it.

On the drive toward Birdie's church, the low tunes coming from the radio drowned out the noise in my head. Though my mind was chaos, the Worship music made it quiet. It was Birdie's station, the one she'd programmed on our first date. Every time I got into my car and heard it playing, I reached for the dial to change it, but I never did.

BIRDIE

59

I COULDN'T TELL YOU WHAT THE SERMON WAS ABOUT. I TRIED. I really did. I sat beside one of my church friends, since my mom was at work today, with my eyes forward and hands folded in my lap like always. But the words coming from the pulpit floated over me like a cloud I couldn't grab onto. Every now and then, I'd catch a phrase... *sovereignty... steadfast love...* and I would nod automatically. But my mind kept going back to one single word.

Fragile.

The doctor had said it all very gently. "Your connective tissue is weaker than average."

I was weaker than average.

I pressed my fingers against the side of my neck. It had been a week now, and it was just getting to a place where it didn't hurt so bad anymore, but my awareness of it was off the charts. Before, it was subconscious, but now it was a constant thing. I almost thought of nothing else. I could even swear I felt the artery running through, surging right beneath my hand.

In his car on the way home, Russell squeezed my knee, checking on me without making a show of it, I was sure. I gave him a half smile in return. I wasn't unhappy about being there with him. I just felt—I didn't know. Far away.

The sun seemed to agree with me, because the sky was dull and overcast, the kind of day that made everything feel muted. Kevin and Sarah were going to meet us at my house later so the guys could tinker with my car. The idea of normalcy had sounded so encouraging. Yesterday. Today it felt exhausting.

"You won't believe who showed up at the house this morning," Russell said as we pulled into the drive.

"Who?" I asked, though I wasn't sure I cared.

"Roger Milton."

That got a little more of my attention. I'd enjoyed hearing Russell talk about the nice man he'd met the other day. "Oh?"

"Fresh from church. Suit and everything. Told me again how he hasn't found a mechanic he trusts since some guy named Marvin passed away."

I hummed.

"He said I remind him of him."

"That's sweet."

"Yeah, but then he starts talking about trees and fruit and storms and roots."

I glanced over at him. "He's a church-man, so he would."

Russell laughed. "He thinks I've got deeper roots than I realize."

I nodded slowly. "You do."

He looked at me for a second like he wanted to ask something else, but instead, he shrugged and grabbed my church bag from the backseat. "He brought me his car this morning. I'm actually looking forward to working on it next. Might turn into something bigger. Remember when we heard that ad on the radio about—"

I tried to listen. I did. But the words kept slipping through my fingers again. The fog had returned. Russ was trying to discuss something he was excited about, something positive, and I was ruining it.

Why does it feel like You're everywhere except where I need You?

Inside, the house felt much too quiet and still.

Russell put my bag down beside the counter and began opening cabinets and the fridge. "I figured we could put together something light before they get here. You should probably eat."

"I'm not that hungry."

"You need to eat anyway."

He wasn't wrong. I reached for a plate while he kept talking—something about donating cars to single moms and how maybe there was something like that he could build here. He sounded hopeful. Encouraged. And so alive. I loved that about him. But I felt like I was watching him from underwater, or like this was all a dream and I was a silent observer.

I opened the cabinet for the peanut butter, and a fly buzzed past my ear. I flinched. The fly landed on the counter and just sat there. I stared at it. Of course there's a fly. Of course.

Russell was still talking. "—and Kevin brought up a lot of things I hadn't thought about, and I was—"

The fly lifted and buzzed again, and circled around me until I jerked my head to one side reflexively. I thought I even registered a small crack. My breath caught as I realized what I'd done. The harsh movement of my neck… it took me back to Dr. Jeffrey's office, and the bees, and the pain, and the blood clot.

And the stroke.

Dear God, I'd had a stroke. Because of my weak and pathetic connective tissues, I had to be careful with my life or I could have one again.

My heart started to race, and I could feel panic rising up inside me. Over a freaking *fly*.

"Stop," I whispered.

Russell paused. "What?"

The fly landed on the edge of my plate. I smacked at it. Missed. Then it buzzed louder, flying away. My throat went tighter. Why couldn't anything just be normal? Why couldn't my body just work? *Why can't I sit in church and feel You like I used to?*

"Birdie?"

I grabbed the plate without fully meaning to, like I was a puppet of something else. The next second, it was sailing across the kitchen. It shattered against the far cabinet, ceramic exploding against wood and tile with a violent crash.

Russell went completely still. The fly had vanished. And suddenly, I couldn't breathe.

"I can't do this," I choked.

"Hey—"

"I can't do this!" My voice cracked, rising higher, the pressure in my vocal cords pressing against my healing dissection. "I did everything right! I rested, I prayed, I trusted You! And I'm still unhealthy!" The words were out before I could catch them. Tears blurred my vision. "I don't want to be fragile," I sobbed. "I don't want to be the girl with the thin arteries and the follow-up appointments and the restrictions! I don't want to be scared every time my neck pops or my head hurts!"

Russell took a cautious step forward. I barely noticed.

"I asked You to heal me," I whispered, looking upward like the ceiling might open, like He might be looking back. "I asked You to fix it. And You didn't. You didn't."

The fear spilled out then. The real one.

"What if this is the rest of my life?" My voice broke

completely. "What if You're tired of answering me? What if You're just... not going to?"

The thought felt blasphemous and yet terrifyingly real. What if this Father leaves, too? What if I was on my own in this broken down body? What if Russell took a page from this book of abandonment and it was only a matter of time before he left, too?

But that was only part of what I was truly afraid of now.

I pressed my hands over my face. "I don't want to die," I said, the final confession small and raw. "I don't want to have another stroke. *I* don't want to be the one to leave. I want to stay with everybody."

The room was quiet except for my breathing, ragged and uneven. I didn't even register Russell moving until I felt him. His arms wrapped around me, firm and sure, pulling me against his chest. I folded into him. He didn't try to shush me or correct my theology or fix anything. He just held me tightly until all I registered was the rightness of his embrace.

My fists clutched the front of his shirt. "I'm scared," I whispered into the material.

"I know," he murmured, his voice rough.

"I don't feel strong."

"You don't have to right now."

I sobbed harder at that, because I always had to. I had always been the strong, faithful one. The girl who bounced back with a smile and a Bible verse. But I was so, so tired.

His chin rested against the top of my head. "You're not alone," he said quietly. "Not in this."

I didn't pull away. Didn't want to. If I let go, I was afraid everything would come apart again.

So, I stayed there, pressed against him, crying into his chest while the remnants of one of my mother's dishes lay scattered across the kitchen floor. And somewhere in the mess of fear and doubt and plate shards, I whispered the only prayer I could still manage.

Please don't leave me.

I didn't know if I was talking to God, or to Russell, or to both.

RUSSELL

60

SEEING BIRDIE UNRAVEL LIKE THAT DID SOMETHING TO ME. THE tears she unwillingly shed in response to her fear over her injury ate away at me. I was powerless against the tear in her neck, and the defects in her genes. I couldn't save her from her own body. Instead, she had to learn to save herself, a little at a time. But how did she do that if she couldn't let go of what she was afraid of?

My Sweetie Bird had come undone. I just couldn't wrap my mind around that. She was the girl who quoted Scripture like it was etched into her bloodstream. She was steady when everyone else tilted sideways. But in the kitchen, with a broken plate at our feet and tears soaking my shirt, she had been anything but steady. She'd been terrified. And that scared me more than the word *'stroke'* ever had.

After her breathing evened out and her cries transitioned into quiet sniffles, I helped her to the couch. Now drained, she appeared smaller. I cleaned up the broken plate while she sat there. Birdie had taken on a new vulnerability I had never seen.

I scooped the pieces into the trash and came back, wiping my hands on a dish towel. "I can call Kevin," I offered gently. "Tell them we'll reschedule."

"No."

"No?"

She shook her head, but it was stiff, cautious. "No. I want them to come."

"Bird—"

"I mean it." She swallowed and pushed a loose strand of hair behind her ear. "I think I needed that. Just to rage for a minute and get it out, I guess." Her eyes were red, but clearer now. "I don't want to hide. If I let fear keep me from the people I love, the enemy wins."

I leaned toward her, our knees touching. "But are you sure you're not compromising your health? There's a difference between fear and awareness."

The last thing I wanted was to push her too hard. The doctor's voice about restrictions and monitoring and rest still echoed in my head. I didn't fully understand the scope of her diagnosis, but I knew it was not going to be quick or easy.

She gave me a faint smile. "We're not going cliff diving. We're sitting in the driveway while you fix my car."

True. "You won't be lifting anything."

"I won't."

"You won't overdo it."

"I won't," she also agreed.

"You'll tell me if you feel weird." I would insist on it. "No hiding anything from me. I can't help you if you don't share."

"I promise, I will."

I crossed my arms, not convinced.

"Russell, I already promised."

I almost argued, but I put my arm around her instead. She

leaned in. "You scared me," I admitted, hoping my honesty didn't set her off.

"I scared myself." The admission surprised me. "I'm sorry I'm not being a good girlfriend right now."

That surprised me more. She said what? "What do you mean?"

"You were so happy." Her voice wobbled a little. "Talking about Roger and the car stuff and all that. I couldn't even focus enough to listen. I just broke."

"That's not true."

"It is."

"No." I took her hands in mine. "As long as you're here, I'm already happy."

Looking up at me, her eyes filled again, but this time tears didn't fall. The emotion was different. "You mean that?"

"I do."

"And are you still here?" She searched my face, her question carrying weight. She wasn't talking about being there physically.

There was no hesitation from me. "Yes. I'm right here." I leaned forward and pressed my forehead to hers.

She let out a deep sigh. "Okay. Good." She shifted back, sitting straighter. "I want you to tell me about everything again later, okay? About Roger, your garage idea, all of it. I promise I'll pay attention."

A corner of my mouth lifted. "You don't have to."

"But I really want to." She nudged my knee with hers. "And I don't want you thinking I don't care."

"I don't think that."

We heard a car pull up outside. Right on time. Birdie swiped her hands over her face.

"Ready?" I asked, standing with my hand out.

"Ready." She stood and took it.

A car door shut, then another. Kevin's laugh drifted toward the house before he even knocked. I glanced at Birdie and she met my eyes. There was still fear and exhaustion, but her resolve had bloomed afresh.

When the knock came, she called out with confidence, "Come in."

RUSSELL

61

Kevin and I didn't need long to get Birdie's car running smoothly again. We handled the engine, the belts, the oil, and the little tweaks that made a difference, while Birdie and Sarah hovered nearby with snacks and lemonade. I cracked a smile as I took a sip of it. It was sweet and tart, a little ridiculous, but somehow perfect.

"So, how you been?" Kevin asked, leaning back against the curb, wiping his hands with a rag.

I wiped the excess off my mouth and set my glass to the side. "Fine."

"Yeah. That *'fine'* is about as convincing as when Sarah says it." He laughed. "By the way, what was it about that car charity program you were thinking about? We never did get a chance to talk about it last week."

Because my girlfriend had a stroke and almost died, and it fell to the wayside. "It's this organization from somewhere out east that helps people, donating cars to single moms and widows, stuff like that."

Kevin whistled low. "Really? Do you think they operate this far out? I wonder if they could give Jenna a car."

"Jenna, the angry pregnant one?"

A chuckle. "Yeah, she's due in February. It's coming up fast."

"Birdie told me she's working at DQ."

"Yep, and she walks there."

"That's not safe. She shouldn't be doing that." I recalled Roger, and how I hadn't let him walk home today. "What if…"

"What?"

"Well, I was thinking maybe *I* could do something… for Jenna."

A slow nod. "Ah… I see what you mean. Well, you'd need a name for it."

"For what?"

"Your ministry," he said with a silly grin.

"My what?" I exclaimed. What was he on about?

"That's what the program is. It's a ministry. And if you wanted to put together something like that of your own, you'd need a name for it."

"I don't know about any of that. I just fix cars, man."

"I can help you get it going, but come springtime, you're on your own when I leave for college." He clapped me on the shoulder. "You've got good inspiration here. Just make it your own. Do what *you* feel led to do."

"Yeah. Maybe I'll try."

My surprised appreciation of his faith in me was short-lived. He took on a more serious tone. "So, how have you *really* been?"

I shrugged, turning to watch Birdie toss a granola bar to Sarah. "Just… happy to be out," I said, knowing he would get it.

"I hear that. The world is a different place after you've seen some of the uglier bits," Kevin said. He glanced down at the cross around his neck. "You ever wonder why I wear this thing?"

I raised an eyebrow. "The cross? Not really."

"Well, I'll tell you anyway. It belonged to my cellmate. The one who got killed."

His words were heavy, and I felt each one. "What was that really like?"

He shrugged, fidgeting with it. "Could've been me. Almost was me, if we hadn't switched beds that night. I… I don't even want to think about what would've happened."

"That's crazy."

"You're telling me." He balled up and tossed a rag he'd been messing with. "I'm grateful I'm here though. That I made it."

I nodded slowly, seeing him in a different light. He had lived in the fire and come out, scarred but still standing.

"So, when did you get into all the God stuff?" I nodded toward his necklace.

"When I didn't die." He laughed. "But we can talk more about that later. My question is, when did *you* get into all the *relationship* stuff? It's still strange to think of my boy Russell with a steady girlfriend."

"Yeah." I chuckled. "It's strange for me, too."

Birdie and Sarah, engrossed in their own conversation, picked up around them and disappeared inside the house. Kevin then turned to me, expression going from encouraging to serious. "Russ, man. I didn't want to bring anything up at the hospital or talk about it in front of the girls… But I've been wanting to ask. What are you doing with Birdie?" His eyes bore into me.

"What do you mean?"

"I mean, she's not like the girls you're used to. Not by a long shot."

Bitterness rose quickly. I didn't need him to remind me of that. "I'm very much aware, thank you."

"So, why are you with her?"

"What is this? You're not satisfied with just sticking your nose into her car, you've gotta have it in our relationship, too?"

He gave a humorless laugh, shaking his head. "I just hope you genuinely care about her and this isn't something it shouldn't be. I know Sarah couldn't stand to see her friend hurt, and neither could I."

"I'm not going to hurt her," I argued. Although, hadn't I had the same worries? Was this a cruel sort of confirmation, some kind of sign that I should be reconsidering my position in Birdie's life?

"You sure? Because I see you're still hanging out with Dominick." He glanced at my forearms, recognizing the additional design as his.

"So?" I could've said that was then, this is now, but I didn't. I didn't stand up for myself at all because I think a part of me wanted to hear this. Wanted to feel less-than, because that's what I was used to. It made sense that Kevin would question me, because he knew the way I was.

"So, you just got out of prison. Do you want to go back?"

"Man, you sound just like my dad. Give it a rest."

He shook his head. "I can't believe this. What about Birdie?"

"What *about* Birdie?"

"You're going to lose her."

Red crept into my vision, pulsing and strong. "What did you say to me?"

"You're risking your relationship with her if you fall into your old ways."

Condescending jerk. "Not so long ago, they were your ways, too."

"I know, and that's exactly why I'm telling you this. Birdie is not the type to stick around if you get back into all that stuff. I'm sure you realize that."

"I love her," I said, desperate.

"You've said that. And does she love you?"

"I..." didn't actually know.

"It doesn't matter either way, just be kind, man. Think all this through. You have to love her enough to walk away if you're not going to love her enough to change."

My heart bottomed out, free falling into a dark pit. Anger warred with fear, one fueling the other inside me.

"I almost lost Sarah when I started doing that crap for Blake Tanner, and it wasn't worth it. I may have been making money, but I'd never go back to all that nothing when I have everything now. I have what matters."

"Well, good for you. Not all of us are that lucky."

"You're so stubborn, dude. It's got nothing to do with luck and everything to do with choices. And there's *nothing* wrong with your life. You have so much going for you. Way too much to throw away now."

"Easy for you to say now that you're all high and mighty."

I didn't even register when we both stood up, but Kevin stepped into my face. Big mistake. He watched my fingers curl into a fist. "I know exactly who you are, Russell. I've got your number big time. You must think I've forgotten we're cut from the same cloth, but you're the one who's forgotten that. The fact that you're mad about me getting out of it makes me think it's because you want out, too, and you're too proud or too stupid to see it through. We all know you didn't need to steal. You didn't need the money like I did. Your home life was a cake-walk, but you loved that money and everything else."

"Nothing wrong with money," was all I managed to get out.

"It isn't called the root of all evil for nothing. Not only that, there's everything wrong with how you were earning it, plus what you were spending it on. Believe me, I learned this the hard way firsthand. The point is you loved money more than you loved yourself or your family, and I don't want to see you love your old habits more than the good things you've got now. Birdie deserves way better than that."

I hadn't even thought about my old habits in a long time, since Birdie and I became serious. I credited that to her, but maybe Kevin was right about the old me still being there, because the tether of calm I held onto inside me broke. My coiled fist went flying and didn't stop until it collided with Kevin's face. Shock registered as he staggered back. Immediately, blood leaked from the cut where my knuckles had sliced skin against bone, dripping down his cheek. Rage clouded his features, and he came at me with fists of his own.

"Do it." I tipped my chin up, daring him to retaliate.

Kevin's rage was palpable, his chest hard at work. Years of one way of life swirled in his eyes, threatening to take over and lash out as mine had. So, he wasn't as perfect as he thought he was. He was still no better than me.

But Sarah was faster than his response. "Kevin, stop!" Her voice called out, preceding her presence by only seconds. She quickly wedged herself between us, her back to me, putting her hands on his face. "You don't want to do this."

A visible shift occurred as his anger melted away. He grabbed hold of her wrists, nodding. "I'm sorry," he whispered solemnly between soft kisses. Then he looked around her at me. "Russell, I—."

She cut him off again. "Shh, let yourselves settle. Let's go inside. You need to clean up." The two of them retreated into the house without another word.

I leaned against the back of Birdie's car, panting, dripping blood from my own knuckles.

I'd totally lost it.

Before that moment, I hadn't even realized that I was jealous of Kevin Sloan. We'd shared the same life before, but he was the only one who came by it honestly. He was right. There was nothing wrong with how I was raised; I simply fell into money and liked it too much. Guilt and fear churned together in my head until I couldn't even think straight.

I wanted Birdie out here with me. I needed her to see, to care, to hold me like Sarah did Kevin. And then she was there, standing beside me, hands on her hips, eyes blazing. Relief hit me until I registered the look on her face. She was not there to comfort, but to reprimand.

"What was that, Russell? You go around punching your friends now?"

Surely, she didn't mean to sound like she was defending him, right? What about me? What about my bleeding hand?

"Why are you acting like this?" she demanded.

Something snapped inside me, unleashing. Releasing every doubt I'd secretly harbored since we started all this. "I'm not acting. This is me. A loser with a bad temper and nothing going for me. What you see is what you get so take a good look."

Birdie shook her head. "You're wrong. That isn't you. Your mistakes don't define who you are."

"You just haven't ever seen the real me." She'd only seen me between mistakes until now. This was her first time seeing me actually make one.

Way to go, Russ. You sure showed everyone.

Her hands reached out, clutching my wrists. "Yes, I have. I know exactly what the real you is like, and this isn't it."

"How can you say that?"

"Because I love the real you," she said, eyes wide and unwavering.

I wanted to tell her everything, to pull her in, wrap her in comfort and fix every bit of hurt I'd caused in so little a time, but I couldn't. Not when I felt too much like the failure I'd always been.

"We shouldn't do this right now. I just need to go."

"Well, where are you going? I can go with you."

"No, Birdie, you can't. I can't be good enough for you right now. Who knows, you might get hurt next." I stepped back, turning toward my car.

"Russell," she called, voice cracking. "It's not about doing things perfectly. It's about being here with me like you said you were." She caught up to me and grabbed my uninjured hand, sliding her fingers through mine. "Don't drift away from me now. Don't take back what you said before."

I stopped, turned to look at our hands, but I couldn't look at her. There was no way I could stand to see those eyes of hers, pleading as I knew they would be, searching for something impossible that she believed me to be capable of.

Choosing flight over fight, I slid into my car, certain that enough damage had been done for one day. I needed to escape before I managed to cause more.

BIRDIE

62

He left.

Russell got into his car and drove away. He fought with Kevin, fought against me, and then left. I'd gone after him, sliding my fingers through his, trying to anchor him, tried to tell him it was about being *here*, together. But he had swallowed my words and turned his back on them.

On me.

And I guess he's really not coming back.

I slumped back toward the house, guilt and worry pressing in from all sides. Thank God my mom was working today. At least I didn't have the added bonus of her reaction on top of everything else.

"I'm so sorry, Birdie. Really, I am." On the couch, Kevin sat opposite me with Sarah by his side. She'd doctored him with a butterfly bandage and a bag of peas, which he now held against his cleaned but splintered cheek.

"It's not your fault. I'm sorry he hit you. I still can't believe it."

"No, it is my fault. I said too much too soon. I was trying to look out for you, and him really, but I completely set him off."

"I know you meant well, Kevin. Don't feel bad." I turned toward the window, looking for his car, hoping it would come back any second. But the street remained empty, and my chest remained full of pain.

"He's still bitter," Kevin continued. "Even more than he used to be. For a while, I thought he was really coming back to the Russell I knew before we got into…" He shook his head. "But I don't think either of us know him fully anymore. I should have kept my opinions to myself."

I sank onto the couch and pulled my knees close, staring out the window. My phone rested in my hand, blank and silent. Nothing. No text, no missed call. Nothing from him. I'm not sure I expected anything, but I wanted something. And I wanted to reach out, to tell him I understood his pain, that I forgave him for leaving, and that I just wanted him to come back. We couldn't fix anything if he wasn't at least present. But a knot of fear kept my fingers still.

Maybe he needed to cool off. Maybe he thought I was too upset to want to see him. Or maybe he… resented me, like he might resent Kevin. I didn't know, and that uncertainty gnawed at me. I wanted to withdraw and start shutting down my feelings just in case this ended badly, but I also wanted to believe in him, in *us.* I loved him. Because of that, I owed it to both of us to keep my head.

Right on cue, the ache in my neck returned, deep and stubborn, as if summoned by stress alone.

Perfect. Just perfect.

RUSSELL

63

After leaving Birdie's house, I drove and drove. The city faded behind me, replaced by open roads and the steady hum of tires on asphalt. I didn't stop until I ended up in Mont Belvieu, standing outside Abby's front door.

I knocked once, twice. Then the door flew open with such vigor her hair flew back. "Russell! What are you doing here?" she demanded, eyes blazing.

"Hey, sis."

"*'Hey, sis.'* That's what you have to say?"

"Can I come in?"

"You pain in the… Ugh. Get in here."

The house was quiet. "Where is everyone?"

"Asleep. Miguel is on shift."

"No wonder. You know, you shouldn't be answering the door this late."

"I can't be calling him from the fire station every time some hoodlum knocks on the door. I can handle myself." She patted her concealed carry. Then, with a glare that could wilt a spruce tree, she asked again, "Now what are you doing here?"

I shrugged. "Running away."

Her eyes scanned me, then landed on my right hand. "Russell…"

"Relax. It's not what you think."

"It's not? Is it about that girl?" she pressed. I nodded. She sighed. "Come here. Let's wash it before you get gangrene or something."

She led me to the kitchen sink and soaped up a clean dish rag, then watched me while she let the water warm up. "Alright, what happened?" Then she got to work on my hand. It stung like heck.

"I got into a fight with Kevin," I admitted.

"Sloan? Seriously? Why would you be fighting with him?"

"He started lecturing me about Birdie."

"What was he saying?"

I grimaced, unable to stop the flood. "How I could ruin her, how she deserves better than me, how my past might ruin everything, and how I might not be good enough."

She sighed, wringing out the rag, not even looking up.

"I don't know why I bothered getting this serious about someone anyway. Maybe it's best if she thinks the worst of me. Might be easier that way."

"How serious are we talking?" She watched me for my response, her eyes prying into the deepest parts of my heart. But I could give no answer. Nothing I could put together would describe it well enough. "Oh, so it's big serious."

"Doesn't matter. I really blew it. She probably never wants to see my face again." I had left her, so I deserved her disgust. I'd betrayed her only hours after giving her my word to stay.

Abby dried my hand, holding it in hers. "Russ, listen. Even if you need to pause during an argument, it doesn't mean you can't handle the relationship. You can take a step back without throwing in the towel. Think before you speak, come back together, and work it out. Move on. It's how Miguel and I stay married."

The knot in my chest didn't come loose, but it felt less constricting. "Really?"

"Granted, this is a practice we've honed and refined over the years. It wasn't just a one-time thing. Don't let me get your hopes up, but don't let yourself bring them down either. Just wait and talk to her after you've both had some space."

"I probably shouldn't go back anyway. I can start over somewhere else, where I haven't already burned a dozen bridges."

"Russell, I love you, so I don't say this lightly. Don't be an idiot!"

"Insulting me now? Go ahead and join the club."

"If you run away now, from the best thing you've had in years, then you're not half the man you need to be. She really would be better off without you."

"How would you know?"

"How many times have you shown up at my doorstep after some kind of fallout?" I grimaced, avoiding eye contact. "And how many of those times were because of something shady?"

"A few of them."

"Almost all of them. All but one." She blinked at me. "Yes, this is that one. Every other time you've come here, you've been hiding out from something. This time, you're here hiding from yourself for the sake of someone else. Even though running is running, it looks to me like you're running for better reasons than you used to. Congratulations, Russ, you're growing up."

I rolled my eyes, barely understanding half of what she said. "I don't know what I'm supposed to do, but if you have all the answers like you act, then please, enlighten me."

"I don't have all the answers, and you may not want to hear this, but God makes a huge difference." Her gaze was loving and firm. "Russ, if you're going to run, do it in here." She tapped her temple. "And run with prayer. Let Him guide your steps. Look after the heart you love with, the people you're supposed to lead. Birdie, like all women, needs a man who is strong for her."

I didn't know how to respond. She regarded me, waiting, until her agitation ceased.

"Open your eyes, Russell. Present-You doesn't have to constantly atone for Past-You's mistakes. They're over and done with. You don't need to prove yourself anymore. You need to grasp that God has already forgiven you for everything you've ever done, so you have an obligation to yourself to let it go. All you need to do now is just be here, there, with her. Show a little of the grace God has shown you."

I swallowed hard, those words causing a deep-seated reaction in my gut. "I don't know what to do."

"I already told you, brother. Take some time, then talk."

I nodded, feeling lighter than I had since leaving Birdie's driveway. Abby had given me perspective, clarity. A roadmap, basically.

"I know it's late, but do you think I could—"

"I'll put your blankets out," she said, walking past me. Her tone said she was annoyed, but her face said she was pleased.

"Thanks," I said a few minutes later, as she stood over me, making my familiar couch-bed on her sofa.

"You're always welcome here, Russ. I'm glad you still come. I know there's worse places you could be and more damage you could do if you put your mind to it. I'm just happy to see you finally coming around to being sensible."

"What do you mean now?"

She gave me that look. "I know you went home, shall we say, under the influence, right after you got released. That Dominick loser is not your friend, Russ."

I rubbed the back of my head. "I know that. Now."

"Yeah? Do you?"

"I actually considered going to his place today."

"I bet. Old habits die hard. But you see? Those are your finer sensibilities that brought you here instead."

"I guess."

She picked up a pillow, swinging it into my face before tossing it back as she left. "Goodnight, buttface. I love you. Life will not seem so tough in the morning."

"Goodnight, brat. Love you, too," I bellowed, feeling the lightness spread. Having somewhere safe to go and someone safe to talk to had never made this much of a difference in my heart before. I didn't know I had those *'finer sensibilities'* she was talking about, but when I realized how much relief I had over *not* going to Dominick's house, I figured she must be right. As usual.

I greeted the couch with a heavy sigh, falling into it like I had so many times before. Palming my phone, I swiped through notifications. None were from Birdie. That was okay, for now. Abby said to take time, so I would try. Even though everything in me urged to text her, to reconnect and to reassure myself things weren't damaged beyond repair, I would heed my sister's advice.

But there *were* messages from my parents:

DAD

Why aren't you home yet? It's past curfew.

Why aren't you answering the phone?

MOM

I don't know what's going on, but please be careful. Come home.

DAD

At least I can see that you're someplace safe. But Russell, you don't always have to run to your sister. Your mom and I love you, too, you know. We're always right here at home for you. Goodnight. Maybe you'll tell me about it tomorrow.

I tossed the phone aside, disgust in myself creeping up my throat. Birdie hadn't exactly chased me down like I'd subconsciously hoped she would, but my parents had, and I wasn't sure what to make of it. They saw where I went, and they were giving me grace. Maybe that was proof enough that taking a pause worked. Maybe things would actually be okay.

Even so, my thoughts kept circling back to Birdie. Missing her, worrying about what she thought, beating myself up for leaving. It all swirled into a really crappy, restless night. I tossed, turned, and finally fell asleep somewhere between exhaustion and regret, haunted by everything I hadn't said.

RUSSELL

64

Come daybreak, I started the drive back home, and talking to Birdie couldn't wait until I got back to town. Halfway down the highway, with fields stretching wide on either side and the sky going soft with early morning light, I hit her name on my phone's call screen.

"Hello?"

The relief that flooded my chest nearly made me pull over. "Hey."

"Hey." Her voice was careful, but she hadn't ignored the call, so that was something.

"I wasn't sure you'd pick up."

"I wasn't sure you'd call."

I exhaled slowly. "Birdie, I'm sorry."

"I'm sorry, too," she rushed in, almost tripping over the words. "I've replayed it all night and day. I keep wondering if I should've done something more yesterday."

"You couldn't have," I said firmly. "I wouldn't have let you. I didn't like what I saw in myself and didn't know how to deal with it. I didn't know how to be my worst in front of you… So, I ran."

"Oh, Russell." Birdie sighed. "I thought I had it figured out. As long as I was minding my own business, I assumed that nothing bad would come looking for me. No one would have the opportunity to hurt me and leave if I didn't let them in. Just focus on my career so I could focus on other people, and not have to worry about myself. I thought I was being selfless, wanting to care for others, but I don't know. Maybe it was actually the most selfish thing I could do.

"But regardless of my efforts, somebody snuck past my defenses and into my heart. You made me care about you, and then you left. You looked me in my eyes, while I stood in that driveway, scared and confused but still wanting to comfort you, and you turned and left. Drove away. I didn't know when I would see or talk to you again, or if you'd *ever* come back. I've experienced plenty of pain in my life, Russell, but I won't lie to you—*that* was pain."

"I'm so sorry, Birdie. I scared myself, I think. I needed to get out of the situation, so yes, I left. I needed clarity I didn't have until I spent the worst night of my life on my sister's lumpy couch. That thing used to mean refuge to me, but it's different now. I hated every minute of it. Refuge, as I know it now, is getting closer to you, not further away. I don't want to run anymore, especially not from you."

I wanted to say it. The words were right there. *I love you.* They pressed against my teeth, ready to fall, but something in me balked. This moment deserved more than speakerphone and highway noise.

"I'm sorry, Birdie," I said again instead.

She sniffled.

"Don't cry, Sweetie Bird. Please."

"When I replay the day in my head, I still feel like I didn't do enough to stop you from leaving."

"No. You couldn't have stopped me, and trying would've only made things worse. I was determined to go."

"I don't know if it makes me feel better that I couldn't have stopped you, or worse that I would've felt pathetic for trying."

"Don't think of it that way, please. It's my shortcoming that drove me away, not you. Never you."

"But I'm not perfect either, Russell. I keep telling you this. Even from the first time we met, you had this version of me in your head, standing on a pedestal, and I've had to hope that the reality never let you down."

"It didn't. You didn't. And my snap judgment the first day we met has nothing to do with how I feel about you or why I feel it. That's just all you, Birdie Jo Rene Lewis MacLean. It's everything you are and everything you've taught me."

"What could I possibly have taught you?"

"The meanings of grace and self-sacrifice, for starters. And the true meaning of love."

A small gasp escaped her. "Really?"

No, no, no. Don't hear that part. It's not perfect yet. "Well, you and my sister, Abby, if I'm being honest."

"She sounds like an awesome woman."

"She is. You'll love her." I cleared my throat, wanting to make her laugh again before I got too mushy. "Don't forget you also taught me portions of math, science, social studies, and language arts."

I luxuriated in her laughter, having saved the moment. "Yes, we can't forget all that," she agreed.

"No, we can't."

She sighed again. It was better than a sniffle.

"I really am sorry," I said, one final time.

"I know you are."

"How do you know?"

"Because a truly repentant heart has its own sound. It's hard to explain, but I can hear it."

It was my turn to chuckle. "You have such a beautiful way of thinking and saying things."

"Enough about me." I would swear I could tell she was blushing. "Why don't you tell me everything I didn't hear yesterday?"

I did. I told her everything about everything she hadn't gotten to hear before. All the ideas that had percolated in the last twenty-four hours about what I might be able to do myself.

"And he thinks you could start something like that here?" Birdie asked.

"I guess. It's been bouncing around in my head ever since."

"Aw, Russell, this sounds like you," she said cheerfully.

"It sounds terrifying."

"Most amazing things are."

We both laughed, and it felt easy. Natural. Like we'd found our rhythm again.

"You and Kevin did a good job on my car yesterday, for what it's worth. I didn't get a chance to thank you for it."

Bringing it up brought back those ugly feelings, but I knew how to deal with them. "I shouldn't have hit him."

"No," she agreed gently. "But he's not done with you, I hope you know that."

"I don't deserve friends like that."

"Maybe not," she teased. "But God seems to think you do."

The last stretch of road into town came into view. We'd been on the phone for three hours, talking about everything and nothing, and I still wasn't ready for the call to end.

"Bird?"

"Yeah?"

"Before things turned south yesterday, Kevin put a little idea into my head."

"Oh, no. Sounds dangerous."

I laughed. "Do you think Jenna would be open to a really big baby gift?"

"Define really big."

I took a breath. "Like... a car?"

"Russell."

"What?"

"That is a *very* big gift idea."

"I know."

The line was momentarily silent. "You'd really do that?"

"I don't know how yet, but I want to try."

"Yesterday I said if I let fear keep me from the people I love, the enemy wins. And if you let shame keep you from doing good, he wins there, too."

I smiled at the road ahead. "So... you think I should go for it?"

"Why not?" I could hear the smile in her voice. "We'll figure it all out together."

Together. The word settled deep, where it belonged. Her forgiveness felt better than a million bucks.

When I finally pulled onto my street, I was happier than I had in ages. I still hadn't said the three words burning in my chest, but I knew that was only a matter of time. Kevin's idea wasn't the only one in my head. I had a special one of my own, too.

BIRDIE

65

Jenna made sure we came while her mom was at work. "That way she can't try to question it," she'd told me over the phone. "She would wonder why I suddenly need one so badly."

Jenna still hadn't told her mother *anything*, and she only got away with hiding her pregnancy this long because of their opposing work schedules and really baggy T-shirts. Still, with her due date right around the corner, Jenna would have to face the music any day now.

I did not envy her, but I knew it would work out somehow. God had her and this baby, even if she didn't have Him.

Russ and I drove separately, though he followed close behind me the entire way across town. I kept checking my rearview mirror, half to make sure he was still there, and half because I liked knowing he was.

Russell's little black Civic parked behind me on the curb in front of Jenna's duplex, freshly washed, the inside detailed twice over. Russell and Kevin had spent evenings under the hood, muttering about belts and brakes and things I didn't understand, making sure it would stay in tip-top shape for a long time to come. I'd contributed in the only way I knew how—snacks, moral support, and a small piece of encouragement currently attached to the keys in Russell's pocket.

When we stepped out, Jenna was already standing in her doorway. Her face was swollen, like she hadn't slept much. Or like she had, but had cried a lot first. Still, her chin was tipped up at a stubborn angle I knew so well.

"You're something else, you know that?" she called, arms folded across her chest. "Both of you."

I smiled. "Hi, Jenna."

She walked down the steps slowly, eyes flicking from me to Russell to the car. Her expression didn't change, but I saw the way her fingers trembled before she shoved them into her hoodie pocket.

"I knew it was coming, and still…" She shook her head, choking up, unless my eyes deceived me. "I didn't ask anyone for a car," she said softly.

"I know you didn't," I answered softly in return.

Her gaze shifted to Russell. "Are you sure you want to do this?"

"Yep." He didn't hesitate pulling the keys from his pocket. I watched Jenna's eyes drop to the keychain before he even held them out.

"I picked it out," I beamed.

"I can tell," she chuckled.

It was simple—silver, round, engraved with *'Philippians 4:13'* on one side, and the scripture itself on the other. Enamel flowers entwined with vines followed the circular edge. I'd found it tucked into a corner rack at a little shop downtown and knew instantly it was the one.

Jenna had yet to make a move. “It still doesn’t feel real. Are you sure you’re serious?”

“Dead serious,” Russell said.

Suddenly, she snapped the keys from his hand. “Good. No take-backs.” Her voice wobbled on the last word, and she coughed like she could cover it up.

Russell laughed discreetly. “No take-backs,” he agreed.

She turned in a slow half-circle, looking at the car again like it might disappear. “It runs?”

“Better than mine,” I offered.

“Hey,” Russ objected mildly. “I worked on both, so they’re both great.”

Jenna released a breath that was suspiciously close to a sob. “You guys are insane.”

“Maybe.” He shrugged.

She took two quick steps and threw her arms around me first. It was tight and sudden and desperate. I felt her inhale sharply against my shoulder, fighting it.

“Jenna—”

“Don’t,” she whispered fiercely, more to herself than me. “I’m not doing that.”

“It’s okay.” I patted her back. “You can.”

“I’m not doing it,” she repeated, pulling back abruptly. Her eyes were glassy, but no tears had fallen.

Then she turned to Russell.

There was a second, just a flicker, where her tough front tried to reassemble itself, but it didn’t last. She stepped into him and hugged him around the middle, pressing her cheek into his chest. He froze at first, looking unsure of what to do with that much emotion, then his arms came up around her carefully.

And that's when she broke. One sob followed another. "Sorry," she choked out. "I'm not usually like this."

"It's okay. Don't worry about it."

She sniffed hard. "Sorry for the text thing, by the way."

I winced at the memory, but Russell was unfazed. "Don't worry about that either. All is forgiven."

Jenna pulled back, scrubbing her eyes and face with the sleeves of her hoodie. "Yeah, well, thanks for not holding it against me. I know it wasn't cool."

He gave her that small, confident smile he'd been wearing more often lately. "We all do things we shouldn't sometimes. Doesn't mean you can't be forgiven."

She looked between us. "I don't deserve you guys."

Russell had thought the same thing about us not long ago. I really wanted to hug her again, but I had a feeling she wouldn't like if I tried. So, I flipped my hair. "I know."

Jenna rolled her eyes but she was smiling.

A few minutes later, she slid into the driver's seat, hands gripping the steering wheel like it was sacred. She started the engine and let out a half-laugh, half-cry when it purred to life.

"Okay," she called through the open window. "If this thing dies in a week, I'm haunting you."

"It won't," Russell assured her.

Jenna pulled away slowly, just to circle the block once for fun.

"It's a good thing she knows how to drive a manual," he said.

"Yeah. But you could've taught her if necessary."

"I guess I could've. I'll have to keep that in mind for next time."

When she disappeared around the corner, the street went quiet. I folded my arms against the sudden chill that had nothing to do with the breeze. Russell stood beside me, hands in his pockets, watching the empty road. I looked at his flowering flames and, as always, they made me smile.

"You have a way with the ladies, it seems," I said.

He glanced at me. "What do you mean by that?"

I tilted my head. "Somehow, you get them all to cry in your arms."

A slow grin tugged at his mouth. "I don't try to."

"I know." I bumped my shoulder against his. "That's the problem. They flock to you."

"Flock do they?" He laughed under his breath. "Too bad you're the only bird I'm interested in."

I could not keep a straight face. "Oh, wow. Well done."

Watching him give without hesitation, without running, without second-guessing himself, worked through me with a warm comfort. This had to be what growth looked like. Like running engines, smiling faces, keychains, and a man who really stayed.

RUSSELL

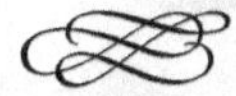

66

It had been a week since I handed over my keys to Jenna. Seven days of walking to work. Seven mornings of Dad offering a ride and me telling him no thanks.

"You sure?" he asked again that Friday, coffee mug in hand.

"I'm sure."

"It's cold out there."

"I've got a jacket."

He looked at me, trying to see around the corners of my decision, but eventually nodded. "Suit yourself."

I didn't mind walking, cold or no cold. It gave me time to think. Time to pray and feel the ache in my legs and remember why I'd chosen it. After another couple of paychecks, I'd be able to buy something new to me anyway. It could be something temporary, as long as it was functional. It didn't need to be pretty.

Two minutes after waving bye to my dad, I watched him come back inside.

"Russ. There's something out here you should see."

Curious, I got up from the bar stool and followed him

outside. In the driveway was a familiar red and chrome Studebaker, all glossy and bright like it had rolled right out of the 1960s. It gleamed even under the gray sky. The curved hood, proud grill, and white-wall tires were all showing off.

And leaning against it, hands folded over the top of a cane he didn't need, stood Roger Milton.

Dad was impressed. "Oh, that one is a beauty. I never got a good look at it when it was in the garage."

Roger's weathered face split into a grin. "Belonged to my wife, Edith. She loved this crusty old thing."

"I see nothing crusty about it," Dad replied, walking closer. "It's in such great shape."

Why was he here? My stomach tightened. "I was sure I gave it everything it needed. Is it running okay?"

"Like a dream. Better than brand new." Roger said with gusto.

"You didn't bring it here for more tinkering?"

He pushed off the fender and reached into his coat pocket. "No, sir."

Before I could process what was happening, a set of keys came sailing through the cold air toward my chest. I caught them on instinct.

"She's yours," he said.

I stared at the keys resting in my palm. "What?"

"One good deed deserves another."

I shook my head and tossed them back. "That's crazy. I can't take your car."

He caught them easily, like he'd expected that. "Without Edith around to drive it, it's mine to give." His eyes lifted skyward. For a moment, his bluster failed, and I saw the grief sitting deep in the creases of his face. "And I believe she would approve."

"No, really. I'm already saving up to get something on my own."

"Boy," he said gently, "I've seen you walking to work every day this week. It's freezing out. Didn't you hear it might snow?"

"My dad can drive me," I muttered.

Dad crossed his arms but didn't contradict me.

Roger lowered his voice like he was about to let me in on a secret. "Or you can drive yourself."

I exhaled sharply. "I gave up my car because it was the right thing to do. That doesn't mean I expect something back."

"Good, because that's not how this works." He took my hand this time and folded the keys into it, pressing my fingers closed around them. "Luke six, verse thirty-eight," he said. "'Give, and it will be given to you. Good measure, pressed down, shaken together, running over, will be poured into your lap. For with the measure you use it will be measured back to you.'"

His eyes held mine. "You sowed something, Russ, and your heart's changing. Don't insult the Giver by refusing what He grows."

I swallowed. Hard.

"I'm not trying to pay you back," Roger continued. "I'm trying to keep the goodness going. You focus your money on fixing up your next donation. Let this old thing be your legs in the meantime."

Dad cleared his throat behind me. "Russell… that's quite a gift."

The wind ripped through my jacket, sharp and cold. I thought about the week of walking. About Jenna's face when she turned the key of her new car for the first time. About Birdie's smile when we'd watched her drive away. Then I looked over at the red paint shimmering under the breakthrough morning light. Did I really deserve a gift like this?

"This is too much," I said, though my voice lacked my prior conviction.

Roger chuckled. "It's exactly enough. Edith always said generosity isn't a transaction, it's a seed. You plant it because you trust God with the bounty."

The words hit deeper than I expected. That's the thing: I hadn't given Jenna my car to get anything back, I knew that for sure. I'd done it because my gut—my *spirit*—had told me it was right. Things changed when I stopped letting shame and doubt dictate my choices.

And now here was something *I* hadn't asked for, much like Jenna. Something I couldn't have earned. It was grace, plain and simple. My fingers tightened around the key. "If I take this, it's not stopping with me."

Roger's smile widened. "I would be disappointed if it did."

Dad's hand clapped my shoulder. "I'm so proud of you, son. And it looks like you've got yourself a ride."

I walked toward the Studebaker, running my hand along the smooth exterior. When I opened the driver's door and slid inside, the leather smelled of polish and years past. The engine turned over with a low, steady thunder, and I had to admit—I freaking loved it.

I glanced through the windshield at Roger, and his face was pure joy. The look on his face was telling. He'd clearly decided to do this long before pulling into my driveway, probably even that first time.

Maybe sowing and harvesting didn't always look like money or literal crops, but like walking in the cold for a week and waking up to grace rumbling in your driveway. I couldn't believe this feeling or everything it'd taken to get here, but I had every intention of planting again and again.

BIRDIE

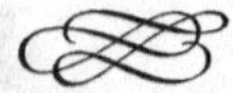

67

AT FIRST, I THOUGHT IT WAS RAIN TAPPING THE WINDOW, BUT when I pulled the curtain aside, the world outside was white. Not iced or sleeted. *White.* Snow—actual snow—drifted in lazy spirals against the glass, settling over the rooftops and tree branches like powdered sugar. I gasped, feeling like a child. "Beautiful!"

My phone rang, and it was Russell.

His voice was cheerful and demanding before I could even say hello. "Are you looking outside?"

"Yes, sir, I am!"

"It snowed."

"And it's still going! Isn't it just the loveliest thing?"

"It hasn't snowed here for how long? A decade?" His voice held a boyish excitement I'd never heard from him before, let alone directed at weather.

Gosh, he is so cute.

I laughed. "You sound like me."

"Don't get used to it. I'm still way cooler than you."

"Debatable."

He didn't take the bait. "Get dressed."

"What? Why? It's too early."

"I'm coming to get you. We're going sledding."

My heart leapt at the idea of wind in my hair, laughter echoing across some unsuspecting hill. And then just as quickly, my heart sank.

"Russell, I can't."

A pause. "Why not?"

I lightly brushed the side of my neck, the tender place that had dictated so much of my life lately. "Three months, remember? I have to wait until my dissection is healed before doing much of anything. I don't want to break off another clot and stroke out again."

The words were as heavy and ugly as they seemed.

"Right. I'm so sorry. I wasn't thinking."

"It's okay." I smiled even though he couldn't see it. "Trust me, there is nothing I would rather do than go flying down a hill on a plastic tray right now."

"A plastic tray? I was picturing something far more dignified for the likes of you."

"Oh, of course. A gilded sleigh, perhaps."

"With chrome," he added.

I laughed, and for a moment, the disappointed faded. He was quiet for a few seconds, and I could almost hear the gears turning in his head.

Then: "I have the perfect idea."

"Do you?"

"Stand by. And do get dressed."

"Russell?" I looked at my phone, but he was already gone. "What in the world is he up to?"

Too curious to wait around, I jumped (carefully) out of bed, took my time in the shower, and got dressed—*you're welcome*—

then went downstairs to brew some tea. Decaf because of my new blood thinners, but I could pretend.

My mom wasn't even awake yet. The sun was barely starting to peek above the horizon, and my first thought was *I hope it doesn't immediately melt everything.*

When I got back upstairs, warm tea in hand, I walked to the window to look out and sip. As I raised the blinds, I nearly dropped my mug. There were letters carved into the snow, spelling out my full name. All of it. And that wasn't all...

I LOVE YOU
BIRDIE JO RENE LEWIS MACLEAN

My breath caught. There was Russell, standing in the yard, hands on his hips, surveying his masterpiece. My heart lurched.

Tea forgotten on my dresser, I grabbed my coat, scarf, and boots in a semi-flurry, trying to stay calm enough not to trip over myself as I made my way outside. The icy air hit my cheeks and made my nose sting. This was a far cry from our perpetual beach weather, but I didn't care. I loved it!

Russ saw me, and his grin came to life. I hit a frozen patch on the back porch steps as I descended.

"Easy," he said, catching me just in time. *My hero.*

"I really like your snow message."

"I'm glad you do."

I brushed snow from his jacket. "I thought you were going sledding."

"I couldn't do that without you. Plus, I didn't know where to get a golden sled at the last minute. I do have something pretty special with chrome to show you though. Later."

Ooh, this man made me feel some things. "You have me properly curious."

He led me to two patio chairs he'd already cleared off, a small table between them with a steaming thermos. He poured out some warm tomato soup—an odd breakfast, but oh-so-comforting. Chilly air carried the loose snow bits from high up and dropped them all over us. A decent amount had accumulated on the angular roof of the turkeys' coop, and they were pecking away at what they could find beneath the snow, chirping like they always did. It was a winter wonderland if ever I'd seen one.

I leaned against Russell's side and he leaned back. My hand slipped into his coat pocket, seeking warmth and found something else. Something small and velvety.

I froze. Slowly, I pulled it out. "Russell…"

He froze, too.

I looked down at the small box in my hand, then back at him.

"Is this what I think it is?"

"No." He let out an amused breath that turned to fog in the cold air.

I raised an eyebrow.

"Don't worry, I'm not asking you a question," he told me. "I'm giving you something. My promise. And we can seal it with a pinky, if you want, but I had something else in mind…"

He took the box and opened it for me. Inside was another silver charm, one I had never seen before. Two intertwined otters, holding each other, and forming a heart shape. Just like the plushie. "I know your body's still healing, and this is still pretty new for both of us. I know we don't know what the future will look like. But I do know this—I'm not going anywhere. Not even if you have a million strokes—which you won't. Not even if we never kiss—which I'm open to if you want. Not if Russell's

Rides never takes off and I'm a bag boy at H-E-B for the rest of my life. Not even if—"

"Wait. Russell's Rides?" I smiled.

"I'm just testing it out. Kevin said I need a name…" he trailed off, voice going shy. It was too cute. "Anyway… This promise isn't about marriage. It's about who I already belong to."

Oh, boy. Tears came and they didn't stop.

"I want you to wear this," he continued, voice low, roughened up by emotion, "so that on the hard days, when your body feels like it's betraying you, you remember that I didn't, and that I won't. Ever. No matter what life does to us, we won't drift away from each other. I love you, Birdie Jo Rene Lewis MacLean."

Be still my heart. Oh Lord, what a special man you have given me.

"I love you, too, Russell Benjamin Grandy," I whispered, pressing my face into his chest. I wrapped my arms around him, leaning in as much as I could, sharing in his warmth and that security. I was safe, I was happy, and I was so in love.

Thank you, God.

EPILOGUE

BIRDIE

JANUARY ARRIVED, CRISP AND CLEAR, A PERFECT DAY FOR graduation. A small handful of women were ready to bid farewell to the South Texas Life and Recovery program, and we were all here to celebrate the huge accomplishment.

Across the room, on the stage, Daisy clutched her certificate with both hands, tears streaming freely as her kids held on to her waist. The room erupted in applause. I clapped until my palms stung. I couldn't be happier for her.

Silently, to myself, I sent up a prayer for Gia. She should have been here, too, but wasn't. Instead, she had just re-enrolled into the program, more determined than ever to do what it took to get her kids back for good this time. I was so proud of her—everyone was. Next year, it could be her up on that stage at graduation, but I had learned something the hard way…

It didn't matter how much I believed in something or wanted it. The effort had to come from them. It was between each woman and God, and all I could do was offer support. And you know what? It still felt amazing. It felt better, in fact, to be less attached. I cared a great deal about my job, and I cared about all our moms and kids, but I knew that ultimately God had to handle it all. I was merely a vessel to assist. Healing wasn't linear, but it was possible, for everyone. I knew that now.

Lord, guide her steps. And keep teaching me how to support Your cause.

I smoothed my hands over my dress and glanced down at the latest charm rounding out my beloved bracelet. I smiled. They were not only adorable otters, but the promise of an amazing man. *Our* promise. He wasn't ever going anywhere, he'd told me. And I believed it wholeheartedly, because I wasn't going anywhere either.

"Look at you."

I turned at the sound of my mom's voice. She stepped beside me, eyes kind and proud in a quiet, motherly way. She reached for my hand and paused, looking at my wrist. She hadn't really taken the time to do that before.

"It looks complete now," she said with a gentleness that was so unlike her.

I smiled. "Yes, ma'am."

"He's different," she noted, glancing across the room to where Russell stood near the back wall, laughing with one of the volunteers.

My stomach fluttered. "Different how?"

"Grounded. He used to carry himself like he had no idea who he was. Now he has confidence. He shines." She squeezed my hand. "He loves you well. And I'm really happy for you both."

Something in me settled *all* the way down. I hadn't known just how badly I'd wanted my mom's approval for Russell, even though I'd gone all this time thinking I'd never get it. He so deserved it. He really had changed for the better, and so had I. I wasn't clutching to ties of the past that held me back from truly living anymore.

Later, after the photos and cake and congratulations, Russ and I stepped outside alone together. The courtyard was wrapped in white string lights, glowing beautifully against the bare winter branches. The air was still chilly but gentle. Inside, laughter hummed against the glass door.

"Are you finished packing?" he asked me as I settled onto a wooden bench beneath the splendor.

"Yes, but it still hasn't sunk in that I'm moving out."

"It will once you get there."

I drew in a slow breath. "I'm excited, but nervous, too."

"You and Jenna will do great. Two peas in a pod."

I smiled at the thought. We were really doing this. A new apartment, for the two—very soon to be three—of us. Same city, new home.

"The apartment next door is still vacant," I teased. "You sure you don't want to be neighbors?"

He laughed, twirling one of my ringlets around his finger. "As tempting as that is, I need to stay where I can save for now. And where I have a free garage to work in."

"I think your parents are kinda happy to have you there anyway."

"I think I'm kinda happy to be there, too," he admitted, and I knew that wasn't easy for him. "And hey, at least I have my door back." I laughed. "Mostly, I think they just like getting a ride to church in the Studie."

"You love that car."

"I do."

"It needs a name."

"Yes, she does. Got any ideas?"

"It's a girl, huh?"

"Aren't they always?"

I tapped my chin. "How about Dottie?"

"That is cute, but actually… I'm going to name her Grace."

"Grace?" I smiled. "It's perfect. I love it."

"Me too."

I slipped my hand into his. "My mom approves, by the way."

"Of what, exactly?"

"You."

"Really?"

"She said you're grounded, basically seem to know what you're doing in life, and that you love me well."

"I intend to."

Around us, the courtyard grew silent. For so long, I'd had reasons to wait, reasons to guard myself and my heart. Reasons that sounded spiritual when I said them out loud, but if I was honest, they were rooted in fear. I'd given myself a false sense of security trying to fix problems that were never mine to solve. I had feared my body betraying me again. I had feared loving deeply and losing everything. I feared that, if I gave too much, I'd have nothing left. I had wrapped those fears up in language about conviction and wisdom and timing, but conviction doesn't tremble. Fear does.

And I wasn't afraid anymore.

Just like the ladies at STLR, my health was in God's hands. My future was in God's hands. And my heart was, too. It didn't need a cage around it in order to survive. God didn't spare my life so I could live half of it.

Russell was saying something about budgets and driveways and saving for the future, and I watched his mouth move, and I knew it was okay. I knew what I wanted to do.

I reached up and touched his cheek. He stopped mid-sentence. "Birdie?"

"I don't want to live afraid."

Concern flickered across his face. "Are you okay? You're not feeling—"

I shook my head, smiling. "I don't want to be afraid of my health or my feelings. I'm not afraid of being hurt or left behind anymore. I don't need false convictions to keep me safe, because I know God has my back." The lights reflected in his eyes. I leaned forward, and understanding settled over him. I wasn't rushing or reckless. I was certain.

I kissed him—my first. Lips meeting lips, heart meeting heart. A promise meeting a promise. I felt his sharp inhale, and for a heartbeat, he froze, before his hand cradled my jaw.

When I pulled back, he leaned his forehead against mine. "That was even better than I imagined it would be."

"You mean, I'm a good kisser?"

He laughed, brushing my cheek with his palm. "Not just that, but everything I know it meant to you, it also meant to me. It felt like my first kiss, too."

Inside me, my soul was roaring. Around us, life was moving forward. My work mattered. Helping people was my calling, because God helped us first. Maybe my health wouldn't let me ride the scariest roller coaster in the world, but I could tend God's sheep, and I could love without fright disguising itself as faith.

"I love you, Sweetie Bird." Russ slid his arm around me. He had gone from being the boy with an attitude who intrigued me to the man of God beside me. The future didn't feel like something I had to survive, but something I couldn't wait to walk into.

"I love you, too, Russell Sprout."

ACKNOWLEDGMENTS

Thank you, God, for getting me through this book. It took a lot longer than I wanted because life did not respect my deadlines. I almost lost sight of it entirely, but You, and those You put in my path, pulled my gaze upward and together we made it happen. Your timing is always right. I'm *so* glad You know better than me. Oh, how grateful I am for the prevailing love of my Father.

Thank you, Lori, for being a champion of my writing, and for always trying to make me smile. It works :)

Thank you, Stephanie, for going walking with me even when you *really* don't want to. Anything is fellowship when you're there. (We're going tonight, right??)

Thank you, Kristina, for every early morning, every sales pitch, every encouragement.

Thank you, Emilie, for knocking another beautiful cover out of the park. This is my favorite one yet! I know I say that every time, but it's always true!

Thank you, Kendra, for somehow always being able to understand where my head is, what the heart of the story is, and how to connect those two crazy concepts. You are so special to this series.

Thank you, Abigail, for being a faithful reader and a sweet friend. Keep letting God move in your life and just watch what He does with it!

Love you all & God bless — Heather

ABOUT THE AUTHOR

HEATHER CAMACHO'S mission is to tell stories of love and faith, dedicating her craft to sharing the testimonies, truths, and promises of the Word with readers worldwide.

A Midwesterner turned Texan, she resides on a small ranch in the southern coastal region with her husband, three kids, and their many animals.

When she isn't writing, reading, or homeschooling, she enjoys sewing clothes for her children, making quilts for her friends and spending time with her horses.

WWW.HEATHERCAMACHO.COM

facebook.com/HeatherCamachoAuthor
instagram.com/heather.author
threads.com/@heather.author
amazon.com/author/heathercamacho
goodreads.com/heathercamacho
tiktok.com/@heather.author